CRUSH THE WICKED

The First Jerrod Gold Novel

James C. Gray

CRUSH THE WICKED

The First Jerrod Gold Novel

OTHER BOOKS BY JAMES C. GRAY

CROSS EXAMINATION

The Second Jerrod Gold Novel

HOSTAGE POLICY

The Third Jerrod Gold Novel

Available in Trade Paperback and Kindle on Amazon.com

Desert Enigma Publishing, LLC
P.O. Box 2555
Dayton, NV 89403
D.E.Publishing1@gmail.com

CRUSH THE WICKED

The First Jerrod Gold Novel

Cover Art by: Travis Miles
www.ProBookCovers.com

Printed by: Kindle Direct Publishing,
An Amazon.com company

Also available in Kindle eBook on Amazon.com

Complete Bible verses courtesy of: The World English Bible (WEB),
a Public Domain Modern English translation of the Holy Bible.
www.ebible.org

ISBN-13: 978-0-9863595-0-7
ISBN-10: 0986359505

DEDICATION

LTC John Gerald Ransier
US Army (Ret.)

1919-2011

Combat Veteran — World War II and Korea
Recipient — The Bronze Star with the Valor Device

Rest In Peace, Colonel

ACKNOWLEDGMENTS

To the law enforcement professionals
who inspired this work.

To those who mentored me and
those who allowed me to mentor them.

To my dear friend, Berni, who read the very
rough early drafts and gave me her brutally
honest and invaluable input.

To my wife, Cindy, who encouraged
the completion of this project
and suffered in silence the many times my
attention would wander as the
creative minutia of this work evolved.

“The Victor of any battle is not determined
by the first blood drawn;
but rather by the last blood spilled.”

CHAPTER 1

SEPTEMBER 1985 -- Tuesday

The fetid stench of decomposing human flesh in the confined space gave Detective Jerrod Gold a sensory perception more *feel* than *smell.*

"The air in here is burning my face," he said.

"That's the nastiest decomp ever," his senior partner Detective Craig Wallace said as he held his hand to his nose. "As bad as anything I saw in Vietnam."

"I didn't sign up for this shit," Jerrod Gold said.

"I just bought these slacks and now I'll probably have to burn 'em," Craig Wallace said.

The detectives wore navy-blue nylon raid jackets with gold-colored cloth badges on the left chest, VALLE VERDE PD stenciled on the right chest and POLICE in large letters were on the back. They stood together at the foot of a crumpled bed in the dank twelve-dollar per night hotel room and silently studied the scene:

The dead man laid on his back in a bed fitted with filthy stained sheets. He wore jeans, but no shirt or socks. He had been dead for more than a few days. The warm, stagnant air in the tiny room had no-doubt helped speed the decomposition process.

The bloated body had red and black patches on the torso and arms. Many areas of the body had blisters where bubbles of gas from decomposition lifted the skin from the underlying tissue.

Although the body was that of a white man, his face was discolored black. His eyes were swollen shut, his cheeks grotesquely bloated, and his lips engorged. An untrained person may have assumed he had been severely beaten.

Thin ribbons of blood trickled from the corners of the dead man's mouth and nostrils as decomposition gasses built pressure inside the body and fluids purged out.

There was no trauma to the body and no evidence of a struggle in the room. The windows were closed and locked from the inside. The only door to the room showed no sign of forced entry.

A thin black leather belt draped the dead man's upper left arm, and an insulin syringe was laying on the bed to the side of his left leg. A cigarette lighter and a stainless-steel teaspoon were on the nightstand left of the bed. The handle of the spoon was bent, a small piece of brown-tinted cotton stuck inside of spoon bowl, and black soot coated outside the bowl. The paraphernalia was used by intravenous drug users to "cook" or prepare the crudely processed and low-quality "black tar" heroin popular in the Valle Verde area.

The dead man had numerous small puncture marks visible along the veins of both inner elbows.

Jerrod looked at Craig and nodded. They said simultaneously, "Heroin OD."

Craig motioned to a pile of vomit on the floor near the foot of the bed.

"Looks like he puked after 'fixing'," Craig said.

He theorized the dead man had barfed after injecting himself with the drug — a common experience for heroin users.

Craig adjusted his eyeglasses to examine the pool of vomit closer.

"That puke isn't from the dead guy," Valle Verde PD Patrol Officer Mark "Marko" Otero said. The dark blue-uniformed officer was standing in the doorway. "I got here just as the hotel manager opened the door for Rusty. Rusty stepped into the room and a few seconds later I heard him toss-his-cookies. He ran out of the room and past me with puke still hanging from his mustache. He was dry-heaving in the parking lot right before you guys got here."

"Rusty" was Patrol Officer Russell Browne and he was nowhere to be seen.

"We should rename him 'Crusty Rusty,'" Jerrod said.

"We should rename him 'Ralph,' because that's exactly what he did in our crime scene," Craig said.

Jerrod bent forward at the waist and did an exaggerated imitation of a person vomiting while bellowing, "Rrrraaaaaalllllllph."

The detectives and Marko snickered as only the sick minds of experienced cops could do in the midst of a revolting death scene.

"The Coroner's Office was called and are on the way," Marko said.

Typically, dead bodies were not allowed to be disturbed until the coroner's investigator arrived. The detectives had no intentions of violating that protocol.

The death investigation procedure at that point was to photograph the scene and find out who the dead man was. They would try to determine when the man was last seen alive to narrow down the time-of-death.

Craig offered to take the pictures and opened a case containing a 35mm camera. Jerrod jumped at the chance to get out of the foul-smelling room and knock on a few doors.

Jerrod talked to a neighbor, a middle-aged woman who spoke broken English. He learned she had last seen the man alive about four days earlier. She told him she started smelling "something bad" about two days before but hadn't called the hotel manager until the smell got "real bad" that evening.

Jerrod found the hotel manager and learned the dead man's room was rented to Anthony Ratich. He knew Anthony "Tony the Rat" Ratich well. He had arrested him several times while still in Patrol for minor theft, public intoxication, and drug possession charges.

Mesa County Sheriff's Coroner Deputy Ted Lindsey, with his wheeled gurney and supplies, was escorted to the room by Marko.

"I didn't need anyone to lead me to the room. I could have just followed the smell from the parking lot," the deputy said.

"I've got a call. See you guys later," Marko said as he turned to leave the room. The detectives and the deputy thanked him for his help.

Ted Lindsey stretched on a pair of latex gloves as Jerrod told him what he had learned from the neighbor and manager.

The deputy surveyed the scene and said, "Looks like another OD. We've had a couple of these this week. One guy was dropped off DOA at the Valle Verde Hospital ER and a young female was found dead in a junkie pad out in the foothills. She was a first-time user according to her friends."

The deputy moved the hypodermic needle to the nightstand and said: "This is going to be a 'two bagger.'"

He took a white plastic body bag from the gurney and unfolded it on the floor to the right side of the bed.

"Would you gentlemen please each grab a leg," the deputy asked the detectives. "The gloves are right there." He motioned his head toward a white cardboard box on the gurney.

Jerrod glanced at Craig and noticed his mustache twitch as he curled his upper lip at the thought of actually having to touch the oozing dead man.

The detectives put on latex gloves and, careful to avoid stepping in Officer Rusty Browne's most recent meal, peeled the body off the gooey sheets and into the white body bag.

The deputy zipped the white bag and unfolded a larger and heavier black body bag.

"Why two bags?" Jerrod asked. "Kind of wasteful. Isn't it?"

The deputy looked up at the detectives. "Listen, I drive the same van every day and I'll be damned if this dead guy's stinking *au jus* is going to leak all over the inside of it. Now please help me put the white bag in the black bag."

Jerrod and Craig looked at each other and did as the deputy had directed. They helped lift the black body bag onto the gurney.

Jerrod collected the syringe and spoon from the nightstand and placed them in an evidence bag. Craig picked up the camera case.

The detectives left the remainder of the disgustedly contaminated room for the hotel staff to deal with.

Jerrod and Craig helped the deputy move the gurney to the parking lot where it was loaded into the white coroner van.

It had still been daylight and warm when the detectives had arrived at the scene, but it had since become dark. The cool fog from the Pacific Ocean had rolled in and started covering everything in dew.

"I'll call you if something weird comes up at autopsy," the deputy said. "But it'll be a couple weeks until we get the toxicology report back and then we'll know just what was in his system."

The detectives thanked him, and they parted without shaking hands.

"I couldn't think of a more pleasant way to spend a Tuesday evening," Craig said as he watched the coroner van drive away. He pulled out a green and white pack of Salem 100s, lit a cigarette, and took a long draw from it. "I no-showed for my daughter's softball game tonight and I'm going to catch hell from Sandi when I get home."

"I can book the evidence," Jerrod said. "And call Hanson so you can at least get home before your girl goes to bed."

"Hanson" was Detective Sergeant Pete Hanson — the detective's supervisor.

"Thanks, pal. I appreciate that," Craig said.

He reached into his jacket pocket and pulled out the roll of color film containing the gruesome death scene images. He glanced at the film canister before handing it to Jerrod. Craig rubbed his hands together to signal he was forever cleansing himself of the sights he had witnessed that night.

"No problem," Jerrod said. "See you in the morning."

Craig nodded and walked away to his city-issued unmarked Chevrolet sedan.

CHAPTER 2

Jerrod drove his unmarked maroon Dodge sedan from the hotel death scene parking lot. He loosened the knot on his tie while he tried to ignore the endless chatter on the police radio.

Derek and The Domino's song, "Layla," came on the radio and he turned up the volume to better hear the opening guitar riffs and to sing along with Eric Clapton's pleading lyrics.

He drove from the hotel on the north side of the city of Valle Verde, population 35,000, toward the downtown area where the police department building was located.

"Valle Verde," a Spanish term meaning "Green Valley," was situated in a flat valley floor where fertile soil, an ample water supply, and a moderate climate created an ideal location for the growing of produce. Apples, strawberries, lettuce, broccoli, and cauliflower were the primary crops in the city built around the growing, harvesting, processing, packing, and shipping of fruits and vegetables.

Jerrod had lived his entire life in Valle Verde. He subconsciously noticed familiar sights as he drove: A park he had once played baseball. A neighborhood market his mother had shopped. A pizza parlor where a birthday had been celebrated. The sights sent flash-like memories of events and activities through his mind of the lifetime he had spent living in that city.

He stopped for a traffic light and his attention focused back to the details of the death investigation. He made a mental checklist of tasks that still needed to be completed.

He drove down Main Street to the downtown area, one block east onto Fremont Street, and south again one block on Front Street to the Valle Verde Police Department building.

Or as the cops simply called it, "The PD."

The PD, a tired, one-story, white-painted block structure that had been built in the Art Deco-style of the 1930s, had a narrow driveway surrounding the building perimeter where police vehicles parked in assigned spaces.

To the building's front were a set of steps leading to a double glass door and a small public lobby. The building interior consisted of a dispatch center staffed around-the-clock by a dispatcher, a six-cell jail, booking area, evidence room, records section, and private offices for the chief of police and captain.

The largest room in the building, the squad room, was where the four sergeants and twenty-four officers assigned to Patrol duties worked.

The squad room was truly multipurpose: The dull, gray-painted room had a single large conference table with a cracked Formica top and wobbly wooden chairs which acted as the gathering spot for all roll-call briefing, report writing, evidence processing, phone calling, and meal eating by patrol officers.

A coin-operated soda vending machine stood in one corner and the windowless room was ringed with dented and scuffed gray metal gym lockers.

Jerrod entered the squad room from a back door and found Officer Rusty Browne at the big table writing a report. The pudgy and red-haired uniformed officer looked up and smiled meekly at the detective.

"Hey, Rusty. How are you feeling?"

"Marko told you. That bastard. I'm going to kick his ass."

"No biggy, man. I'm real glad I didn't eat anything before I got to that scene or I may have chucked too. It was pretty disgusting."

"Thanks. I can't even change my boy's diaper without wanting to lose-my-lunch. And that scene was *way* worse."

"No problem. How old is your little guy... Jimmy? And how's he doing?"

"He's three now and he's okay, I guess. He has some behavioral issue we're dealing with. Katy had to quit work to stay home and take care of him."

"Give Jimmy a high-five from me. And give Katy a big hug too. I'm sure this hasn't been easy on either of you."

"Thanks, Jerrod."

Jerrod walked around a bank of lockers and placed a key into the knob of a flimsy wooden door.

A small brown plastic sign above the door read: Detective Bureau.

The door opened into a narrow room separated from the squad room only by a thin wall.

He sat down at his desk and telephoned Detective Sergeant Pete Hanson at home.

"Hello," the sergeant answered.

"Hey, Sarge. It's Jerrod. I'm back at the PD. Just called to let you know the dead body call was most probably a heroin OD. The scene was pretty straight-forward, and the coroner will call when the tox report comes back in a couple weeks to confirm."

"Anything I need to notify The Brass about?"

"Nah. There's nothing odd about the scene that they need to know about tonight."

"Okay. See you in the morning. Thanks for the call."

"Good night, Sarge."

Jerrod marked the insulin syringe, heroin spoon, and film canister with the investigation case number and dropped them off in a property room locker.

He locked the detective bureau door and walked through the squad room to the back door.

Fastened to the interior of the door was a white sign with bright red lettering he had seen so many times he no longer noticed. The sign read:

WHAT YOU SEE AND WHAT YOU HEAR.
WHEN YOU LEAVE, YOU LEAVE IT HERE.

As Jerrod walked into the parking area, a black-and-white Chevrolet patrol car pulled around the building and Marko Otero yelled, "Meet me at The Corner."

"Okay," Jerrod yelled back as he got into his car.

Jerrod drove the nearly fifty feet to "The Corner" where he found Marko already parked and getting out of his patrol car.

The Corner Hotdog Stand was a Valle Verde landmark and a special place to several generations of valley residents.

The Corner was a simple, but successful, family-operated business: It had been in the same location since 1957 and it shared the parking lot with the PD at the busy corner of First and Fremont Streets. The structure of The Corner was no bigger than a small bedroom and its exterior was painted royal blue and crisp white. A red neon sign of a hotdog and bun shined from its roof.

It was open every day of the year except Thanksgiving and Christmas.

The menu at The Corner was simple: they sold chili dogs and little else. They served premium boiled hotdogs on specially ordered steamed buns topped with a stripe of yellow mustard and a secretly formulated ground-beef chili.

Finely chopped white onions were optional. Locals made their chilidog order by announcing either "with" or "without" — the staff knew what they were talking about.

Ketchup was not available as a condiment.

A customer at The Corner could order a soda, milk, or coffee to wash down their entree. A variety of bagged chips were also available at the counter.

There were no tables or chairs at The Corner and most people either took their chilidogs home or ate them at their car. It was the go-to place for a quick meal before or after a movie or sporting event. People who had once lived in Valle Verde and moved elsewhere often detoured to The Corner when in the area to treat themselves nostalgically.

Most of the VVPD officers were reared locally and were frequent customers at The Corner. Many people joked that it was the safest place in Valle Verde due to its proximity to the PD and the number of on-duty officers who visited there.

The strong coffee in Styrofoam cups was sold for a mere twenty-seven cents and had helped many officers survive some long, cold night shifts on Patrol.

Marko ordered coffee. Jerrod asked for "two without" and a coffee.

As Jerrod unwrapped the paper from the first chilidog, he said: "Did I ever tell you about the time I ate sixteen of these in one sitting?"

"No. But I'm sure I'm going to hear about it now," Marko said.

"Well, I was a sophomore in high school and was out one night with the boys. I'll admit there had been some under-age drinking that night. We all got hungry and walked to The Corner where I ordered four chilidogs."

Marko sipped his coffee. Jerrod finished eating the first chilidog and unwrapped the second.

"After finishing them, I was still hungry, so I got four more. Eight chilidogs still wasn't enough, so I ordered four more. After they were gone, my friends dared me to eat four more and offered to pay for them. I took the challenge, and the rest was... history."

"Must have paid dearly for that stunt the next day," Marko said.

"It wasn't pretty," Jerrod said. "Two 'dogs have been my limit ever since."

A female police dispatcher's voice on Marko's portable radio announced a burglar alarm sounding in a downtown business. Marko keyed the microphone and announced he would handle the call.

"Later, *Dude,*" Marko said, imitating the surfer voice of the Sean Penn character in the movie *Fast Times at Ridgemont High,* as he turned to jog to his patrol car and sped out of the parking lot.

The experienced patrol officer didn't spill a drop of coffee getting into his black-and-white.

CHAPTER 3

Jerrod finished his second chili dog and got into his car to head home. He lived only five minutes from the PD and used that time to attempt, in vain, to erase the sights and smells of the death scene from his mind.

He lived in a simple two-bedroom 1950s-built house with a detached single-car garage in the quiet residential eastern portion of Valle Verde. He had purchased the house the previous year.

As he turned the corner onto the narrow street where his house was located, he saw a white Volkswagen Rabbit convertible parked in his driveway. It effectively blocked *him* from using *his* driveway.

He parked the city-issued car at the curb in front of the house, walked the narrow concrete pathway that divided his neatly trimmed lawn, and unlocked the house front door. He pushed open the door and peered into the living room. Stretched out on the sofa, wearing a pair of turquoise shorts and a tight white tank-top, was the most wonderful woman he had ever know.

"Welcome home," *she* said. "Long day?"

She was Natalie Segura, his on-again and off-again girlfriend since high school. He called her "Nat."

"Just another day at the... you know," he said, intentionally avoiding completion of the cliché.

"Hungry?"

"I had a couple 'dogs with Marko, but I can still eat."

The television was on, and Natalie had been watching MTV. The Tina Turner music video for the song "Better Be Good to Me" was playing as he walked through the living room.

Jerrod washed his hands in the kitchen sink and opened an ice-cold bottle of Heineken he had grabbed from the refrigerator. He sat down at the small kitchen table as Natalie took a plastic-wrap covered plate from the refrigerator, placed it in the noisy counter-top microwave, and turned the dial to heat the meal.

"My mom made *mole poblano pollo* today and asked me to bring you a plate."

Jerrod had experienced Mama Segura's cooking many times. In fact, he thought to himself, she made the best Mexican food he had ever tasted. No restaurant he had ever visited could come close to Mama's homemade delicacies.

“How was your day, Nat?” he said as he savored the tender chicken coated with a thick spicy and bittersweet chocolate sauce.

“Nothing special,” she said as he sat at the table. “The hospital is what it is.”

Natalie was an Admissions Clerk at the Valle Verde Community Hospital.

“I saw Hector at my mom's this afternoon,” she said.

“Hector” was Hector Medina, a kid Jerrod had met at the Segura home several years earlier.

“I haven't seen Hector for a few months. What's he been up to?”

“I don't know. He was leaving when I got there, and we really didn't get a chance to talk.”

“Hector must have been about eleven when he first showed up at your parent's house,” he said. “That was a year or so after we graduated, so he must be about... eighteen now.”

“That's about right,” she said. “He didn't speak a word of English then, but he learned quickly and seemed to do okay in school.”

As he savored the last delightful tastes of *mole* from his plate, he said, “I'll cruise the old neighborhood tomorrow and see if I can find Hector.”

Natalie nodded.

“Excuse me, Jerrod,” she said. “Nothing personal, I love you and everything, but what's that smell?”

“You don't even want to know, believe me.” He stood up from the table and said, “I'm going to take a shower.”

Jerrod went into the master bedroom where he removed his gold seven-pointed Valle Verde PD badge in its belt holder, a Beretta 9mm semi-automatic pistol in a black leather holster, and a set of chrome handcuffs from his belt. He placed them in an unlocked drawer of an oak chest-of-drawers. He removed his dress shirt, tie and suit pants and balled them up for a trip to the cleaners.

He stood naked in front of the bathroom mirror sink as he brushed his teeth. He examined his tall frame and pinched the slightest hint of the dreaded “love handles” which had appeared on his midriff. He noticed his brown hair was getting just a little longer than department regulations allowed. While most of the other VVPD cops sported full mustaches, Natalie preferred he stay clean shaven.

He started the water and got into the shower. He attempted to scrub the stench of the death scene from his hair and skin and memory.

After he had thoroughly cleansed himself and was simply enjoying the relaxing pulsation of the shower water beating on his back, he noticed the plastic shower curtain being pulled open.

“May I join you?” Natalie asked.

“Of course.”

Natalie let her deep-blue silk robe fall from her shoulders and drop to the floor. She stepped over the rim of the tub surround into the warm water with him.

Natalie was painfully beautiful. She had shoulder length black hair and deep brown eyes. She was average height with a perfectly proportioned figure and a natural bronze complexion that made her look tanned all year. Her lips were luscious, and he tasted them as they kissed and embraced under the warm shower water. They left the shower and continued to kiss as they dried each other with large soft white bath towels.

They moved slowly to the bedroom where they made the beautiful and generous love they had both enjoyed so many times before.

CHAPTER 4

Natalie was sound asleep with her head on his chest as Jerrod lay awake. Sleeping was never easy for him, and his mind raced with random thoughts:

His relationship with Natalie was unusual. They had dated since their junior year in high school. They were very much in love and had a great time together. But there was something missing. They rarely argued but had broken up several times. They would tell each other they were going their own ways but would inevitably get back together again.

They had never discussed getting married.

He had dated other girls during their breakups but hadn't brought any of them to his house. Although Natalie still lived with her mom, he had given her a house key and never bothered to change the locks during their separations.

She would often just show up as she did that night.

He was very confused and had no real answers for his own questions.

Jerrod switched thoughts to the kid Natalie had mentioned earlier — Hector Medina. He recalled the many times, when he was still working in Patrol, Hector would walk into the PD lobby and asked the dispatcher if he was in. If he was in the building, the dispatchers would "buzz" open the lobby door and he would walk himself through the interior PD hallways to the squad room to see what Jerrod was doing.

He chuckled, and nearly woke Natalie up, as he remembered the many occasions, he had given Hector five dollars and asked him to go to The Corner to get a chilidog and a cup of coffee for him. The 'dog and coffee, with sales tax, would have come to just a dollar-eighteen, but Hector somehow never returned any change.

And he had never asked Hector for the change either.

His mind slowly began to shut down and he drifted off to what typically would be a restless night of sleep.

CHAPTER 5

Armando Mendoza went every week and he always went alone.

He parked in the gravel lot and took the package from the passenger seat. The heels of his boots crunched against the white gravel until he reached the lawn.

It was overcast and the cemetery gloomy. The grass was damp with dew.

He walked past the other markers without noticing them. He knew where he was going. He had been there many times over the previous two years.

He found the grave. He brushed away a few dried leaves and plucked some wild blades of grass. He touched the cold marble headstone with his palm. It read:

MARIA LOURDES MENDOZA

BELOVED WIFE AND MOTHER

1942-1983

He unwrapped the cover from the package. Eleven perfect white roses. He took a deep smell from the flowers before placing them in the permanent vase.

He whispered in Spanish: “I miss you.”

CHAPTER 6

Valle Verde PD detectives worked from eight to five, Monday through Friday. They were allowed one unpaid hour for lunch.

Jerrod Gold arrived at his desk that morning as his usual time... exactly one minute before eight.

Craig Wallace was already at his desk in the small detective bureau office enjoying one of the many Salem 100 cigarettes he would smoke that day. He was going through the variety of crime reports generated by Patrol the previous day.

"Anything good in there?" Jerrod asked as he gestured to the stack of reports.

"Not a thing," Craig said.

"Where's Hanson?"

"Staff meeting."

"What's happening, Willie?" Jerrod said to the third detective assigned to the bureau: Guillermo "Willie" Sanchez.

"*Nada, amigo.*"

Willie, thirty-five with a sparse mustache and jet-black wavy hair, wore a big wristwatch with a heavy gold band. He had a habit of shaking the over-sized watch to move it back into position if it slipped up onto his forearm. The watch band would give a subtle metallic rattle each time he adjusted it.

"Missed a 'stinker' last night," Jerrod said to Willie, referring to the death investigation.

"No, I didn't. Craig told me about it. Pass. I don't do well at decomps."

"Neither does Rusty Browne," Craig said. "Poor bastard."

"That was nasty, dude," Jerrod said. "Just nasty."

The narrow room designated the Detective Bureau contained four desks — one for each investigator. The desks assigned to Jerrod and Craig were situated together so the two detectives faced each other as they worked.

Willie's desk was in the back corner facing the two mated desks.

Pete Hanson, being the supervisor, had his desk near the only window in the room that could be opened.

There were no partitions to provide any sort of privacy. Any conversation, however hushed, was easily overheard... and often commented on.

Three metal file cabinets, a bookcase, a small metal table with an IBM Selectric typewriter on it, and a wooden coat stand near the door completed the office furnishings.

On top of one of the file cabinets, there was a time-worn, but always reliable, coffee maker and a beat-up AM-FM radio with a tag marked "Evidence" attached to it. Both the coffee maker and radio were always on during business hours. The radio was tuned to the one local station all four investigators could agree on — FM 94.3, KHJB, "The Valley's Rock."

As the coffee brewed and the music played, the detectives quietly conducted their normal morning routine in order of priority: Drink coffee, read the new reports, drink coffee, check their open case files, and drink more coffee as they made follow-up phone calls and mentally formed a work plan for the day.

They were fully aware that any plans made could be changed in an instant should they get called-out to investigate a fresh crime.

The three detective's areas of responsibility were straight-forward:

Craig was the most senior detective, so he got the serious cases — homicide, robbery, and major assaults.

Jerrod was the junior detective and he handled mostly property crimes — burglaries, thefts, embezzlement, vandalism, and document fraud including forged and non-sufficient-fund checks.

Willie was the only fluently Spanish-speaking detective, so he got a mixed-bag of cases involving victims or witnesses who did not speak English. He received a token five-percent bilingual incentive on his paycheck for his efforts but received twenty percent more work because he had that valuable language skill.

Jerrod was able to speak a respectable form of "street-Spanish" that had served him well in Patrol. He had considered brushing-up his skills and taking the city bilingual test to get the extra cash but changed his mind after seeing how badly Willie got used-and-abused.

Sergeant Pete Hanson's job was to review and assign all new cases. A few of which he took himself. He handled the administrative duties for the Bureau, such as payroll and performance evaluations. His main duty was to be the buffer between them and The Brass.

The Valle Verde PD was a relatively small department and was organized by two distinctions: Sworn and Non-Sworn.

The sworn personnel included: Twenty-seven police officers, five sergeants, and The Brass.

The Brass was a generic, and not always respectful, title for any police personnel above the rank of sergeant. They were so named because they wore shiny brass rank insignias on their uniform collars and shoulder epaulettes. There were two lieutenants, one captain and the chief of police.

Non-sworn personnel included: Dispatchers, records clerks, and a property clerk.

About a half-hour into the shift, Sergeant Pete Hanson came into the bureau and sat down at his desk. He was a tall and athletic man with Nordic features. He had short blond hair and a wide mustache.

"Anything good come out of 'staff,' Sarge," Craig asked.

"Nothing that applies to you guys," he said. "There's a new directive to Patrol from the captain prohibiting the game of 'Grommet Wars' the troops have been playing. You guys heard of that, 'Grommet Wars?'"

"Never heard of it," Jerrod said.

"Nope, me either," Craig said.

"*No Se,*" meaning "I don't know" in Spanish came from Willie.

What the sergeant didn't know at that moment was all his detectives had just lied to his face. They knew exactly what "Grommet Wars" was. Willie had answered in Spanish so he could later claim a language-barrier defense should he ever get called on it.

"Well then, let me enlighten you," the sergeant said. "'Grommet Wars' is apparently a game Patrol plays in which they make surprise strikes on each other in the chest with their department-issued wooden batons and get points for breaking the plastic buttons off the victim officer's uniform shirt. There are bonus points if you break another officers pen in their uniform pocket or cause another officer to drop or even spill a cup of coffee or soda."

Jerrod's chair creaked as he leaned back.

"Points get deducted if you strike the badge or name plate as they are considered 'out-of-bounds.' Most of the patrol guys wear ballistic vests and no one's been hurt during the game... yet. But the captain wants it stopped."

Craig sipped his coffee.

"Additionally, some of the troops have found that if they loosen the black rubber grommet that holds the baton in the ring on their duty belts and then swing the baton like a baseball bat — the grommet will fly off the baton fast enough to make a serious impact on an unsuspecting victim. That may explain the black skid marks on the squad room and hallway walls and the dents in the lockers."

"I wondered where those marks came from," lied Craig.

"Me too," lied Jerrod.

Willie remained silent. But his silence was a lie all the same... through omission.

"Sounds brutal," Jerrod said.

"Glad we're safe in here," Craig said.

Willie shook his watch but remained mute. He looked around Craig and made eye contact with Jerrod. Jerrod nodded to him and looked at Craig. Craig nodded back.

The three detectives were silently thinking the same thing: The Brass had *way* too much information. It sounded like there was a "snitch" somewhere in the department.

The sergeant said, "And a reminder, you are expected at the police range this afternoon at one o'clock for firearms qualification. Officer Otero will be expecting you.

Craig sighed. "I have some follow-up this—"

The sergeant interrupted, "Death, or at least a verifiable hospitalization, are the only excuses I will accept from you three mutts if you miss range day this time."

"Yes, sir," the detectives responded collectively.

Jerrod said to no one in particular, "I've got to go out to talk to a witness in an employee theft case and a few other follow-ups, so I'll see you guys at the range. I think I'll stop at Garcia's and get a burrito-to-go before we shoot. Anybody want anything?"

"Nah, I'm going to have lunch with my wife today," Craig said.

"Get me a *carne asada* burrito and a Coke," Willie said. "I'll pay you back later. *Gracias, amigo.*"

"*De nada,*" Jerrod said.

Jerrod collected some case files from his desk and his suit jacket from a hanger on the coat rack. He turned and started to walk through the bureau doorway when he nearly ran face-first into one of The Brass – Captain Andrew Wheaton.

"Sorry, sir."

The captain smiled. "What's the hurry, Detective?"

"Just can't wait to get out there and crush-some-crime, sir."

"Go get 'em, son."

"Yes, sir," Jerrod said as he stepped to the side and gestured for the captain to pass through the doorway first.

CHAPTER 7

Jerrod got into his unmarked car and pulled away from the PD.

The song, "The Heat is On" by the former Eagles band member Glenn Frey was on the radio. He sang along and wondered out-loud if the Eagles would ever get back together.

He laughed at himself for almost crashing into Andrew Wheaton. He recalled the very first time he had seen the captain and how that man had been responsible for him becoming a police officer:

His parents separated in 1974 – during the summer between his freshman and sophomore years at Valle Verde High School. They sold the house they had shared for over ten years in the only neighborhood he could remember living in. He moved with his mom and younger brother to a new neighborhood on the east side of the city.

His father, Jerrod "Jerry" Gold, moved to Las Vegas, Nevada about six months after the separation.

Jerrod recalled that he didn't care much for school and was, at best, an average student. He enjoyed playing baseball and being with his friends from the team but was pretty much a loner with no real direction or ambition to do anything past high school.

During his junior year, the entire class was assigned to attend a series of presentations by local private businesses and government officials during "Career Day."

Jerrod attended several presentations and sat down in one from the Valle Verde Police Department.

The presenter was Captain Andrew Wheaton.

Jerrod recalled how struck he was by Captain Wheaton's appearance: His crisp, dark blue LAPD-style uniform caught his eye first, followed by his shining gold badge, and polished leather gear and boots. He was immaculately groomed with short, light brown hair, and neatly trimmed mustache. Andrew Wheaton stood with perfect posture as he spoke and had a command-presence no one could ignore.

Captain Wheaton spoke about his eighteen years with the VVPD. He described how rewarding law enforcement was as a career and the opportunities available to young police recruits.

Captain Wheaton added that the police department sponsored a police cadet program in which boys and girls aged seventeen to twenty-one could wear uniforms, ride-along with patrol officers, and assist with special events and programs.

Jerrod was sold. From that moment, he had no greater desire than to become a police officer. The very next day, he walked to the police department and applied to become a Valle Verde police cadet.

Jerrod completed his follow-up interviews and remembered he had told Natalie he would try and find Hector Medina.

He went to the neighborhood in which Natalie and Mama Segura lived — narrow Victorian-style homes on small lots located just a few blocks from the PD. As he cruised the streets, he was met with some glares from the neighborhood tough guys — none of whom were Hector.

He drove past The Corner and smiled as he mentally tallied the change from the five-dollar bills he had never received back from Hector. It occurred to him he could have claimed the kid as a dependent and taken a tax deduction for all the cash Hector collected from him.

On his way to the police range, Jerrod stopped at Garcia's Mexican Food to get burritos for himself and Willie.

As he entered the restaurant through a wooden-framed screen door, he took in the distinctive aroma of the roasting pork, chicken, and beef being prepared for the many customers who would visit the tiny restaurant that day.

A heavily accented male voice from behind the counter said, "Welcome, Detective."

"*Hola,* Sal. How are you?" He said to the owner of the establishment — Salvador "Sal" Garcia.

"Life is very good. What can I get you?"

"Dos burritos de carne asada y dos Cokes. Para llavar. Por favor," he said, asking for two grilled thinly-sliced marinated beef burritos and two Cokes, to go, and then thanking him.

"Coming right up," Sal said.

Jerrod was the only customer at the time, so he sat at a small table while he waited for his order. The screen door opened, and he looked up as a man walked in. He was carrying a clipboard and wearing a white polo shirt with "Mesa County Health Department" imprinted on it.

As the health inspector adjusted his eyes from the daylight, he said to him, "How have you been, Gary?"

He had played baseball with Gary Pell from Little League to the high school varsity team. They had run around together in school but hadn't seen each other in a few years.

"Hey, Jerrod, Gary said. "Doing good, thanks."

As Gary walked over to the table, Jerrod asked in a hushed voice, "Tell me, should I make up a reason to run out without my burritos or is this place safe?"

Gary laughed and said, "No this is just a routine inspection. We didn't get a complaint. I eat here myself from time-to-time. Nothing to worry about."

"Let's get together for a beer and catch up a little," Jerrod said.

Gary agreed and they exchanged business cards as they shook hands.

"Order's ready, Jerrod," Sal yelled from the kitchen.

He paid for the burritos and cokes, thanked Sal, and said goodbye to Gary. He privately hoped the health inspection went well as he walked to the restaurant doorway.

A large barrel-chested man in his early thirties with thick black hair, a full beard, and a scowling face reached for the exterior screen-door handle at the exact moment Jerrod reached for the interior handle. The eyes of the two men met and, after a pause, Jerrod let go of the handle. The large man yanked the door open and walked inside — the two men never losing eye contact.

Jerrod nodded and expressionlessly said, "How you doing?" as the man walked by him without responding.

"Welcome, *Oso*. What can I get for you?" Sal said.

Jerrod walked out of the restaurant thinking how appropriate the name "Oso" was for the large man — as Oso meant "bear" in Spanish. "That was one asshole of a bear, if I've ever seen one," he said quietly to himself.

Jerrod didn't notice the blue Oldsmobile parked at the curb in front of Garcia's or the man behind the steering wheel who intently watched him walk by.

Jerrod drove toward the police range located near the very north boundary of the city limits.

If the City of Valle Verde were viewed from the sky, it would resemble a rough-edged pie cut into three pieces. The first block of Main Street originated at a concrete bridge spanning the Valle Verde River. The river acted as both the city and southern most Mesa County boundary. Main Street was six blocks long and was the commercial center of the city.

Located on the east side of Main Street's 300 block was the City Plaza. The Plaza was an inviting square of beautifully maintained lawn and landscape. The United States and California flags fluttered from a forty-foot flagpole.

Main Street ended at a "Y" intersection with two major traffic arteries named after the parallel roadways on either side of the National Mall in Washington, D.C. Constitution Avenue branched off Main Street to the right and ran north-west. Independence Avenue ran left, south-west, off the "Y."

Saint Daniel's Roman Catholic Church, with its beautiful red-brick facade and tall, majestic twin spires, stood at the intersection with Independence Avenue and marked the north end of Main Street.

Jerrod pulled onto the paved lot at the Police Range located parallel to the main runway of the Valle Verde Municipal Airport. He parked next to the only vehicle there — a black-and-white VVPD patrol car.

He could hear gunshots and found Marko Otero practicing his marksmanship with his duty handgun.

Jerrod watched Marko move to a spot approximately seventy-five feet from a fresh paper silhouette target. He unholstered his revolver, swiftly raised the handgun to the shooting position, and fired six rounds in a few seconds.

Jerrod strained his eyes and saw six holes in the very center of the target. The distance between the bullet holes could have been covered by a playing card.

Marko reloaded and holstered his blued-steel Smith-and-Wesson .357 Magnum revolver.

"That was pretty impressive," Jerrod said as he looked again at the target.

Marko shrugged.

"Want half a burrito? It's from Garcia's."

"Pass. Thanks. Already had lunch."

As Jerrod unwrapped his burrito and opened one of the Cokes, he asked Marko, "How come you still carry that old 'wheel-gun'? My Beretta holds fourteen rounds of 9mm ammo, and I can reload fourteen more in no time if I need to."

Marko chuckled as the said, "It's not what *you shoot*, my boy. It's what *you hit* that matters. If you need more than six rounds, you should come to the range more often."

Jerrod nodded and chewed.

"There's another issue with that Beretta you should know about," Marko said. "Remove the magazine, clear the action, and hand it to me."

Jerrod pulled the Beretta from its holster, ejected the magazine, pulled the slide back to clear the live cartridge from the firing chamber, locked the slide back, and handed the pistol to Marko.

Marko double-checked to make sure the handgun was unloaded and unlocked the slide.

"With the slide forward, or 'in-battery,' this auto-pistol operates fine," Marko said as he pointed the muzzle down range and pulled the trigger. The hammer moved back and fell making a solid metallic slap.

Marko then placed the palm of his left hand on the muzzle and pushed against the barrel – causing the barrel and slide to move back an eighth-of-an-inch. He pulled the trigger, but the hammer didn't move.

"This pistol is now 'out-of-battery'," Marko said. "Once the barrel and slide are in this position, the handgun is useless. This can happen with any type of auto-pistol – not just your Beretta. Keep this in mind the next time you stick your gun into some bad-guy's ribs. It may not fire if you want it to."

"I'll remember that. Thanks." Jerrod said.

The other detectives subsequently arrived, and they all passed the qualifying course.

As they collected the empty brass cartridge cases from the range pavement, Jerrod asked Marko, "You remember Hector Medina. That little kid I used to send to The Corner all the time."

"Yeah, I remember him," Marko said. "I'm pretty sure I saw him a couple weeks ago near Natalie's house. He's not a little kid anymore."

"Nat saw him yesterday and I tried to find him this morning, but I was UTL," Jerrod said.

"UTL" was police slang for "Unable To Locate."

"I'll keep an eye out and ask him to drop by the PD if I find him," Marko said.

"Thanks. I'll owe you one."

CHAPTER 8

Jerrod left the range and cruised the neighborhood around the PD again in another unsuccessful search for Hector Medina.

He went to the PD and made a few follow-up phone calls from his desk until his shift was over.

At home, he found no white VW Rabbit convertible blocking his driveway. He changed into shorts and a t-shirt, put on running shoes, and jogged the five-mile course he had measured with a car odometer. After the run, he had a beer and prepared a simple meal for dinner before settling on the sofa and watching TV.

Alone.

CHAPTER 9

At about ten-thirty, Jerrod's phone rang and woke him from the light sleep he was having on the sofa. He had drifted off while watching a rented VHS movie.

He picked up the phone and before he could answer, heard Marko's voice say: "I found Hector. He's okay. You need the come to the PD right away."

At the PD, Jerrod found Marko standing over Hector Medina at the squad room table. Hector's face was bruised, an area around his left eye was swollen, and he had abrasions on his left hand and arm.

"We got a 'man-down' call and found Hector trying to walk away from the scene," Marko said. "Looks like he got worked-over bad. The EMTs checked him out, but he refused to go to the hospital."

Hector shot a glare at Marko.

Jerrod thanked Marko and told Hector, "Come with me."

Hector got up and walked behind him into the detective bureau. Hector flopped into the chair next to Jerrod's desk and hung his head.

Hector was no longer the little kid Jerrod had met years before. He could see Hector's chest, shoulders, and arms had become muscular through the recently dirtied tight white t-shirt he was wearing. He had short cropped medium brown hair and sported a few days of sparse beard on his face.

Jerrod could see no visible tattoos on Hector which might have indicated a gang affiliation.

However, he did notice one odd thing: Hector was wearing a new pair of red and white high-top Nike Air Jordan basketball shoes. Those shoes had been on the market for about a year, and he had never seen a pair except on TV or in magazines. He knew those shoes were expensive at nearly sixty-five dollars a pair.

Jerrod started the conversation by asking, "How old are you now?

"Eighteen," Hector said.

"You been drinking tonight?"

"I had a few beers."

"Any drugs?"

"I don't do that shit."

"So, what happened tonight?"

"I got jumped for no reason. I don't know."

“Do you know who jumped you?”

“I don't know them and I'm not a snitch.”

Jerrod thought to himself that the entire time he had known Hector, he had never asked him to give him any information and Hector had never offered to give any.

“Are you working?” Jerrod asked.

“Lumping,” Hector said.

A “lumper” hung-out at the produce truck shipping docks and got paid in cash to load and unload produce into the large transport trailers.

“Tough work,” Jerrod said.

“It's okay,” Hector said.

“What else have you been up to?”

“I quit school and just take care of my mom now. She's sick.”

“Want a ride home?”

Hector nodded.

They walked through the squad room and out to Jerrod's unmarked car. The ride was silent except for a few terse directions by Hector to a house in an older downtown neighborhood.

Hector pointed out his house but asked to be dropped off around the corner.

Jerrod drove to the next intersection and pulled over to the curb.

Hector opened the door and Jerrod said, “Keep in touch. Call or come by the PD anytime. Okay.”

Hector nodded and smiled weakly back. He got out of the car without saying anything and walked around the corner toward his house.

Jerrod drove home with an uneasy feeling about Hector. He knew how tough the life of a street-kid could be and the peer pressure placed on young Latinos. He worried that Hector would get himself into trouble and hoped he would call him if he did.

Although he wasn't related to Hector, he still felt a sense of responsibility for him.

CHAPTER 10

Thursday

Jerrod Gold arrived at the detective bureau at his customary time. Pete Hanson and Willie Sanchez were at their desks. Craig Wallace was gone.

"Where's Craig?" Jerrod asked no one in particular.

"He had a dentist appointment this morning," the sergeant said. "He'll probably be in later."

Jerrod shrugged and the detectives quietly proceeded with the morning routine.

At about eight-thirty, the sergeant's desk phone rang, and the two detectives stopped to listen.

The sergeant said into the phone receiver, "I'll get Jerrod and Willie out there right away."

"What's up?" Willie asked as the sergeant hung up the phone.

"That was Dispatch. Patrol is out at the ER with another heroin OD... but this one's alive. Get out there and find out what you can."

The hospital was a four-story plain-concrete blob of a building just outside the Valle Verde city limits. Jerrod parked in one of the "Police Only" stalls near the ER entrance between two VVPD patrol cars.

They walked through the ambulance double-doors and were greeted by a young security guard who directed them to an ER treatment room.

In the room, they found a skinny, freckled woman with a mat of wild Lucille Ball red hair laying on a gurney. Jerrod estimated her to be about thirty years old — but they had been an extremely hard thirty years. Her right wrist was handcuffed to a gurney rail and an IV tube was attached to the back of her right hand. She appeared to be sleeping peacefully.

The woman was being guarded by two VVPD patrol officers — Kevin Arneta and Kevin Holcomb.

Kevin Arneta was average height but was built like an Olympic power lifter. He was of Filipino-Samoan descent with dark features, short wavy black hair, and no facial hair.

Kevin Holcomb stood eight inches taller than his partner and had a trim, athletic build. He had light-brown crew-cut hair and a bushy mustache.

Both officers had grown up together in an area near Valle Verde named Plumdale. Most locals referred to Plumdale as “Plumtucky” due to its rural location and redneck reputation.

The two officers were outstanding multi-sport athletes together in high school. They decided on a whim to join the VVPD and both started their law enforcement careers on the same day. Although they had been in patrol less than three years, both had established themselves as very capable officers.

Kevin Arneta and Kevin Holcomb were inseparable both on and off duty. Most people referred to them by nicknames: Kevin Arneta was “Big Kevin,” and Kevin Holcomb was “Tall Kevin.”

They were known together by a single name, “The Kevins.”

“We got a radio call of a ‘woman down’ in a hotel room,” Big Kevin said. “When we got there, the door was unlocked, and this lady was flat on her back on the floor with no one else around. She looked dead and we started securing the scene until we heard her take a shallow breath. I tried to wake her by rubbing my knuckles on the middle of her chest like the EMTs do and by pinching her on the tender part of her inner upper arm. She didn't budge. I pinched harder on her arm, and she still didn't move. We pulled back her eye lids and we saw that her pupils were constricted down to little pinpoints. Then we knew it was a heroin OD.”

“That's when we called for an ambulance,” Tall Kevin said. “In the ambulance, the EMTs started an IV and gave her a shot of Narcan. That woke her ass up. She started yelling for a minute or so and then drifted back off. They gave her another shot, and she started yelling again.”

“Narcan” was a brand name for the drug Naloxone which was commonly used to counter the effects of opioid – including heroin – overdoses.

“We found her ID,” Big Kevin said. “Her name is Stella Leiter.”

Jerrod thanked the officers and walked over to the gurney. He said: “Stella, wake up. We need to talk to you.”

Stella Leiter's eyes opened slightly, and she said in a groggy voice, “Where am I?”

“You're in the emergency room at the hospital. You've had an overdose,” Jerrod said.

“I don't use drugs.” Her voice had a slight drawl to it. Texas, or maybe Oklahoma, Jerrod suspected.

“You're lucky to be alive, so don't start bullshitting us now,” Willie said as he shook his watch.

“I don't want to go to jail.”

"No one's going to jail," Jerrod said. "But we have some questions for you."

"Only if you promise I won't go to jail."

"No Jail. Now, where do you buy your *junk*? Jerrod asked, using a street-name for heroin.

"I didn't buy it. My boyfriend gave it to me."

"Who's your boyfriend?" Willie asked.

"I don't want to get him in trouble."

"Give us his name or we can reconsider the jail thing," Jerrod said.

"Those orange jail jumpsuits will really clash with that red hair of yours," Willie said.

Stella glared at Willie and paused for a moment. She then said, "His name is 'Valdemar.'"

"Valdemar What?" Willie demanded.

"Valdemar Reyes."

"Valdemar Reyes? Val Reyes?" Jerrod asked.

"Yes," she said.

"When did he get out?" Jerrod asked. He knew Val Reyes was supposed to be serving a six-year prison sentence for a series of burglaries three years earlier.

"Few weeks ago," she said.

Jerrod knew Val Reyes very well. He was a long-time heroin addict who supported his habit by breaking into houses and stealing cash and small items. Jerrod had arrested him after his last crime spree.

"How did you OD?" Willie asked.

"Well, Val and I were 'fixing' as usual and I just kind of nodded off," she said. "The next thing I knew, I was here. I can tell you there is some new black tar on the street that is so potent people have to 'shoot' little pieces twenty times a day instead of three or four. I guess I took too much."

"When did this new heroin hit the street?" Willie asked.

"A few weeks ago," she said. "Around the same time Val got out. We've already lost some people."

"I know of three deaths in the last week," Jerrod said.

"Is it packaged any different than before?" Willie asked.

"No. The little rat-turd tar balls come in clear plastic just like it always has. There is no way to tell if it's new or old shit when you get it."

"Where can we find Val?" Jerrod asked.

“I don't know. We had to pay for the hotel room for a week in advance, so he might go back there. I really don't know where else he might go.”

Jerrod handed Stella his business card. “I need to talk to Val. He knows me. Have him call me the next time you see him.”

Stella squinted to read the card.

“Anything you want to ask us?” Jerrod asked.

“Yeah,” she said. “What the fuck happened to my arm? It hurts like hell.” She pulled back the sleeve of the hospital gown and exposed a dark purple six-inch bruise on her right inner upper arm.

Jerrod glanced at The Kevins and saw sheepish grins spread on their faces.

“Maybe the nurse can get some ice on that,” Willie said.

Big Kevin removed the handcuffs from Stella’s wrist and the two officers walked out of the room with the detectives.

“Nice save, guys,” Willie said to The Kevins. “We would probably have another dead junkie if you hadn't got her to the ER.”

“I'll follow-up with Dispatch,” Jerrod said. “And see if there is any information about whoever called the PD about poor Stella.”

The Kevins talked to the hospital security guard and told him that no police hold was being placed on Stella. She was free to go when she got discharged from the ER.

“Would you mind catching a cup of coffee in the cafeteria while I see if Natalie is working?” Jerrod asked Willie. “I need to talk to her about something.”

“No problem,” Willie said.

Jerrod walked to Admissions where he saw Natalie interviewing a patient. She gestured to him to have seat until she was done.

He waited a few minutes until she came over and hugged him.

“Can you get away for a few minutes,” he asked. “I need to talk to you about Hector.”

They walked into the employee break room, got coffee, and sat together at a small table in the otherwise unoccupied room.

“Marko found Hector last night and it looked like someone beat the shit out of him. He was dinged up but refused to come to the hospital. He wouldn't tell me who was involved and wasn't very chatty, so I ended up just driving him home.”

“I'm really worried about him,” she said. “It's dangerous out there for those young guys and I'm afraid he might be with the wrong crowd.”

“I don't know what to do,” he said. “He's a big boy now, but I'm worried about him too.”

“I'm sure you'll figure something out.”

“Will I see you tonight,” he asked.

“Probably.”

Willie was in the cafeteria reading *People* magazine with a photograph of pop sensation Madonna on the cover. He was so involved in the article; he was startled when Jerrod sat down next to him.

“Find your girl?” Willie asked.

“Found her. Let's head back to the office.”

Willie took one last peak at the *People* before throwing it into a pile of other magazines on the table.

“Well, I'll be damned.” Jerrod said as he drove away from the hospital. “Val Reyes is back out already.”

“I don't remember much about him,” Willie said.

“What's the point of giving that guy a six-year prison sentence if he's going to get out in three and be our problem again?”

Willie shrugged.

“At least I got a free steak dinner the last time he was out.”

“How did that happen?” Willie asked.

“I was still in Patrol during Reyes' last crime spree. The detectives at the time suspected him as the suspect in over twenty burglaries based on the ‘M.O.’ used.”

Jerrod turned left onto Constitution Avenue and headed downtown.

“Val Reyes had a simple, but distinctive, technique when he broke into houses: He would approach houses during weekdays and knock on the door or ring the doorbell. If a resident answered, he would ask for someone with a fictitious name and then politely excuse himself as having gone to the wrong house.”

Jerrod stopped for a traffic signal.

“However,” he continued, “If there was no answer at the door, he would go to the back of the house, find a small rock, break a hole in a window big enough to reach his hand in, and unlatch the window to get inside the house. He would only steal valuable items small enough to carry in his pockets.

"The detectives suspected Reyes because he used the same M.O. before. They got an arrest warrant for him after he failed to show up for a probation interview and piss test for a previous drug charge.

"The detectives offered a free steak dinner to any officer who arrested Reyes. They handed out fliers with Reyes' picture and description on it. I had never met the guy, so all I had was the picture and description."

Jerrod slammed on the brakes to miss a car making a quick left turn.

"The following afternoon," he said. "I was patrolling downtown. I had a young police cadet riding with me. As we cruised through the narrow parking lot behind some businesses, I saw a man with a dark jacket and dark pants walking slowly away from us. I pulled the black-and-white up to the right side of the man and tried to get a look at his face. The man didn't glance at the patrol car — which was really weird — because, you know, *everybody* looks at a patrol car when it drives by.

"I said to the cadet, 'I think that's Val Reyes.'"

"As soon as I stepped on the brake and threw the shifter into 'Park,' Reyes turned and started running in the opposite direction. I jumped out of the car and started chasing him around a corner and toward Main Street. I was trying to get my portable handset out when I heard the cadet broadcast the foot pursuit, that I was chasing Reyes, and accurately giving the direction the pursuit was headed from the patrol car radio.

"I chased Reyes onto Main Street and was getting close to him when he started pulling jewelry from his pockets and throwing it on the sidewalk. People were jumping out of the way as we ran up the sidewalk for about a block."

Willie shook his watch.

"Reyes veered off the sidewalk and across heavy Main Street traffic near Saint Daniel's Church. He kept looking back at me, but I could see he was running directly at another patrol car. The other officer skidded his car to a stop right in front of him and Reyes hit the front fender at full speed. He flew over the hood of the black-and-white and landed on the other side. Somehow, he didn't get hurt, but the patrol car got a big dent in its fender. It was right out of a movie. Frigging awesome.

"Jewelry spilled out his pockets while we handcuffed him and stuffed him in the patrol car backseat."

Jerrod drove south onto Main Street.

"It was rush hour and Main Street traffic was at a stand-still for the few minutes it took to collect the jewelry items from the roadway. Some people who saw the chase picked-up the jewelry from the sidewalk and handed it to me when I walked back to my car.

"I found my patrol car safely parked out of the parking lot roadway and being guarded by the young police cadet."

“We may not have caught Reyes that day if that cadet hadn't been with me. He’s off at the Police Academy now and is going to be a damn good officer when he gets out.

“The detectives connected the jewelry we recovered to a few of the house burglaries that had been committed in the previous few days and they returned the items to the owners. Reyes took a plea deal for about ten of the ‘burgs.”

Jerrod drove past The Corner and into the PD parking lot.

“The odd part of the whole thing was Val Reyes himself. He ran from me but didn't put up a fight when he got caught. He was polite and articulate during the booking process and was, well, professional about the whole thing. I kind of liked the guy.”

He parked the car behind the PD.

“The detectives made good on their steak dinner promise, and I invited the cadet to join us.”

CHAPTER 11

"Some people might think these heroin ODs are a good thing," Sergeant Pete Hanson said after Jerrod and Willie briefed him on Stella Leiter's information. "'Cleaning up the streets,' you know. But we need to find the source of this new heroin before we get overrun with dead junkies."

"Yes, sir," Jerrod said.

Jerrod walked to the Dispatch Center and spoke to the dayshift and lead dispatcher, Albert "Al" Kees.

Al had been with the VVPD for over fifteen years and handled the sometimes-manic dispatch position with ease. He juggled radio traffic, incoming calls, and a conversation with an inquisitive detective with grace and humor.

Jerrod asked Al, "Did you take that 'woman down' call this morning that turned into an OD case?"

"Sure did."

"Did you get any ID info from the caller?"

"Nope," he said. "Wouldn't give his name. Spoke clear English. Middle-age. Lots of auto traffic noise in the background. Probably called from a pay phone. He just said there was an unconscious woman at the hotel, and he gave me the room number. He hung-up when I asked for more information. Sorry."

"Al, all incoming telephone calls are tape recorded, right?"

"Yep."

"Can I get a copy of the call on a cassette tape? I have an idea who the caller might be, and I may need to confront him with his own voice when I find him."

"Yeah. I can make a copy. But it's a pain-in-the-ass. I need to find the call on the big reel." He pointed to a cabinet with a Plexiglas face housing a tape recorder with two fourteen-inch reels of quarter-inch magnetic tape. "I can dub it for you. May take a day or so. Bring me a blank cassette tape, okay."

"Will do. Thanks. I'll owe you one."

"You already owe me about three, Jerrod."

"Got me there."

Craig Wallace had come to work after his dentist appointment and was at his desk. He said, "I need to go and look for a gang-banger victim on a stabbing case. Want to get out for a while?"

"Hell yes," Jerrod said. "A real criminal investigation. Sure. I want to play."

"Good. You can drive."

They left the office and unsuccessfully checked two residential addresses for the gangbanger.

"No luck." Craig said. "Case closed. Moving on."

"That was so exciting," Jerrod said. "Now I know what *real* detectives do."

As Jerrod drove back to the PD, he made a quick right turn into the parking lot of a liquor store and pulled into a stall.

"I'll be right back, Jerrod said. "Need anything?"

"Pack of–"

"Salem 100s?" Jerrod interrupted.

"No. Marlboro box. Screw you. Of course, Salem 100s."

Jerrod went into the store and returned a few minutes later carrying something in a brown paper bag. He got into the car and tossed a fresh pack of cigarettes to Craig.

"Thanks. What's in the bag?" Craig asked.

"A bribe for a public employee."

The two detectives went back to the PD and found the sergeant and Willie at their desks.

The radio was playing "Relax" by Frankie Goes to Hollywood. The mood in the detective bureau was upbeat and jovial.

Jerrod carried the paper bag to the Dispatch Center. Al was busy handling phone calls and radio traffic.

During a brief break in the action, Jerrod said, "Here's a token of my deepest thanks for all the assistance you have given me in the past and will continue to provide in the future."

He partially revealed a six-pack of Michelob beer from the bag and said, "There are six beers in here. I already owe you three favors and the tape-thing is one more – so that makes four. That will leave me two beers credit."

Jerrod pulled a blank cassette tape from his pocket and said, "If you can get me the dub of the OD caller by the end of the day, I'll just consider us even. Deal?"

“You're an ass, Jerrod.” Al said while shaking his head. “How did you turn this into ‘I owe you.’ Okay, deal. You should really sell cars, man.”

Jerrod gave him an exaggerated toothy smile and carefully placed the paper bag and its contents on a counter as he mouthed the words, “Thank you.”

Jerrod telephoned the California Department of Corrections and learned Valdemar Reyes had been paroled from the State Prison at Soledad twenty-two days earlier. He had been given two days to report to his parole officer in Mesa and had no-showed there. Jerrod asked if they wanted him picked up for parole violation and the CDC put a “Parolee At Large” or PAL hold on him.

He went to the Records Division and found a copy of Val Reyes booking photo from the arrest three years earlier. He prepared a flier listing Reyes’ description with the photo and the PAL hold. The flier also asked that he be called should Reyes be arrested. He made a dozen copies of the flier.

Patrol was having its three o’clock roll-call and Jerrod sat with the group of officers at the squad room table. After the shift was briefed by the sergeant, he handed out the flier of Val Reyes and told the officers about the series of heroin ODs and Reyes' possible involvement.

Borrowing from his past and to encourage some enthusiasm, he offered a steak dinner to the officer who arrested Val Reyes. He asked to be called at home if he was picked up after business hours.

The remainder of the workday came and went as the detectives left the office one by one.

At a few minutes before five, Jerrod was the last one in the office when his desk phone rang. He answered and was somewhat anxious of what may be coming when he found it was Al from Dispatch on the line.

“Got your tape. Come and get it.”

He walked to Dispatch to get the cassette tape and noticed the bag of beer had been placed under the desk for protection from prying eyes.

“Thanks, Al. We’re even now”

“Not by a long-shot, pal.”

Jerrod went back to the bureau and played the tape. He listened to the voice of the male caller and then had no doubt in his mind that the caller had been, indeed, Valdemar “Val” Reyes.

The song “Simply Irresistible” by Robert Palmer was on the radio when Jerrod turned it off and locked up the detective bureau for the night.

CHAPTER 12

Jerrod parked his unmarked car in the street in front of his house and went inside. He put his police equipment in the dresser drawer and changed into some jeans and a red t-shirt. He grabbed a bottle Heineken from the refrigerator and walked through the laundry room door to the back yard.

The sun was still bright, and it was relatively warm for a fall afternoon. He decided it was a good time to wash his personal vehicle, so he pulled his silver Toyota 4x4 pick-up from the garage and into the driveway. He got a bucket from the garage and was filling it with water when he noticed his next-door neighbor quietly smoking a cigarette.

The neighbor, Charles Horvat, had been living in the house next of Jerrod's when he bought the house about a year earlier. There was no fence separating the driveways for each house leading to the detached garages, so, in essence, they shared a backyard.

Charles Horvat, in his mid-sixties with a full-head of white hair and a short-cropped beard, had come over and introduced himself on the first day Jerrod moved into the neighborhood. Jerrod enjoyed talking him, especially about their favorite baseball team — the San Francisco Giants.

Charles was always friendly and cheerful, but in conversation he tended to use terminology that may have been acceptable in the 1940s and 50s but would be considered very offensive in 1985.

"Good evening, Colonel," Jerrod said to his neighbor while referring to him by his title as a retired US Army Lieutenant Colonel. He had served in combat in both World War II and Korea before retiring in 1967.

"Good evening, Jerrod," he said. "Got time for a 'snap?'"

A "snap" was his term for a cocktail.

"Sure," Jerrod said as he realized the truck would get washed some other time.

Jerrod left his beer and followed the colonel into the kitchen.

"How about a 'Fat-Burner?'" the colonel asked.

A Fat-Burner was the colonel's name for a gin-and-grapefruit juice cocktail.

"That would be fine, sir."

The colonel filled two tall clear glasses with ice, poured in about two ounces of Tanqueray gin and topped them off with white grapefruit juice. He stirred the drinks with a long-handled iced tea spoon.

They both tasted their drink and Jerrod said, "Perfect, sir."

"Join me in the living room."

They walked into the small living room and the colonel settled into a large brown-leather reclining chair. Jerrod sat on a nearby delicate hand-carved sofa. The sofa was an antique the colonel's late wife, Meredith, had inherited from her family.

Meredith had died after a lingering illness about a year before Jerrod bought the house next door.

Jerrod had been in the immaculately kept house several times. The only evidence of the colonel's long military career was a modest shadowbox his wife had made for him shortly after he retired, and which contained the trappings of his military uniform.

Jerrod had studied the contents of the display before and it included: the HORVAT name plate, silver oak leaf collar brass, a gold eagle hat piece, marksmanship badges, and eleven service medals.

One of the medals was a bronze-colored five-point star with a white, scarlet red, and ultramarine blue striped ribbon with a small bronze "V" attached to it. The "V" device was only awarded for acts of valor or heroism in combat.

Jerrod knew The Bronze Star was a very distinguished combat medal and he had asked the colonel on a couple occasions how he had earned it. The colonel was coy about it and only offered he had received it "for something that happened in Korea." He would end the subject by saying, "I'll tell you about it some other time" and then pivot to some corny joke somehow related to his time in the military.

The colonel caught Jerrod's glance at the shadow box and said, "I've got one for you."

Jerrod groaned and dropped his head knowing a bad joke was on the way.

"It was about 1947 and I was a brand-new first lieutenant. I was in uniform traveling across country by train with an entire company of men. We stopped in St. Louis where I stepped off the train to stretch my legs.

"I was approached by a 'colored' prostitute who asked me, 'Where are all the black soldiers at?' I told her the train car I was riding had only white officers, but that I had black privates.

"She said with a straight face, 'Ain't we the fancy one,' before sauntering away."

Jerrod tried but couldn't contain his laughter. He also couldn't handle another joke from the colonel, and he knew he would get another one if he asked about the combat medal again.

"How's that young lady friend of yours — Natalie?" the colonel asked.

"She's fine, sir," he said. "She's still working at the hospital."

"When are you going to make an honest woman out of her?" the colonel asked.

"Well, sir, that's... complicated."

Sensing Jerrod's discomfort, the colonel said, "Are you taking her out this weekend?"

"Going to play-it-by-ear, sir. We may go out."

"Spend all the time with her you can, son. I spent my entire adult life with Meredith, and we traveled all over the world together, but I still wish I had more time with her."

"Thanks, sir. I was thinking a quiet weekend would be nice, but we should definitely go out."

"Have a wonderful time, if you do."

The two men finished their drinks quietly. Jerrod broke the silence. "Should get moving, sir. Thanks for the drink. The Giants are playing 'The Bums' at Candlestick this weekend. Maybe we can catch a game on TV."

"The Bums" was a derogatory term all serious Giants fans used when referring to the rival Los Angeles Dodgers.

"Sounds good, Jerrod."

The fog had started to roll in, so Jerrod put the bucket away and poured out the remainder of the warm and flat Heineken.

His conversation with the colonel, specifically about "making an honest woman" of Natalie, had struck a nerve. He wasn't upset at the colonel about the question he asked, but, rather, *was* disturbed by his lack of an answer.

He asked himself, when, if ever, he and Natalie would either permanently commit to each other or go their separate ways. If he were to ask her to marry him, she might say "no." Was he that afraid of rejection? Maybe. But then, what if she said "yes?"

He often wondered if his disjointed thoughts about Natalie had something to do with his parents' divorce and the aftermath.

He suspected he could spend a few thousand dollars in therapy to sort things out and maybe get some answers. But that would all have to be some other time.

CHAPTER 13

Jerrod felt his stomach growl. He looked in the refrigerator and found it lacking anything to eat more substantial than peanut butter and jelly. He decided to take the colonel's advice to spend some time with Natalie and take her out for dinner.

He telephoned the Segura residence and Mama Segura answered. Through her broken-English and his broken-Spanish, he learned Natalie was still at work.

He called the hospital switchboard and asked for Admissions. Natalie answered the phone.

"I guess I know what you're doing?" he said.

"One of the swing-shift clerks called in sick and I'm going to cover half her shift."

"That's too bad. I was going to take you out tonight. There's nothing to eat in this house. Come over when you get off."

"I will."

Jerrod decided to treat himself to a nice dinner — alone. He showered and shaved, put on a pressed blue dress shirt with his favorite jeans and grabbed a dark sport jacket.

Out of habit, he started to put his police equipment on, but changed his mind and left them in the drawer.

He drove downtown with no real destination in mind. He remembered an upscale Mexican restaurant owned by someone he knew. The restaurant was named "Nopales."

Nopales, taken from the Spanish term for the edible paddle of the prickly pear cactus, had been in business for about two years. The owner, Magdalena Mendoza, was a friend of Natalie's from high school. Everyone called her "Maggie."

He parked in the nearly full parking lot just off Main Street and walked into the restaurant. The place was packed with patrons and most of the tables were taken. The bar stools were all occupied, and more people stood holding their drinks. A four-piece *mariachi* band roamed the restaurant playing beautiful melodic Mexican songs on request.

He waited at the reception stand for a few moments and looked for familiar faces in the crowd. He was just considering leaving and trying another restaurant that was less crowded when Maggie hustled over to the stand. She had a frazzled look and her long black hair, pulled back into a bun, was coming loose.

"Jerrod. How are you? Welcome," she said as they hugged.

"Busy place, Maggie." he said. "Business looks good."

"Thank you," she said. "It's been a good Thursday night. Where's Natalie?"

"Working late," he said. "I'm solo tonight."

"Wait here," she said.

A few minutes later, Maggie walked back toward him and motioned for him to follow her. She directed him to a small table-for-two. He sat in the seat with his back to a wall and the best view of the restaurant — something all cops instinctively did in public places.

"Something to drink, Jerrod?" Maggie asked as she collected the second set of silverware, napkin, and place mat.

"How about a can of Tecate with a lime. No glass. Please."

"You got it. Your waiter will be right over," she said as she turned and rushed away.

Long before meeting the Segura family, Jerrod had acquired a fondness for good Mexican food from his grandfather.

Frank Gold had traveled the world as a teenage musician in the 1920s. He settled in California in the 1930s when he married a young woman, Jenne, right out of high school.

Frank and Jenne — later better known as "Gramps and Gram" to the grandkids — soon started a family. Jerrod's father, Jerry Gold, was the second-born of four kids.

The Gold family crisscrossed the state during the Great Depression as they followed the harvest of various crops with a group of fieldworkers and produce processing laborers known at the time as "fruit tramps." They lived where they could find shelter and scraped by to survive. He performed the long hours of back-breaking work along with a variety of ethnic groups — mostly of Eastern European, Asian, and Latino descents.

Although the workplace had been far from racially integrated at that time, Frank Gold became especially fond, and often imitated, the work ethic and lifestyle of his Latino co-workers. He respected their sense of family, their strong religious faith, and their ability to live off the items that were available to them — and all without complaint.

He learned from them to appreciate the things you had and not worry about the things you didn't.

After a stint in the Navy during World War II, Frank Gold found regular work in the fertile fields and produce empire established in Valle Verde. He soon made a permanent home there with his family.

Many years later, he would talk about those difficult times and the life lessons he had experienced.

After he retired in the mid-1960s, he often traveled to Mexico and took in as much of the culture there as he could.

Every time his grandfather ate in a Mexican restaurant, he had ordered a can of Tecate with a lime.

Jerrod scanned the menu, but already knew what he was going to have.

His young server, Rafael, came to table with the beer and a wedge of lime. He placed the beer on the table and asked if he was ready to order.

"I'll have the *chili verde* with corn *tortillas*, please."

"Very good, sir," Rafael said before dashing away from the table.

Jerrod squeezed the juice from the lime wedge onto the top of the already-opened red and gold can of pale lager *cerveza*. He picked up the saltshaker and sprinkled salt onto the lime juice just as his grandfather had always done.

He raised the can of beer and whispered, "To you, Gramps," before taking the first satisfying taste of the lime, salt, and cold beer mixture.

Frank Gold had died about six-months earlier after losing a battle with cancer.

Jerrod enjoyed the live music and watched the crowd while waiting for his meal. He took another sip of beer and as he peered over the can, he noticed a huge man with a full beard standing near the bar watching the crowd. He hadn't been there when he first came into the restaurant.

The large man looked familiar, but he couldn't immediately place him. After a few moments, he recognized him as being the unfriendly bear of a man he had met at the door at Garcia's the day before.

Sal Garcia had addressed him with the accurately descriptive nickname: Oso.

He watched Oso as Oso watched the crowd. He saw him scrutinize each person who entered the restaurant, and it was apparent he was not a guest.

He worked there.

His interest in Oso's activities became background when his meal arrived. He took in the aroma of the seasoned slow-roasted pork in its green chili sauce along servings of rice and whole pinto beans. He tore the hot corn *tortillas* into quarters, picked up delicate pieces of pork with some rice and beans, and ate them without utensils.

He watched Oso again as he ate. He had not left his post near the bar and was undoubtedly on-duty there. He saw a taller and thinner clean-shaven man walk over to Oso, lean close to him, and appear to say something into his ear. Oso nodded his head and the other man walked away toward the front door and out of sight.

Jerrod finished the plate of *chili verde* and enjoyed the last sips of his beer. Rafael removed the empty plate.

"Dessert, sir?" Rafael asked.

"Pass, thank you," he said. "I'll take the check though."

Rafael pulled out a small black folder from his back pocket and searched through a number of checks before pulling one out and placing it on the table face down.

"Rafael, who's the big guy standing over by the bar?"

He looked over and said, "Everyone calls him 'Oso.' He is security here."

"Do you know his real name?"

"No, sir. Just Oso."

"Thank you, Rafael."

"Thank you, sir."

Jerrod glanced at the bill and placed seventeen dollars on the table to cover the dinner bill and a healthy tip.

He got up and walked toward the front door. He saw Maggie talking to a group at a table and waved goodbye to her. She smiled and waved back.

He walked past the bar and found Oso's eyes focused on him. From about four feet away, he stopped, squared his shoulders, and glared back at Oso. The two men locked eyes for a few seconds.

"Do we have a problem... *friend*?" Jerrod said – intentionally not addressing him by his "street" name.

Oso's eyes narrowed and he looked more bull than bear as he took a step toward him. An attack was imminent. Jerrod held his ground and instinctively swept his right hand under his sport jacket – forgetting his Beretta 9mm auto-pistol was not attached to his belt.

Oso glanced at Jerrod's right hand and paused. Maggie stepped between the two men. She whispered something in Spanish to Oso – causing him to back away and resume his post at the bar.

Maggie walked over to Jerrod. Her fake smile was easy to spot. "Thank you for coming in tonight," she said. "Please bring Natalie with you next time, okay." She then took him by the arm and walked him to the door.

"Thanks, Maggie. The meal was great," he said while his eyes were still locked on Oso.

CHAPTER 14

Maggie walked back toward the bar as the expression on her face changed from fake smile to hard frown. She stepped to within inches of Oso's face and said under her breath, "Come with me."

Oso followed Maggie to her private office.

"Sit down."

The wooden chair creaked when Oso sat as he was directed.

She closed the office door and plopped into her plush black leather desk chair.

Oso said, "Maggie—" and was cut off when she thrust the palm of her hand toward him and turned her head, so he saw only the side of her face.

His fists clenched at her rude interruption, but he contained his anger knowing who was in charge of the conversation.

"Shut the fuck up, Oso. Do you know who that man you just had your little confrontation with is? Do you? Are you an idiot? Or what?"

"He's just a stupid city cop," he said. "Screw him. What can he do?"

"By himself, not too much," she said. "But he may be smart enough to use a telephone. And with a telephone, he could get state or federal police interested in us. That's what he can do."

Oso started to say something but changed his mind.

"I know you don't like cops and you don't have to make nice with the ones who come in here. But do not piss them off and bring unwanted attention on us. Understand?"

"I understand, Maggie. Sorry."

"Get back to work," she said as she flipped her hand at him and turned her head away.

Oso lifted his huge frame and carefully positioned the chair back to where it had been. He left the office and closed the door quietly.

Maggie leaned back in her chair and stared at the ceiling for a few moments. She jumped to her feet, looked into a small mirror on the wall, fixed her frenzied black hair back into a neat bun, put on her public smile, and marched back into the restaurant.

CHAPTER 15

As Jerrod drove home, he found himself perplexed by what happened at the restaurant. *Why would Maggie, a successful woman with a thriving business, hire a hothead like Oso for any position at her restaurant?*

There was more to the story, and he intended to learn what it was. Finding out more about Oso would be first on the list.

In his home, he turned on the TV and changed into a pair of green surgical scrub pants Natalie had "relocated" from the hospital for him. He switched on the small front porch light.

He was watching *Magnum, P.I.* when the twin beams of headlights swept across the drawn curtains covering the living room picture window. A car with a small engine pulled into the driveway and the headlights shut off. He walked to the front door and opened it as Natalie reached the front step.

He held the door open, and she pushed past him into the living room. Her expression told him something was wrong.

"Is everything okay?"

"Jerrod. We need to talk."

"Sure," he said as he invited her to sit down on the sofa.

Holy shit was the first thought through Jerrod's mind. The questions in his brain came fast and furious: *What the hell was wrong? Are we done? Has she met a new guy? Is she sick? Is she pregnant? What could this emergency be?*

He turned off the TV and sat with her.

"What's up, Nat?" he said as he felt his heart starting to beat faster.

"You know I've always wanted to be a nurse, an RN, right?"

"Of course," he said as his heart rate returned toward normal.

"I was talking with one of the new ER nurses today on break."

"Okay," he said.

"She went to a nursing program in San Diego and there's a new class starting in a month or so."

"I thought you were looking at the program at Mesa Community College. That's right here. Why San Diego?"

Her speech started getting faster as she said, "Mesa's program is a part-time deal. The San Diego classes are full-time. I have a cousin who lives near there. I talked to her..." and she started to cry.

Jerrod moved over and hugged her. She held him and cried onto his chest.

"No decisions need to be made tonight," he whispered.

After a minute, they let the embrace relax and he smiled while looking into her familiar brown eyes. He motioned to her with his hand that her mascara had run. She excused herself and went into the bathroom.

Jerrod resisted the temptation to turn the TV back on as he was accustomed to it being on at all times when he was home.

Natalie returned from the bathroom with a clean face and a handful of tissues. As she sat back down, he was reminded she was more beautiful without make-up.

"What do you want to do?" he asked.

"I don't know." She sighed. "There's a lot of things that would need to be done if I left here for a year or two. My mom is going to be the biggest issue."

"What can I do?"

"That's the thing," she said as her eyes welled up with tears again. "I don't know where we are in our relationship."

"Seems to be fine to me," he said.

"Sure. Fine for you. You have your job. You have your house. You have everything you've always wanted."

"That's not fair."

"I'm twenty-six and still live with my mom, for Christ's sake." Her emotions shifted toward anger.

"Look, I can't make any decisions for you, but I'll support whatever you decide," he said as his heart rate started to rise again.

"I don't want to fight with you," she said. "We can talk about this some other time."

"Okay. I love you and don't want to fight."

She sat upright on the sofa, looked him in the eyes, and asked, "Are we ever going to get married?"

Jerrod was caught off guard and stammered as he searched for an answer.

"I don't know... maybe... our relationship is... odd."

"'Odd.' Really?"

"Well, not 'odd.' Wrong word. Take it back. 'Unusual.'"

Natalie just shook her head and they sat in silence for a few minutes.

"Got anything to drink?" she asked.

"Beer. Vodka. No wine, though. He was glad she changed the subject.

"Vodka with orange juice."

Jerrod went to the kitchen, filled a glass with ice and poured in some vodka. He went into the refrigerator and found an open bottle of orange juice. He removed the top and smelled the contents. It seemed okay to drink. He topped off the glass with juice and opened a bottle of Heineken for himself.

He returned to the sofa and handed the drink to her. She sipped at the drink and then took a large gulp.

"I don't know what to do with you," she said.

"You can do anything you want with me... baby."

They both laughed and the mood lightened.

"I had dinner at Nopales tonight."

"Nopales? Without me? Really?"

"The food was real good, but I had a little confrontation when I was leaving with a big dude named 'Oso' who works for Maggie."

"What happened?" she asked as she took another gulp.

"We just had a little stand-off near the bar. He was glaring at me, I said something to him, he made a move, Maggie stepped in, and I left. That's all."

"'That's all?' Two guys trying to prove who had the longest dick or what?"

"It wasn't like that. That guy, Oso, well, there's something else going on there."

"Glad you made it out alive," she said with a huge grin. "You'd might have lost the 'dick' thing, by the way."

"Ouch."

Natalie nearly spilled the rest of her drink when he tackled her on the sofa.

CHAPTER 16

The detectives considered Fridays, especially payday Fridays, to be special holidays.

Friday was their day to close as many cases and tie up as many loose ends as possible before getting out of the office on time in order to enjoy the precious weekend off.

Jerrod Gold had a different agenda. The incident at Nopales was gnawing at him. Something just didn't smell right. His objective that day was to identify Oso and find out all he could about him.

It was personal.

The detectives went through their morning routine.

Willie Sanchez was on the phone and whispered into the receiver, "I love you."

"I love you, too," Pete Hanson said.

"I love you more," Jerrod said.

"I love you the most," Craig Wallace said.

"Screw all you guys. That was my wife," Willie said... after making sure the receiver was hung up.

Jerrod announced he had some follow-up to do and would be back by lunch. He grabbed a couple case files to make it look official.

He knew Garcia's Mexican Food opened at ten and he walked through the screen door to the restaurant at five-after-ten. He was greeted as usual by Sal Garcia. No other customers were in the restaurant.

"Hello, Detective," he said. "What can I get for you?"

"Sal, I have a question for you. You're not in any trouble, so don't worry."

"Good. How can I help?

"A man came in the restaurant the last time I was here, Wednesday. A big guy. You called him 'Oso.'"

"Yes. Oso. Yes. He comes in here all the time. He always gets the *asada* like you do, Jerrod."

"Do you know anything about him, Sal? What his full name is, where he works, where he lives, or the kind of car he drives? Anything?"

"No. Not really. I saw him get into a blue car a few weeks ago. Another man was driving. I don't know if it was Oso's car or not."

"Does he come in here often?"

“Nearly every day. At about eleven. Almost every day. What did he do?”

“Nothing at this point. I was just curious about him, that’s all.”

“Okay.”

“Thanks, Sal. Please don't mention this conversation to anyone, okay.”

“Sure. Okay. Do you want something to-go? Breakfast burrito, maybe?”

“Not this morning, but thanks,” Jerrod said. “See you later.”

“See you later.”

Jerrod looked at his watch and it was ten-fifteen. He decided to find a safe place to park and watch the restaurant for a while. He backed his car into a stall in a parking lot across the street which gave him a good view of the business and the streets around it. He rolled down his window and was pleased, for a change, when he felt the chilly bite of the ocean-cooled fall air that would keep his car from becoming an oven.

He sat for nearly an hour and was getting ready to leave when a medium-blue colored four-door sedan pulled up to the curb in front of Garcia's. He recognized the unmistakable build and full beard of Oso as he climbed out of the car from the front passenger door and walked into the restaurant. Another man stayed seated behind the steering wheel of the car.

He started the car and placed a small pad of paper on his lap. He tested a pen to make sure it worked. He pulled out of the parking stall and drove through the lot so he could take a long look at the blue car by approaching it from the rear.

He waited for cross traffic to pass and then pulled onto the roadway. He drove just under the speed limit and started taking mental notes about the features of the car by speaking out-loud.

“It's an about '78 or '79 Olds Delta 88. California Plate. 3-3-9-Frank-Adam-Sam. 3-3-9-Frank-Adam-Sam. 3-3-9-Frank-Adam-Sam,” he said as he used the police-version of the phonetic alphabet for the letters “F,” “A,” and “S.”

He glanced at the face of the man in the driver's seat and was surprised to see him looking right back at him as he drove by. He estimated the man to be Latino, about thirty-years old, with short black hair and no facial hair.

He picked his speed up a little, signaled, and made a right turn at the next intersection. He drove about a block and stopped at the curb. He wrote, in police brevity, "339FAS" and "med blu 78 79 Olds 88 LMA 30 short blk no facial" on the pad of paper.

Jerrod drove back to the PD and walked directly to Dispatch. Al Kees was on duty.

"Hey, Al. Can you run a license plate for me?" he said.

"Sure. Go ahead."

"3-3-9-Frank-Adam-Sam," he said as he read from the piece of paper.

Al wrote the license number down on a spiral-bound stenographers notepad kept at the Dispatch desk. He then typed the number onto the keyboard into the California Law Enforcement Telecommunications Systems, or CLETS terminal — the only computer in the VVPD.

It took under five seconds to get a reply from the California Department of Motor Vehicle's data base.

"1978 Oldsmobile. Sedan," Al said. "Current owner is a local. Registered to 'Efrain G. Hernandez' with an address on Fourth Street."

"Efrain Hernandez, awesome," Jerrod said. "Can we get a driver's license on that name?"

"Pretty common name," Al said. "Got a birth date or age?"

"No DOB," Jerrod said. "He's around thirty."

"Let's try it," Al said. "I'll use 1955 as the birth year. It'll give a couple years each way."

He punched the information into CLETS.

"Efrain Gomez Hernandez," Al said. "Same Fourth Street address. DOB in 1956. One traffic conviction. No accidents."

"Looks like my guy," Jerrod said.

"Want hard-copies?

"Sure. Print 'em up, please."

Al punched a single key on the keyboard and a noisy tractor-fed printer attached to a box of fan-folded continuous paper printed out the DMV information.

Al pulled the sheets off the printer and handed it to him

"Thanks, Al. I—" he started to say.

"I know, I know. You 'owe me one,' blah, blah," he said with a smile. "Now please go away. I'm busy."

"See you later," Jerrod said.

"Much later. I hope," Al said.

"Do you *always* get the last word?"

"Always."

Jerrod had met his match and decided to just walk away.

Captain Andrew Wheaton was sitting in his office near the Dispatch Center and had overheard the banter between Jerrod and Al.

Jerrod went to the half-door of the Records Section to check the arrest records for "Efrain Gomez Hernandez."

He was pleased to find the Records Supervisor, Ann Rogers, on-duty. Ann was in her early-forties and had been with the VVPD for nearly twenty years. She seemed comfortable with the subtle streaks of gray in her Purdey-style hair made popular at the time by Princess Diana. She had a certain difficult-to-describe elegance about her. Her movements were light and fluid like those of a skilled dancer or gymnast.

Ann also had a very sharp tongue.

"I'll check," Ann said after taking the DMV printout and walking gracefully away to a worn wooden cabinet containing a set of 3x5 index cards. The cards contained the identifying information for anyone arrested by the VVPD going back into the 1940s.

"I found one with a domestic violence arrest from last year," Ann said. "Home address on Fourth Street. Want me to pull the file?"

"Yes, please."

Ann took the index card and glided to a wall containing file folders of arrest records on shelves from the floor to ceiling. She walked her slender fingertips along the files until she found the one she wanted and pulled it from the others. She laid the file on the narrow ledge atop the half-door.

"Thank you."

Jerrod opened the file and was pleased to find three booking photos of Efrain Hernandez attached to the arrest report from 1984. He studied the photo and was reasonably certain it had been the driver of the blue Oldsmobile. He was less sure it had been the man he had seen speak briefly with Oso at Nopales the previous night.

The arrest report listed Hernandez' height, weight and identifying marks. The record listed the prosecution result as "dismissed" and listed a VVPD crime report number.

"Ann, may I take one of these booking photos, get a copy of this arrest report, and the crime report that goes with the DV arrest?"

"Want me to get you some lunch too?" she said.

"Everyone's a comedian today," he said. "I'd get the records myself, but I know you'd throw something at me if I walked in there and started messing up 'the system.'"

"Good point," she said. "Here's the crime report. I'm going to just make a copy of everything 'cause you're going to ask me for them anyway."

"Thank you."

Jerrod got the copies from Ann and walked down the hallway to the bureau. The door was open and found only Craig sitting at his desk.

"Where's Hanson and Willie?" Jerrod asked.

"Willie's helping Hanson on a case. It is a Spanish-speaking thing."

"Sounds interesting. Glad I'm not involved," Jerrod said.

"Where've you been all morning?"

"Out handling my massive caseload of misdemeanors. All my investigative skills being tested daily. In quantity, not necessarily quality. You know."

"I only handle 'big' cases. I wouldn't know," Craig said without breaking character.

"I feel like Dean Martin in an office full of Jerry Lewises this morning."

The detectives laughed and Craig lit a fresh cigarette.

"Those things are going to kill you," Jerrod said as he pointed to the cigarette and feigned a cough.

"I figure I'm going to die from something," Craig said. "I started smoking in the Marines, in-country, in 'Nam, and I survived that fucked-up year in the jungle. I am not afraid of these little things." He held up and admired the cigarette before taking a very long drag from it.

"Oh, okay, I get it," Jerrod said. "Cigarette smoke is now a 'protective force' that can actually *save* your life. That's it, I'm calling the Surgeon's General office and telling him to change the warning label. Better yet, I'm calling whoever makes Salem 100s and pitching a new commercial to them. You'll be the star. Screw police work, I'm going into advertising. Madison Avenue better lookout, I'm on the way."

"Good luck with that," Craig said. "What are you working on... *really?*"

"I don't know... *really*. What do you mean?"

"I know you pretty well by now. You don't fool me, pal."

"I had this weird little confrontation in a restaurant last night with a big dude named Oso. There was no fight or anything, but he was maddogging me as I was about to leave. I said something to him and the next thing I know the owner is walking me outside."

"You got kicked out?"

"No. I know the owner and she just escorted me to the door."

"Sounds like *kicked-out* to me."

"Whatever. It was really weird. There was something else going on. It's just a gut thing. I have to check it out."

"Have fun," Craig said. "Why don't you just take out a new case number and add it to your stack. No wonder you get buried under your pile of cases."

Jerrod didn't answer. He knew Craig was right. He hated the volume of low-priority cases he was assigned and the juggling act he had to perform with them every day. *Detective work was so damn glorious,* Jerrod thought.

Jerrod read the crime report documenting Efrain Hernandez' 1984 arrest. He had been charged with felony domestic violence after brutally beating his nineteen-year-old and eight-month pregnant live-in girlfriend. Her name was Martha Figueroa. She had received cracked ribs, a broken finger, a bruised and swollen face, a concussion, and nearly lost the baby. She spent four days in the hospital, and he went to jail.

The arresting officer had been Rusty Browne.

A follow-up report in the file said all charges had been dismissed when Martha Figueroa recanted her entire statement and said she had been attacked by a stranger. She had refused to testify at Hernandez' preliminary hearing and the District Attorney's Office had, therefore, no evidence to prosecute with. They had no choice but to dismiss the charges.

"Nice guy," Jerrod said to himself.

"What was that?" Craig asked.

"Nothing. Just reading a crime report," Jerrod said as he threw the report on his desk and picked up one from the continuously growing stack of real cases needing attention.

CHAPTER 17

Jerrod answered his desk phone on the first ring.

"Detective Gold?" the caller asked.

"It is."

"This is Andrew Wheaton."

"Good morning... sir."

"Will you come see me in my office?"

"Be right there, sir." He hung up the phone and held his hand on the receiver.

"What's up?" Craig asked.

"Captain wants to see me. I don't know what it's about."

"Better you than me."

Jerrod walked down the hallway and was passing Dispatch when Al Kees gave him the "what do you want now" look. Jerrod held up both palms as he walked by and gave him the "relax, I don't need a damn thing... right now" look.

He walked into Captain Wheaton's office and asked, "Door open or closed, sir?"

"Close it please and have a seat."

Jerrod sat in an uncomfortable wooden chair next to the captain's desk as directed.

"How have you been, Jerrod?"

"Good, sir. Busy."

"I heard part of your conversation with Al. What are you working on these days?"

"Just some follow-up on those heroin OD cases, sir."

"Any good leads on those cases so far?"

"Some leads. We've had two ODs here, one dead and one alive, and the Sheriff's Office has two dead ones as well. One man and a young woman. They've all been in the last week or so, sir."

"Stay on this. You're doing a good job."

"Thank you, sir."

"I remember when we hired you, Jerrod. You were still a few months short of your twenty-first birthday then. You had placed at the very top of the police officer testing and came highly recommended by the officers who knew you. I convinced the chief to hire you despite your age."

"I appreciate that, sir."

"Do you remember the question I asked you the day I offered you the job?"

"No, sir. I was pretty excited about getting hired. That day was my dream come true."

"Well, as I recall, I asked you whether you were either 'very good or just an incredible bullshitter?' Your answer was, and I'll never forget it, 'A little of both, sir.'"

"That was pretty bold," Jerrod said. "For a new guy, that is."

"Yes, it was. But I liked that about you then and I like it about you now. You have become a particularly good officer and I've never regretted my decision back then."

"Thank you, sir," Jerrod said while wondering where the conversation was going.

"Please keep me posted on this OD situation. Will you, son?"

"Yes, sir," Jerrod said as he stood up and left the office.

Jerrod walked back to the detective bureau trying not to read too much into the conversation with the captain.

He had remembered every single word spoken during the 1980 conversation with Captain Andrew Wheaton. He was still very good *and* an incredible bullshitter.

"Want to get lunch? Jerrod asked Craig. "I need to talk to you about something."

"Okay. Let's go," Craig said. "No chili dogs or Mexican food, please. My stomach can't handle that stuff like you can."

The detectives locked the bureau door and left the PD lot in Jerrod's car.

"Where to for lunch? You pick a place that won't upset your tummy."

"Very funny. How about that Japanese place over by your house? 'The Geisha,' or something."

"'The Ginza.' Good call," Jerrod said as he turned the unmarked car east from the PD.

"What did you need to talk about?" Craig asked.

"I just had the weirdest conversation with Wheaton."

"What was weird about it?"

"He wanted to know about what I was working on, and I told him about the OD cases. But why the hell would he care about them?"

"Maybe he's afraid the chief will ask him about the ODs, and he just wanted to have an answer for him," Craig offered.

"Maybe so. I don't know. It was weird, that's all I have to say about it."

"Wheaton *is* weird, but not in a bad way."

"I've never worked with him directly, so what do you mean?" Jerrod asked.

"He was still a lieutenant when I started. He was fine to work for and got promoted to captain in about 1974. He doesn't drink, doesn't fool around on his wife, and goes to church at Saint Daniel's two or three times a week."

"How come he didn't get the chief job when the old chief stroked-out in his office a few years ago?" Jerrod asked.

"Well, that's not really clear. Wheaton became the acting chief when the old chief went down, and it looked like he was going to be the next chief. However, according to the rumor-mill at least, the city manager and the mayor didn't like him much and decided to open the position up to outside candidates. They ended up passing over Wheaton and hiring the new chief.

"Was Wheaton pissed?" Jerrod asked.

"He probably was, but you wouldn't know by talking to him. I haven't ever heard him say anything bad about the new chief. And as it is, Wheaton runs the day-to-day operation at the PD anyway. The new chief rarely comes out of his office."

"Okay. I believe you. But our conversation was still pretty damn weird."

The detectives arrived at The Ginza and were quickly seated. The former house-converted-to-restaurant was small, having maybe ten tables. The food was good, and the price was reasonable.

Craig ordered *teriyaki* chicken and Jerrod ordered a plate of *tempura*. They sipped hot black tea and ate *miso* soup when Jerrod asked, "Any plans this weekend?"

"Not really. The kid has a softball game tomorrow and I think we'll just have a quiet couple days otherwise. How about you?"

"I'll do my lawns in the morning. And I'll probably go out with Nat tomorrow night. I'll just let her pick what we do."

"Smart boy," Craig said.

The entrees arrived and the detectives were quiet as they enjoyed their meals.

As they finished, the waitress asked if they wanted any dessert. Craig passed, but Jerrod ordered some green tea ice cream.

"Where do you store all the food you eat? You should weigh 300 pounds the way you put it down."

"Good genetics, I guess," Jerrod said while intentionally failing to mention the recent discovery of love-handles on his sides.

On the way back to the PD, Jerrod drove by the Fourth Street address of Efrain Hernandez and found no blue Oldsmobile there.

CHAPTER 18

All four investigators were quietly working on their cases at their detective bureau desks as Huey Lewis and The News played “The Power of Love” on KHJB.

Jerrod’s desk phone rang, and he found Al Kees on the line.

“Patrol just picked up that guy you were looking for. Valdemar Reyes. They're bringing him in now,” he said.

“Thanks, Al. Awesome. Who found him?”

“The Kevins.”

“Two steak dinners. Shit. This better be worth it.”

Jerrod was standing in booking when The Kevins brought Valdemar Reyes into the jail.

“Good afternoon, Val,” Jerrod said. “How have you been?”

“Officer Gold, excuse me, *Detective Gold* now,” Val said.

“I have some questions for you,” Jerrod said.

“I want a lawyer,” the wiry parolee said.

“You're only here on a PAL hold,” Jerrod said. “You’re going to be RTC and back at Soledad in a week. You don't need a lawyer.”

RTC was a prison term for “Returned To Custody.”

“I don't have anything to say,” Val said.

“I haven't asked you any questions yet. Just relax. Are you going to be ‘sick’? I can get you something.”

Getting “sick” was a street term for heroin withdrawal.

“I've done it before,” Val said. “I'll be okay. But thanks though.”

“You're welcome,” Jerrod said.

“How did you find him?” Jerrod asked The Kevins. “Did he run?”

“Nope,” Big Kevin said. “We were on a traffic stop and he walked up to us—”

“He told us who he was,” Tall Kevin interrupted. “And said he was wanted on a parole violation. It was that easy.”

Jerrod thanked The Kevins and asked them to book Val Reyes and to put him in a jail cell when they were done.

About a half hour later, Jerrod returned to the jail and brought with him two cans of Coca-Cola he purchased in the squad room vending machine. None of the other cells were occupied.

He unlocked the door to the cell Val Reyes was in and sat down in the bunk directly across from him. He handed him one of the Cokes. Val thanked him.

“What have you been up to, Val?” Jerrod said to start the conversation. “I read the crime reports every day and I know you haven't been 'burging houses since you got released.”

“I seem to get by,” Val said.

“Val, we've had three of your friends killed by the new heroin on the street. Your girlfriend was almost the fourth. You saved her life when you called us. I'm not going to bullshit you. This new stuff is going to kill more people... people you know.”

“I don't know anything about it.”

“Can I see your arms, Val?”

He looked at both of Val’s inner elbows and saw dozens of fresh puncture marks.

“Need to ‘shoot’ what, twenty times a day now so you *don't* OD?”

Val hung his head and didn't need to answer.

“I'm not looking to make you a witness,” Jerrod said. “I just want to find the source of the new *junk* and get a handle on it, so we don't have more dead users.”

Val shook his head and then chewed his lip for a few seconds.

“All I know is it comes up from Mexico,” Val said. “It gets smuggled just over the border in small packages. Someone from here goes down and collects the packages of dope. They bring it to Valle Verde for processing.”

“Go on.”

“This *chiva* is at least five times stronger than what we usually see around here,” Val said. “They process it over and over, but still can't get the dose right. They're making... probably making a fortune on that shit.”

“Who's bringing it here, Val?” Jerrod said as he leaned closer into him.

Val appeared defeated and began to speak but stopped.

“It's just you and me in here, Val. No one will ever know we had this conversation.”

Val was silent. He closed his eyes and shook his head. He licked his lips several times. He looked like he was starting to feel the first physical effects of heroin withdrawal.

“You've always been straight with me,” Val said.

Jerrod nodded and moved closer to him.

“But I can't tell you that. You must be fucking crazy. All I *can* say is it's way bigger than you, Detective.”

Jerrod returned to the detective bureau and briefed Pete Hanson on the information he had just learned from Val Reyes. He said he would, in turn, relay the information to Captain Wheaton.

The sergeant announced he was leaving with his family for Lake Tahoe right after work and would be back Sunday evening. He designated Craig as in-charge should they get called-out to anything over the weekend.

The detectives finished their otherwise uneventful Friday afternoon and went home to enjoy their weekend off.

On his way home, Jerrod drove by the Fourth Street address of Efrain Hernandez and again found no blue Oldsmobile parked there.

CHAPTER 19

Jerrod got home and found Natalie busy in the kitchen preparing some rice and a green salad. She had picked up two beautifully marbled New York strip steaks and all he had to do was grill them.

He changed from his suit into a t-shirt and jeans. He grabbed a Heineken from the refrigerator and took the steaks outside. He started the gas barbecue.

Charles Horvat was in his backyard smoking a cigarette and Jerrod signaled for him to come over.

"Beer, Colonel?"

"Love one."

Jerrod ran into the house and returned a few seconds later with another Heineken.

"Here you go, sir."

"Thank you," he said as he took a drink.

"This weekend's getting off to a good start," Jerrod said.

"Indeed. I see your lady friend is here."

"Yes, she is."

The two men stood in silence for a few moments as the steaks sizzled against the hot grill.

The colonel said, "Did I ever tell you about the twin brothers I was stationed with in New Guinea during World War II?"

"I don't believe you have, sir."

"Well, me and these two brothers, Henry and Harvey Dye, were assigned to an ordnance company together and we became particularly good friends. They were from a tiny town in Louisiana named 'Faye' and both just loved to fish. All they could talk about was fishing. Non-stop."

Jerrod flipped the steaks.

"One day, both brothers caught pieces of shrapnel when a shell exploded, and they were damn lucky they didn't get killed. They spent a month or so in the hospital and were sent home. The last time I talked to them they told me they were the happiest men in the world — they could put on their waders, walk out their back door to a nearby stream, step into the water, and fish all day long."

"That's interesting, sir. But I don't get the point."

"The point is: Old Soldiers named Dye; they just Wade at Faye."

The steaks were grilled to perfection and Jerrod thanked the colonel for "reeling him in" one more time.

In the kitchen, the rice was cooked and the salad in bowls. The steaks went on a platter, and he took them to the dining room table. The table was intimately set for two. A single lighted candle. An open bottle of wine. White cotton napkins folded neatly on the plates.

"Some feast. Our birthdays are both in March, so what's the occasion?"

"No occasion." she said. "Just happy to be with you."

"Thank you." he said.

"You are very welcome."

"Want to go out later?"

"Nope. Just want to stay here."

"That's okay with me."

After they savored their delicious meal, they took their glasses of wine to the sofa. The TV was off. He knew the Giants were playing the Dodgers at that very moment... but he didn't care.

"Want to do something this weekend?" he said. "Dinner? Movie? Marathon lovemaking?"

"All three sound good," she said. "Maybe we can go to Nopales for dinner?"

"Maybe not Nopales," he said. "We can try somewhere else."

"Why?"

"I had that 'thing' there last night. We can go there some other time."

"Fine," she said, in the tone women use to make F-I-N-E sound both like a profane four-letter-word and a threat at the same time.

"Okay. Okay. Nopales it is. But I'm taking my Beretta... just in case."

"I love you," she said.

"I love you, too."

CHAPTER 20

Stella Leiter watched the reflection of her face swirl away with the water of the flushing toilet. Her dash into the bathroom to retch for the ninth time that day had been in vain.

There was nothing left to vomit.

She was starting to feel better from the heroin withdrawals but had lost all interest in the drug after the overdose the day before. She had come to grips with the fact it at almost killed her and the experience scared her straight.

She shook her head as she thought about the path her life had taken since her first introduction to heroin: North Texas. Seventeen years old. A boyfriend her mother hated... and for good reason. She had watched him "fix" and then fall into a deep and comfortable stupor. She finally gave in. She agreed to "skin pop," but he injected into a vein. Her body instantly felt warm and peaceful. It was like slipping into a soothing bath after a grueling day. She felt no pain and had no fears... for about two hours.

She used it again and again trying to revisit the feel of that first time.

It was never the same.

The boyfriend eventually left her, and she found herself both physically and psychologically addicted. Her daily routine evolved into a simple cycle: Wake up. Get money. Score dope. Shoot dope. Sleep. Repeat.

At the peak of her addiction, she needed to score over three hundred dollars' worth of heroin daily to "stay well" and not feel the effects of withdrawals. She no longer cared about that warm feeling and only feared the pain that came with detox.

Other necessities — eating, exercise, and personal hygiene — became far less important than the drug her body craved.

She wasn't able to keep a job more than a week at a time and the money she did make never covered the cost of her addiction.

She supplemented her income by taking cash and small valuables from her family and friends. They soon told her to stay away from their homes. Her mother told her to never come back.

She tried shoplifting and other petty thefts, but those escapades got her arrested a few times.

She eventually turned to hooking — an all-cash business where nobody got hurt. She found she could make three to five hundred a day... if she saw enough men.

Her addiction continued since then and she never again felt the wonderful sensations of that very first time.

She had gone through heroin detox twice previously. Both times in jail. It had taken a few days to recover then. She had once described "cold-turkey" heroin withdrawal to a friend as, "Suffering through the worst case of flu you have ever had... multiplied by ten."

This time it had been not nearly as bad and didn't last as long. Her stomach ached, she had a slight fever, and some chills.

It felt more like a bad cold.

Maybe the injections the EMTs gave to revive her helped. She would never know for sure.

She sat in her hotel room contemplating the rent due the following morning. She had used all the money Val had given her before his arrest.

She searched the pockets of every piece of clothing. Every bag. Every drawer. Beneath every cushion. And under the bed.

She came up with three one-dollar bills and some loose change.

She knew of only one way to make quick cash on short notice. She didn't enjoy doing it. Not at all.

Stella was tired and still feeling ill when she washed her face, fixed her hair, got dressed, and headed downtown.

CHAPTER 21

Saturday

Jerrod Gold had just fallen back to sleep from a disturbing dream when his telephone rang. He glanced at the clock, and it read: 1:33. He fumbled with the receiver and answered the phone on the second ring.

"Jerrod, this is Dispatch," the female dispatcher said.

"How you doing? Social call, I hope?"

The dispatcher was unamused – which woke him up quickly.

"Sergeant Murray wants you to go to the scene of a dead body on the west side. Detective Wallace has already been called and is on his way."

"Yeah. No problem. Where's the scene?"

The dispatcher gave him the location.

"I'll be there in fifteen minutes."

Natalie had been awakened by the call.

"What's up?"

"Dead-one on the west side. I'm going to help Craig. Probably another OD."

"Be careful."

"I promise," he said as he kissed her and got out of bed.

Jerrod dressed and quietly collected his police equipment. He went outside and found it to be a bitterly cold and windy morning. His car was covered in dew, and he waited as the engine idled long enough for the defroster to clear the windshield.

He drove through his quiet neighborhood and the deserted downtown streets of Valle Verde to the industrial area on the west side of the city. He turned onto the street the dispatcher had given him and there was no doubt he was in the right place.

The street was blocked by three VVPD patrol cars with their red and blue overhead lights activated. Several uniformed patrol officers were milling around. Bright yellow CRIME SCENE DO NOT ENTER tape had been liberally strung from power poles to various signs and from the patrol cars to mark the restricted area of the scene.

He parked his car on the roadway just outside the crime scene tape. A frigid wind welcomed him, and he zipped his too-lightweight raid jacket to the collar. He walked to the edge of the scene and was met by patrol Sergeant John Murray.

Sergeant Murray had been with the VVPD for over twenty-five years. He was a well-respected and no-nonsense supervisor who was very much in charge at the scene.

"Good morning, Detective," greeted the fifty-year old gray-haired sergeant.

"Good morning, Sarge," he said. "What do you have for us this fine morning?"

"We got a radio call of a 'man-down' out here at 0105 hours," he said. "Dispatch said a woman reported finding a body after being dropped off here. That woman is over there talking to your partner." He pointed into the scene and at Craig Wallace.

"The body is wrapped in plastic and there's a lot of blood. The coroner has been notified and should be on the way," he said.

"Thanks, Sarge," Jerrod said. "Okay if I go inside?"

"Go right ahead," the sergeant said as he lifted a ribbon of crime scene tape for him to walk under.

Jerrod, as he had learned to do from Craig, paused to scrutinize the area as he entered the scene. He made mental notes of the temperature, wind speed and direction, and the amount of moisture in the air and on the ground.

He also noted smells. That morning it happened to be the overwhelming flatulent smell from the broccoli and cauliflower being processed at a nearby frozen food plant.

He walked toward Craig and found him talking with a woman whose back was to him. As he got closer, he shined his flashlight on the woman and recognized the wild red hair belonging to no other than Stella Leiter — the OD from the hospital earlier that week.

"Good morning, Stella," Jerrod said.

Stella whipped her head around at the sound of her name and said, "You? Again?"

"That's right. Feeling better?"

"Better than the other day. Thanks."

"Morning, Craig," he said to his partner. "What's happened so far?"

"I got here a few minutes before you. Sergeant Murray briefed me on the scene. I was just starting to get some info from Stella here."

Jerrod looked at Stella and asked, "So what brings you way out here in the middle of the night?"

"I'd rather not say," she said.

"Perhaps you'd *rather* go to the police department where you can sit for a while and gather your thoughts." Craig said. "You may need a few hours or a couple days to think, or we can do it right now and you can go home."

"I don't want to go to jail. I'll tell you what happened."

"Go ahead," Jerrod said.

"I got picked up by a 'date' downtown who was willing to pay twenty-five dollars for sex. I got into his car, and he drove me out here. We did... our business... and he paid me. I told him I needed to pee, so I got out of the car and walked near that building to clean up a little."

Stella averted her eyes from the detectives.

"Don't worry about it," Craig said.

"Sorry. I'm not proud of what I do, but it's what I have to do sometimes," she said as tears brimmed her eyes.

The detectives gave her a few moments to collect herself and then continued the interview.

In a soft tone, Jerrod asked, "What happened next, Stella?"

"I walked over to the shadows and got out one of the little towelettes I carry. I squatted down and looked over to my right and saw the roll of plastic."

"Go on," Craig said.

"I finished and threw the towelette on the ground. I stood up and walked over to the plastic and could see there was blood around one end of it. I looked closer and it looked like a person inside the plastic."

"And then what happened?" Jerrod asked.

"I screamed and ran back to the car," she said. "I tried to get in the car, but I guess I scared the guy, and he took off without me. I didn't know what to do. I started walking back to town and found a gas station that was open. I told the man in the station I thought there was a dead body and he called you guys."

Stella started to cry as she added, "I hope it's not one of my friends."

"Stella, you did good tonight," Craig said. "We're going to have you sit in a nice warm patrol car for a few minutes while we look a little closer at things. Is that alright?"

"Sure," she said and added, "Do you have a cigarette?"

Craig held out his pack of Salem 100s and shook the pack until a cigarette protruded enough for Stella to pluck it out with her bony fingers. Craig lit the cigarette for her, and she closed her eyes as she took the first drag. She seemed to calm down as she was escorted to a patrol car by a uniformed officer.

The detectives stopped to study the scene. They asked themselves objectively if Stella's story fit with what they were seeing. Or did it conflict with it? Their experience had taught them to compare the physical evidence against witness statements and to formulate reasonable and logical explanations for everything found at the scene.

A patrol officer, Dave Yamamoto, was guarding the plastic-wrapped body. Jerrod and Dave had gone to school together from elementary through high school and worked in Patrol together. They were close friends.

“Hey, Dave,” Jerrod said.

“Hey, Jerrod. Sorry you guys got called out of your cozy warm beds this morning.”

“Anything to spend some quality time with you, brother.”

“This is just the way we found it. No one else has been around the body except me and Sergeant Murray.”

“Thanks. Let's take a look,” Craig said.

The entire scene was paved with either concrete or asphalt, so shoe soleprint or tire-tread evidence was not likely to be found. There were no signs to suggest the body had been dragged to its location – so it had been carried there. That suggested at least two people were involved.

The body was tightly wrapped, face-down, in a piece of clear plastic sheeting. The material was much heavier than the thin plastic house painters use to cover furniture and other items they didn't want paint to get on. It was more of an industrial thickness. The type used to cover roofs or to line ponds. No tape or rope secured the plastic sheet around the body.

The body’s features were not easy to determine, but it appeared to be of average height and weight. The detectives suspected from the size it was a male. The body was dressed in dark clothing.

A large mass of blood was contained inside the plastic around the head of the body.

“What do you think, Craig?” Jerrod asked.

“I don't know at this point,” Craig said. “I don't think this is another OD. There’s way too much blood. We'll handle this as a homicide until we can show it's something else.”

Jerrod nodded.

“Let's get some photos of the scene as it is now and take a few measurements for a diagram before the coroner arrives, so he won't have to wait too long.”

Knowing Craig’s strategy for handling the scene was the correct course to take. Jerrod went back to his unmarked car and retrieved the case containing the 35mm camera. Craig retrieved a clip board and 100-foot measuring tape from his trunk.

Jerrod methodically photo-documented the scene. He began by taking orientation shots from the perimeter of the scene and then moved closer to the body. He took numerous shots of the plastic-covered body from a variety of angles.

Craig drew a rough sketch of the scene on a piece of graph paper. He plotted the roadway, concrete wall, and the position of the body. Jerrod held the "dumb-end" of the tape as Craig recorded the various distances between the body and permanent landmarks at the scene.

The detectives were taking the last few measurements when the familiar unmarked white van of the Mesa County Sheriff-Coroner arrived.

Coroner Deputy Ted Lindsey was allowed into the scene by Sergeant Murray and was greeted by the two detectives.

"We meet again," Craig said.

"Indeed," the deputy said. "This is my third call-out tonight and I'm beat. What do we have here, gentlemen?"

He was briefed by the two detectives and then pulled a pair of latex gloves from his jacket pocket.

The deputy said, "I suppose you two want some ID from this one so you can see who you are dealing with?"

The detectives nodded.

The deputy carefully rolled the body onto its back. The face was obscured with the mass of blood smeared against the plastic. The deputy looked for the most logical way to delicately remove the plastic away from the body so he could search the pants pockets for a wallet or some form of identification. He gently pulled away the plastic and a gust of wind tore the damp plastic from his gloved hand – exposing the body from the waist to the feet.

Craig was crouched near the body and Jerrod stood behind him as they watched the deputy's movements. He was startled when the wind pulled away the plastic but lost his balance and dropped to a knee when Jerrod yelled from behind him: "Oh my God."

CHAPTER 22

Jerrod knew who the dead man was the instant the plastic pulled back and exposed the pair of white and red Nike Air Jordan basketball shoes.

Deputy Lindsey found a wallet in a pants pocket and a California driver's license confirmed the dead man was, indeed, Hector Chavez Medina.

Even in the cold and wind of that morning, Jerrod's entire body felt hot. His stomach ached and his brain filled with questions: *Why Hector? What did he do to deserve this? What could I have done to prevent this from happening? How am I going to the tell Hector's mother? How am I going to tell Nat? Why am I even doing this job at all?*

"Walk with me," Craig said.

The detectives walked away from the body to a distance far enough from the others their conversation couldn't be overheard.

"That's Hector, man," Jerrod said as he fought a welling of tears in his eyes.

"I know. Get it together," Craig said.

"Why him?" Jerrod said. "What did he do?"

"We are going to find out," Craig said. "That's what *we* do."

The detectives stood together in silence for a few minutes.

"Are you good? I can call Willie and you can sit this one out."

"No fucking way," Jerrod said. "You can call Willie, but I'm not going anywhere."

"Okay. Let's go back to work."

"Give me a second, okay."

Jerrod took a few deep breaths of the chilly morning air and tried to clear his head. He knew Craig was right. Craig was always right.

He took one more very deep breath and walked back into the scene.

CHAPTER 23

Hector Medina's body was fully exposed from its plastic containment.

"No rigor mortis yet," Ted Lindsey said. "He hasn't been dead very long. There's a gunshot wound right on top of his head which accounts for all the blood. We'll know more at autopsy."

Jerrod took another series of photographs of Hector as he appeared with the plastic pulled away. Craig helped lift Hector from the plastic into a black body bag.

The detectives examined the bloodied plastic sheeting once the body was removed and found no apparent bullet hole in it.

It became obvious Hector was shot elsewhere, wrapped in the plastic, and dumped at the scene.

Jerrod rolled the plastic sheet and placed it in a large paper evidence bag. The body bag was lifted onto a gurney and loaded in the coroner van.

"I don't know when the autopsy is going to be," Ted Lindsey said. "'Doc' works his own hours. Could happen today. Could be tomorrow. Or it could be Monday. I'll call you as soon as it gets scheduled."

"Doc" was Doctor Robert Torosian, the forensic pathologist for the Mesa County Sheriff-Coroner's Office.

Craig lit a cigarette and said, "Nothing else to do here. Let's go to the office, freshen up, have some coffee, try to call Hanson, and get a game plan together."

"We'll need to call Willie in," Jerrod said. "I may need some Spanish-speaking help notifying Hector's mother."

Jerrod walked back to his car with the camera case and the paper bag containing the plastic sheet.

Craig told Sergeant Murray they were done and the scene could be released. The sergeant directed two patrol officers to remove the crime scene tape and head back to their beats. Within five minutes, the tape was gone, the cars driven away, and the area returned to its previous quiet.

The only things left behind at the scene were three questions:

The first asked why a young man — through a brutal, senseless, and merciless crime — had his life cut so short. The second question asked who, ultimately, was responsible for committing the deadly act of violence. And the final question asked, simply — what was he going to do about it.

CHAPTER 24

Jerrod and Craig drove to the PD and opened the detective bureau. It was about four o'clock and the PD was eerily quiet.

Craig called Willie at home and asked that he come in to help with the investigation. He said he would be there in a half-hour.

"I should call Hanson in 'Tahoe," Craig said. "But he's five or six hours away and I don't want to screw up his weekend."

"He'll want to know, at least," Jerrod said. "He'll kill *us* if we don't call him. He can decide whether to come back early or not."

"You're right," Craig said. "I'll wait a few hours and see what else happens before I call him."

The coffee was brewed, and the radio was on as they discussed their next moves.

Willie walked into the office, poured some coffee, and was briefed on the investigation.

"Was Hector that kid that always used to come in the PD looking for you?" Willie asked Jerrod. "If so, I remember him."

"That's the kid," Jerrod said.

Craig lit a cigarette. "I'm going to at least cover my ass now and call Wheaton at home to tell him about the murder." He pulled out a list of PD personnel home phone numbers and dialed the home number listed for Captain Andrew Wheaton.

Jerrod and Willie talked while Craig briefed the captain. Craig said into the receiver, "Okay. Thanks. I will, sir," before hanging up.

"What did he say?" Willie asked.

"He said 'to handle it' and not to bother Hanson. He asked for the phone number in Lake Tahoe and said he'd call Hanson later personally."

"Okay," Jerrod said. "We need to notify Hector's mother. Me and Willie can handle that. I know where he lived."

"Okay," Craig said. "See if the family can give us any information that might help."

"I'll need to go home at some point and tell Nat about Hector," Jerrod said. "It's not going to be easy."

"Go home after you talk to Hector's mom," Craig said. "Do what you have to do. Take a shower and get something to eat. This may be an awfully long day."

CHAPTER 25

Willie followed Jerrod in his unmarked city-owned car. Jerrod found the house Hector had pointed out to him two nights earlier and they parked at the curb.

The sun had just started to light the eastern sky as the detectives climbed the four steps on the front stoop of the old, weather-worn two-story Victorian-style house. No interior lights were on.

Willie pushed the button on the antique doorbell, but they heard no chime inside. He knocked on the door and a light came on in an upstairs window.

The door was opened slowly. A woman in her mid-forties wearing a heavy bathrobe said in Spanish, "Yes. Want do you want?"

Willie said in Spanish, "We're the police. We need to talk to you. Is there anyone else home with you?"

The woman said, "My daughter is here. Why do you want her?"

"No. We need to talk to you," Willie said. "May we come in?"

"Yes," the woman said in accented English. "Please, come in." She directed them to the kitchen and offered to make some coffee. The detectives politely declined.

"What is your name?" Willie asked in Spanish.

"Carmen Medina," the woman said.

A younger woman, about twenty-three years old, walked into the kitchen and was startled to see police officers at the table.

"I heard voices..." she said in English. "Why are you here? Is my brother in trouble?"

"Is your brother Hector Medina?" Willie asked in English.

"Yes," she said. "What did he do? He didn't come home last night."

"What's your name?" Jerrod asked.

"Yvonne. Yvonne Medina."

"Please, both of you have a seat," Willie said in Spanish.

"*What's going on*?" Yvonne demanded.

Jerrod had never met any of Hector's family. His stomach was in knots knowing what was going to happen next. He had done it many times. There was no graceful way to notify a family that one of their loved ones was dead. Simple and direct words were used to avoid confusion.

Willie said in Spanish, "Hector was found dead this morning. He had been shot."

The detectives said nothing further as the woman absorbed and reacted to the news.

Carmen began to cry, and Yvonne sat in stunned silence. Yvonne got up and walked over to her mother. She knelt next to her and held her in her arms. The two women rocked together as tears rolled down their faces and they let loose painful sobs.

Jerrod saw a bathroom just off the kitchen and got up to look for some tissues. Finding none, he unrolled some toilet paper and returned to the table.

"Thank you," Yvonne said quietly.

Jerrod nodded back to her.

The women held each other. Carmen excused herself, walked into the bathroom, and closed the door. She turned the faucet on, but her sad wails could be heard over the stream of water.

Yvonne took her mother's chair and sat upright. She dabbed her eyes with the tissue and took several deep breathes.

"Did he suffer?" Yvonne asked.

"No," Jerrod said confidently. He assured her, but at the same time didn't know if he had suffered or not.

"Thank you," Yvonne said. "I'm glad."

"You're welcome," Jerrod said.

"I've known your brother for a few years," Jerrod said. "But I never met your mother, and I didn't know he had a sister."

"I know who you are," Yvonne said. "You used to date Natalie Segura."

"Still do," Jerrod said.

Even at difficult times like this, experienced detectives use small-talk unrelated to the case to build relationships or *rapport* with the people they interview. To the uninitiated, rapport-building would seem manipulative and, frankly, it was... but with a purpose. Building rapport with victims, witnesses, suspects, and even co-workers is how the detectives got the work done by breaking down barriers and creating a sense of cooperation. Especially with ethic groups who tended to distrust law enforcement, rapport-building was even more important. An average detective could learn to build a certain level of rapport with people. Exceptional detectives were born with the skill.

"What has Hector been up to lately?" Jerrod asked.

"He quit school three or four months ago," Yvonne said. "He loaded trucks for a while, but I don't know exactly what he is... was... doing."

"I talked to him a couple nights ago," Jerrod said. "It looked like he got beat-up, but he wouldn't tell me much."

"He just told me he got 'jumped,'" she said. "That's all he said about it."

Carmen came out of the bathroom and sat down in the chair earlier vacated by Yvonne. Her tired face was streaked with tears, but she had otherwise regained her composure.

"When did you last see Hector?" Willie asked.

"He had dinner with us last night," Yvonne said.

"Did you remember about what time it was?" Jerrod asked.

"About 5:30 or so," Yvonne said. "That's when we usually eat. I'm not sure really."

"This could be important," Willie said. "Can you narrow down the time better?"

"Was the TV on, Yvonne?" Jerrod asked.

"Yes. The TV is *always* on during the day," Yvonne said.

"Do you remember there being any particular show on either before or during dinner?" Jerrod asked.

Yvonne thought for a moment and spoke back and forth with Carmen in Spanish.

"It was between 5:30 and 6:00," Yvonne said. "I'm sure of that. My mom made dinner while she watched her favorite *telenovela* between 5:00 and 5:30. We sat down at 5:30 and had dinner. We had chicken and corn with tortillas for dinner."

A *telenovela* was a serialized Spanish-language television show similar to a soap opera.

Carmen said something in Spanish to Yvonne. The women started to cry again. Yvonne walked around the table and hugged her mother.

"What did she say?" Jerrod whispered to Willie.

"She said Hector cleaned up the dishes and kissed her before he left the house," Willie said.

The detectives sat silently until the women were ready to talk again. After a few minutes, Yvonne moved back to the chair and sat down.

"Who has Hector been hanging out with?" Willie asked.

"Just the same neighborhood kids we grew up with mostly," Yvonne said. "I don't know who he hangs out with away from our street."

Carmen said something in Spanish to Willie.

"She said Hector was getting money somehow," Willie said. "He had cash and would give her money from time to time. Twenty or thirty dollars."

"Does she have any idea where Hector was getting this cash?" Jerrod asked.

"She said she didn't know," Willie said.

"My mom got hurt at work about six-months ago," Yvonne said. "Money has been pretty tight here ever since."

"How do you think Hector was making money?" Willie asked Yvonne.

"I don't know," Yvonne said.

"Tell me about those Nike basketball shoes he was wearing," Jerrod said.

"*Those goddamn shoes*," she said as she caught a quick glare from her mother. "He came home wearing those shoes about a week ago. He said they were a gift."

"Did he say who may have given him the shoes?" Jerrod asked. "Those shoes weren't cheap."

"He never told me who gave them to him," Yvonne said. "I think he just bought them."

Carmen said something in Spanish to Yvonne.

"Wait a minute," Yvonne said to the detectives.

Carmen and Yvonne talked back and forth in Spanish so fast Jerrod could only understand every third or fourth word. Although he couldn't understand the content of the exchange, their voices got progressively louder and more animated.

Yvonne put her hand up to stop the exchange.

"My mom said Hector was hanging out with a man, an older man," Yvonne said. "The man would sometimes come by and pick Hector up in front of the house. She never told me this before."

"Do you know who the 'man' was?" Willie asked.

"My mom said she didn't know his name," Yvonne said.

"What kind of car did the 'man' drive?" Jerrod asked.

Yvonne and Carmen spoke Spanish in a quieter tone for a few moments.

"She said it was a blue car. A big blue car with four-doors. She didn't know what kind it was," Yvonne said.

Jerrod's mind flashed for a moment to the blue four-door Oldsmobile Delta 88 that belonged to Efrain Hernandez.

"Do you or your mom know a man named 'Efrain Hernandez' or another man named 'Oso?'" Jerrod asked.

Willie shot him a subtle look. He had no clue where the two names came from.

The two women talked in Spanish for a few seconds.

"We don't know those names, sorry," Yvonne said.

"Do you have a recent photograph of Hector we can have... or just use?" Jerrod asked.

"Yes. We have school pictures of him from about six months ago," Yvonne said. "I'll get one for you."

She returned a few minutes later with four five-by-seven-inch color photos of Hector Medina. He was smiling with a pleasant expression on his face.

"You can keep one," Yvonne said. "We have a lot of them."

The detectives thanked the Medinas and gave them a timeline regarding the autopsy process and when Hector's body could be claimed. Both Jerrod and Willie gave them business cards and asked them to call anytime they had any questions or learned any information.

"I am sorry for your loss. Our loss," Jerrod said.

"Thank you," Yvonne said.

The detectives left the house and squinted their eyes from the diffuse sunlight washing through a thick overcast sky. They walked to the sidewalk and stopped near their cars.

"Who the hell are 'Efrain Hernandez' and 'Oso?'" Willie asked.

"They're names that came up in another thing I'm working on," Jerrod said.

"'Another thing.' Interesting."

"I have to go home and tell Nat about Hector now," Jerrod said as he changed the subject.

"Go take care of business. Take your time. I'm going back to the office."

Jerrod felt the four-minute drive from the Medina residence to his home was more like a cross-country trip.

He had been able to compartmentalize his emotions while talking with Yvonne and Carmen. However, he was unsure he could, or should, do the same when he gave Natalie the news about Hector. He rehearsed the words he would use, out loud, in the privacy of his car.

This was going to be the most difficult thing he had ever done.

He took a very deep breath as he put his key in the front door lock of his house and opened the door.

CHAPTER 26

When he stepped inside, the interior of the house had enough daylight that he didn't have to turn on a light. He walked directly to the bedroom and found Natalie still asleep.

"Nat," he said. "Wake up, honey."

She rolled over and opened her eyes.

"Cold out there?" she asked.

"Yeah. It's cold."

"Come to bed and I'll warm you up."

"I need to talk to you. Please get up and meet me in the kitchen."

She stretched diagonally in the king-sized bed and said, "Okay. Okay."

Jerrod went to the kitchen and prepared a pot of coffee. Natalie visited the bathroom and came into the kitchen a few minutes later.

"Coffee smells good."

"Have a seat, please."

She sat down in one of the wooden kitchen table chairs and he sat down next to her.

"Nat, Hector was killed last night. That was the call-out I had."

He had seen Natalie in a variety of emotional situations over the years – including the day her father died from a massive heart attack just a few months after they graduated from high school.

However, he was unprepared for her reaction to the news about Hector: Her mouth was opened slightly, but she didn't make a sound. Huge tears formed in her beautiful brown eyes and poured down her soft cheeks onto her terrycloth robe. She stood but didn't seem to know what to do or where to go.

Tears welled in his eyes as he got up and wrapped his arms around her. No more words were said as they held each other and openly wept together for several minutes.

Jerrod let go of Natalie and sat her in a chair. He went to the bathroom and got some tissues for both of them.

"Want some coffee?" he asked.

"Sure."

He poured two cups of coffee. Cream and sugar in both. He placed the cups on the table and sat down again.

"How did he die?"

"It looks like he was shot in the head. We don't know much else." Jerrod was intentionally vague.

"Was he robbed or something?"

"We don't know right now."

"This must be hard for you?" she asked. "Hector was your friend."

"I'll be okay."

"I'm sorry," she said.

"Me, too."

They sat in silence for a minute and sipped their coffee.

"Nat, I have to go back to work," he said. "You're welcome to stay here or go home or do whatever you need to do."

"I have to tell my mom," she said. "She's going to be devastated."

"Can you call your sister in Mesa to help you?"

"I'll have her come to my mom's house. Good idea."

"I need to shower and get going. Craig and Willie are waiting for me."

He kissed her and held her again for a short time.

Jerrod got up and walked to the bathroom. He closed and locked the bathroom door. He took a long look in the mirror and said to himself: "Can you do this?"

He showered and shaved. He put on some fresh jeans and a pressed dress shirt. He hung his badge, Beretta, and handcuffs from his belt.

He looked one more time in the mirror and thought: *This has already been the worst day of my life... and it's not over yet.*

CHAPTER 27

At the PD, Jerrod walked into the bureau and found Craig and Willie seated at their desks.

"How did it go?" Willie asked.

"She took it hard," Jerrod said as he slumped into his chair. "She's going home to tell her mom. Not good, man, not good at all."

"Sorry you had to do that, pal," Craig said.

"Thanks."

The room was silent for a few moments.

"I talked to Hanson," Craig said as he broke the silence. "He's cutting his trip short and will be back tonight. He'll call from time-to-time to check in."

"Tell me about the 'other thing' you're working on?" Willie asked Jerrod. "And why did you ask the Medinas about 'Efrain Hernandez' and 'Oso?'"

Craig looked at Jerrod, "Pray tell. Please share your story with us."

"This won't make sense to you," Jerrod said. "This guy, Efrain, owns a blue Oldsmobile Delta 88 and drives another guy, Oso, around in it. Oso works at Nopales as a bouncer or something and I had a little run-in with him at the restaurant Thursday night."

"He got kicked out of the restaurant," Craig added.

"I didn't get kicked out," Jerrod said. "This is my story, not yours."

"So how are those two guys related to Hector's murder?" Willie asked.

"I have no idea if they are related or not," Jerrod said. "There could be a thousand blue four-door cars around this town. I don't know."

Craig completed a list of investigative duties for each detective. Time was of the essence on any major case. The more time that passed, the more evidence was lost, and the more witnesses forget or become unavailable.

Since Hector Medina's body was found in a location that obviously was not the same place he was killed, a second crime scene existed. Somewhere.

Any witnesses having information either directly about the killing or peripherally about the circumstances leading to or following the crime which could direct the investigation had to be located, interviewed, and locked into a story... even if they were lying. Eventually, a pattern or theme would emerge to guide the investigation.

The goal was to create and modify a theory of exactly what happened to Hector supported by the facts. The challenge was to not misinterpret or twist the facts to fit a specific theory.

It was easier said than done.

Craig's desk phone rang. He had a short conversation and took some notes.

"That was Ted Lindsey at the Coroner's Office. The autopsy will be performed at one o'clock this afternoon. They asked that at least one of us attend the entire procedure."

"I'll do it," Willie offered.

"I'll go," Jerrod said. "I talked to Hector the night he got beat up. I know the injuries he had then, and I can help Doc figure out which injuries he may have now that were new."

"You sure about that?" Craig asked.

"I'm sure."

"Okay. You handle it. But tell me if you get cold feet."

"I'm okay."

"Here are the assignments," Craig said. "Willie, we need to go to Hector's neighborhood and talk to the people there who knew him. Find out who he was hanging out with, where he earned his money, and anything you can about that blue car."

"Got it," Willie said.

"Jerrod," Craig said. "Go out to the west side and check the crime scene again. Take another look now that it's daylight in case we missed anything. Take a few more overview photos to get a better perspective of the area. While you're out there, see if any drivers or lumpers hanging around the produce docks know anything."

"Will do," Jerrod said.

Craig said, "I'll stay here and handle any phone calls that may come in and keep the Brass informed on where the case is going. Hanson told me to put out a press release about the murder, but to keep it brief and generic until he gets here. Any questions?"

Willie and Jerrod both shook their heads.

"Go find something we can work with," Craig said.

Willie pulled his car to the curb about a half block from the Medina family residence. He had no specific place to start, so he knocked on the door of the house he was park in front of.

A woman and three small children came to the door. He spoke to them in Spanish and told them he was investigating Hector Medina's death. He asked if they knew Hector and the woman said they did. He asked questions about who Hector hung-out with, where he worked, and about the blue car. The answers to all of his questions were the same: "We don't know anything." He handed them a business card and asked them to call if they heard anything.

Willie went to the next house. Same questions. Same answers.

He went to a total of thirteen houses. Nobody knew anything about anything.

He walked back to his car and found a group of three young Latino men standing in front a house three doors away from the Medina residence. He had not talked to them earlier.

"How you doing?" Willie asked.

He was met with blank stares. He sensed he needed to raise the stakes a little.

"I'm looking into a homicide of someone you know. Hector Medina. Someone shot him in the head and dumped his body on the west side."

He got more silence, but the men glanced at each other.

"If you don't give a shit, I don't either," Willie said as the turned and started to walk away.

"Fuck you, *Coconut*," one of the young men shouted.

Coconut was a comment within the Latino community reserved as an extreme insult. It was a metaphor thrown from one Latino at another accusing them of losing touch with his cultural roots and selling-out to the white establishment — thus considering him, "Brown on the outside, but white on the inside."

Willie stopped, turned around, and rushed back to the young man who just happened to be standing the closest to him. He thrust his face so close to the young man's he could smell the detective bureau coffee on his breath.

"Say it again, motherfucker. Say it again and you'll be wearing your teeth like a necklace."

The young man said nothing but didn't back away either.

"Your friend was killed last night? I plan on doing something about it."

"We're going to take care of it," one of the other men said.

He was the physically largest of the trio and apparent leader of the group. Willie left the first man and moved swiftly to confront the leader. He crowded him just like the other man. Their chests touched as they spoke.

“We knew Hector. What happened to him was fucked up,” the leader said. “I don't know why he got killed, but he didn't deserve it. *We'll handle it, not you.*”

“Tell me what you know,” Willie said.

“I can't talk to you, man,” the leader said.

“Here's my number,” Willie said while handing him a business card. “Call me *before* you do something stupid.”

The leader studied the card and said, “‘Guillermo Sanchez.’ I'll remember you, man.” He then intentionally dropped the business card to the sidewalk.

Willie turned and walked back to his car. The group of men started walking the opposite direction. The third man in the group, the smallest and youngest member, paused a moment, bent as if he had to tie his shoe, reached down, and scooped the business card into his hand. He stuffed the card into his pants pocket as he caught up with the other two.

Jerrod returned to the location Hector Medina's body was discovered. He searched around the area for twenty-minutes and found no additional evidence they had overlooked. He took a series of overview scene photos.

He drove by several produce docks and found no groups of lumpers milling around waiting to load trailers full of lettuce or apples or berries for trips to markets all over the country. He stopped at a dock and talked to a man driving a forklift. He explained the investigation to him, and the man said he didn't know Hector or anything about him.

At a frozen food plant a mile from the crime scene, he saw two men — one Latino in his mid-twenties and one white in his forties. They were standing near a six-bay loading dock with no trailers backed in. He thought he recognized one of them. He recalled his real first name to be Luis, but he went by a nickname, “Lucho.”

He parked his car and walked toward the men. They studied him as he approached.

“I know you,” Jerrod said to the Latino man and hoping to break-the-ice. “‘Lucho,’ right. I think we went to school together.”

“I don't remember you,” Lucho said. “What do you want?”

“A young man was killed last night. His name was Hector Medina. I think you knew him.”

The two men looked at each other and it was apparent from their reaction that they hadn't yet heard of Hector's death.

The white man asked, “How did he die? Accident?”

“No accident,” Jerrod said. “He was shot in the head and dumped about a mile from here.”

The two men shook their heads.

“We knew Hector,” Lucho said. “He was a good kid. Hard worker.”

“When did you last see him?”

“Couple months ago, the white man said. “We heard he found another job.”

“Do you know where or who he was working for?” Jerrod asked.

“We really shouldn't be talking to you,” Lucho said.

Jerrod gave them both business cards and asked them to call anytime if they had information they would share. He had often found witnesses with information they would like to divulge but would stay silent while in groups fearing they would be labeled a “snitch” or “rat.” Occasionally, those witnesses will later make a phone call when they can't be overheard to protect themselves.

Jerrod decided to make a detour on his way back to the PD. He drove to Fourth Street and the address listed on the DMV print-out for the blue Oldsmobile Delta 88. The car wasn’t there.

He drove down the street Natalie and her mother lived. He saw her VW and her sister’s car parked at the curb and felt a deep wave of sadness knowing what Natalie was going through at that moment without him.

CHAPTER 28

Craig was at his desk when Jerrod got back to the detective bureau. Willie was gone.

"Where's Willie?" Jerrod asked.

"I sent him home to clean-up. He'll be back in an hour or so."

"Okay. Did he come up with anything?"

"No. The 'Code of Silence' is in full effect in Hector Medina's neighborhood."

"Find anything out on the west side?" Craig asked.

"Not really. I took a few more photos at the scene and talked to a couple lumpers. They said they knew Hector but hadn't seen him in a couple months. They said he found another job... before they decided they shouldn't be talking to me."

"Okay," Craig said. "This case is going nowhere quick."

Jerrod used Hector's high school photo to prepare a flier for Patrol describing the murder. It asked that any information an officer had, or came across, regarding his death be directed to the detectives as-soon-as-possible.

CHAPTER 29

At twelve-fifteen, Jerrod left the PD and drove to the City of Mesa, the seat for the County of Mesa, to attend the autopsy of Hector Medina. He had been to several autopsies in the past, but never one conducted on someone he knew personally.

The Mesa County Morgue was located within a cluster of buildings which were part of the Mesa County Health Department.

Jerrod knocked on the extra-wide morgue door and after a few moments it was opened for him by Coroner Deputy Ted Lindsey.

"We really need to stop meeting like this, dude," the deputy said.

"You're telling me," Jerrod said.

"Get any sleep?"

"No. You?"

"A few hours."

The first thing anyone noticed when entering the morgue was the smell. A mixture of formaldehyde and bowel were the dominate aromas. It took several minutes inside the morgue for the olfactory system to get overloaded and begin to ignore the stench.

A short hallway separated the exterior door from the autopsy suite. The well-lighted room was square and about the size of an average living room. An industrial-size stainless-steel sink lined one wall. A Formica work surface above a row of supply cabinets lined another. A bank of older casement-style windows were above the counter and a few were opened to connect with the outside world.

On a third wall was a large door which opened to a walk-in cooler large enough to accommodate up to six bodies on morgue gurneys at thirty-four degrees.

The fourth wall had a large garbage can in one corner. The can was lined with a bright red bio-hazard bag. A heavy cord stretched the length of the wall at about five feet from the floor and acted as a clothesline.

Hector's dark jacket, jeans and white t-shirt hung from the cord to air dry. All were stained with blood.

The pair of Nike Air Jordans had been placed neatly together on the tile floor. There wasn't a single drop of blood on the bright white leather uppers.

A middle-aged man in green hospital scrubs stood with his back to the room as he studied three x-ray films on a wall-mounted viewer. Two of the films showed a human head from front and right-side views. A white spot in both films had the unmistakable silhouette of an intact bullet. The third film was of a human torso that even an untrained eye could see there was at least two ribs that had been fractured.

"Good afternoon, Doc," Jerrod said.

Doctor Robert Torosian turned and said, "Right on time. We will begin soon."

Ted opened the large door to the walk-in cooler and wheeled out a stainless-steel gurney which contained the naked body of Hector Medina.

Jerrod unconsciously bit on his lower lip at the sight of his friend.

Ted placed the table under a bright overhead light and the foot of the gurney over one of the large sinks. He pulled a rubber stopper from a drain at the foot of the gurney and turned the faucet on. Water flowed from a rubber tube into the sink and would run continuously for the duration of the autopsy.

Hector was laying on his back. A hard black rubber block held his head off the table.

Coagulated blood covered his face, matted his hair, and streaked his neck and shoulders. A variety of abrasions and bruising were visible on his torso, arms, hands, and knees. He had no tattoos.

His eye lids were open. His eyes were dull and had sunken into their sockets. They had lost all the brightness they once had in life.

"You knew this young man?" the doctor asked.

Jerrod shifted his attention from Hector and said, "Yes, sir. I've known him for about seven years."

"I'm sorry," he said.

"Thanks, Doc," Jerrod said.

"Let's get started" the doctor said. "I had Deputy Lindsey take the body to county hospital to have the films taken. I've already examined him while his clothes were still on."

Doctor Torosian had a structured and methodical technique when performing an autopsy. He worked slowly and precisely so no details were overlooked or left unexplained. He dictated his observations into a small hand-held cassette tape recorder.

Ted Lindsey had a 35mm camera with a detachable flash loaded with film and ready for the series of photographs Doctor Torosian would direct be taken during the procedure.

"The body is that of a healthy and well-nourished young Latino male adult..." the dark-haired and goateed doctor said as he began his dictation. Height, weight, hair color, eye color, birthmarks, and scars. He measured features with a stainless-steel ruler and noted their accurate size and precise position on the body. He directed photographs be taken of particular areas.

Jerrod caught himself detaching his mind from the friendship he had with Hector while focusing on the procedure and the details surrounding his death that were emerging. He would do that several times over the course of the next few hours.

The doctor dampened some rough brown paper towels in the continuous flow of water and scrubbed away blood from areas of the body he wished to examine closer.

He measured and documented the various marks on the body: bruising to the ribs and abrasions on his right shoulder, left forearm, both knees, and the hands. He noted more abrasions and swelling to Hector's face.

At a moment the doctor was not dictating, Jerrod said, "I talked with Hector a few nights ago. Wednesday night. He had been in a fight and would only tell me he had been 'jumped' by someone he wouldn't identify. His face was bruised, an area around his left eye was pretty swollen, and he had some abrasions on his left hand and forearm."

Doctor Torosian looked at the body again and said, "I can see the areas you are talking about. They have some evidence of healing. Many of these other injuries were received much more recently then Wednesday. Some of these newer injuries, particularly the abrasions on the knuckles of his hands and the knees, may have happened a short time before his death."

It became apparent Hector had been beaten again before he was killed. The abrasions on both hands suggested he may have fought with someone more recently than Wednesday. The light abrasions on his knees suggested he had been kneeling at some point.

The doctor walked over to Hector's clothing hanging from the cord and examined the front of the blue jeans. He held the knee portions of the pants toward the light and looked closely at the material. Jerrod joined him. The denim material was relatively clean, but under close examination they noticed small fibers on the portion of both knees that would have contacted the ground if Hector had been kneeling.

The doctor walked over to the counter and opened a drawer. He pulled out a large magnifying glass and returned to the pair of hanging jeans.

He examined the knees of the pants again through the glass and said, "These fibers are not from the pants material. They are from another source."

Jerrod suggested, "If Hector had been kneeling outside somewhere, we could expect there to be some dirt attached or some grass staining visible. But if the knees were clean and there are those fibers, he may have been kneeling on some type of carpet."

"Very possibly," the doctor said.

Doctor Torosian directed Deputy Lindsey to collect the fibers from the pair of pants. The deputy used transparent tape — the same type used by law enforcement to collect powder-enhanced fingerprints at crime scenes — to dab the adhesive side onto the knee area of the denim pants and "lift" the loose fibers from the material. He used separate pieces of tape for each knee and then suspended the tape on white glossy-faced cards.

The doctor examined the lifts under the lens of the magnifier and said, "It appears these fibers have a rusty-golden color to them. Could be from carpet. I don't know. A crime lab should be able to tell you."

Jerrod nodded. The small fibers could connect Hector to the actual scene of the fatal shot. That location could lead to the identity of the killer... or killers.

The doctor completed detailing the position and condition of the various injuries to the body and said, "Let's look at the head wound."

He examined and measured the gunshot wound to the very top of Hector's head. He cleaned away the matted blood from the short brown hair and looked closer to the wound. The scalp had ragged star-like tears in it. The skin and tissue around the wound had a deep red and black coloration to it.

"The gunshot wound appears to be near contact..." the doctor said into the cassette recorder.

"Look at this," the doctor said to Jerrod. "The muzzle of the gun looks like it was placed close to the scalp when it was fired. There is little burned or unburned gunpowder around the wound. That would indicate the muzzle was either in actual contact or just a fraction of an inch from the scalp. The 'stellate,' or star-shaped, wound was caused by the hot gasses from the muzzle entering the wound and tearing the skin as it spread out under the scalp. The heat from the burning gun powder seared the tissue, we call it 'heat coagulation,' which gives the wound that darkened appearance."

It was becoming apparent that Hector Medina had been executed. The evolving theory surrounding his death indicated he had been beaten first and was in a kneeling position when the muzzle of a gun was placed to the top of his head and the trigger pulled.

After directing Deputy Lindsey to photograph the gunshot wound, the doctor said, "Let's go inside."

The doctor used a scalpel to cut the skin in an arching line from the left shoulder, along the mid-line of the torso, around the navel, and to the pubis. He cut the skin from the right shoulder to intersect the first in the mid-chest. He cut back the underlying tissue and folded back the skin to expose the ribcage and internal abdomen. A quarter-inch layer of lumpy, bright yellow fat laid under the skin of the fit young man's abdomen.

The doctor examined the exposed ribs. He manipulated the bones with his gloved hands and two of the ribs on the left side had been fractured. The fractured ribs were located directly under one of the bruises on his torso.

The doctor used a Stryker saw — an electric reciprocating device with a half-moon shaped blade designed to cut through hard tissue like bone, while not cutting softer tissue — to cut away and remove the sternum or breastplate and the attached ribs to expose the under-laying organs.

Doctor Torosian dictated the condition and color of the organs before using the scalpel to detach the organs one by one. Each organ was weighed individually in the pan of a scale suspended from the ceiling.

Deputy Lindsey stood nearby with a clipboard and wrote the data onto a form. Blood samples and a urine sample were taken for alcohol and drug testing.

The doctor removed the stomach and poured its liquid contents into a clear jar.

"Do you know when he last ate?" the doctor asked.

"He ate with his family between five-thirty and six last night," Jerrod said. "Chicken and corn with tortillas, as I recall the sister telling us."

"His stomach was pretty much empty," the doctor said. "That means there was some time between when he ate and the time he died," the doctor said.

"Can you tell how much time?" Jerrod asked.

"Not precisely," the doctor said. "There are many variables such as the kind of food he had eaten and the size of the meal. I can say it could take between two to four hours for the stomach to completely empty, but I can't give you an absolute time."

Doctor Torosian placed a wooden cutting board onto the body's legs between the knees and ankles. He used a large butcher knife to dissect and inspect each organ for anything unusual. He took small samples of each organ and placed them into a glass jar containing a formaldehyde and water solution called formalin.

"He was a healthy young man," the doctor said. "No disease and no trauma to the organs. I was surprised his liver hadn't been lacerated from the fractured ribs."

Jerrod nodded.

"Let's look at the brain," the doctor said.

The doctor used the scalpel to cut the scalp from the back of the left ear, across the top of the head, and to the back of the right ear. He pulled, or reflected, the skin of the scalp forward so that it partially covered Hector's face and the back of the scalp, so it draped toward the table until the skull was fully exposed.

He examined the gunshot wound again and directed more photographs be taken.

"I would expect some more fracturing of the skull," the doctor said. "There must be a very small caliber firearm involved here."

He used the Stryker saw to cut the circumference of skull above the ears.

Jerrod thought the high-pitched whining sound of the saw as it cut through the skull was the most unique, eerie, and disturbing sound he had ever heard.

A wedge device with a T-handle was used to separate the skull cap from the remainder of the skull. The thin protective membrane surrounding the brain, the *dura mater*, strained as it held the brain in the now exposed cranium.

Doctor Torosian examined the skull cap and commented there were only small fractures visible to its interior.

He cut away the dura mater with the scalpel while cradling the brain in his other hand.

The brain, typically a firm pale light-gray mass of tissue, was bloodied, bruised and jelly-like. He gently pulled the brain from the base of the skull, reached in with the scalpel, severed the spinal cord, and separated the brain from the body.

The doctor carried the brain in both hands to the cutting board. He went to the x-ray viewer and reviewed the films of Hector's head.

He returned to the cutting board. He examined and dictated the condition of the brain and the wound to it. Photographs were taken. He used his one of his gloved fingers to probe the wound and said, "There it is."

Keeping his finger in the wound, he used the scalpel with the other hand to cut away the brain tissue until his hand emerged with a nearly pristine bullet.

He held the bullet in his finger and rinsed the blood from it with the water from the rubber hose. He dried the bullet with a paper towel and placed it on a dry paper towel on the cutting board.

The bullet was small, about half the size of the 9mm bullets Jerrod carried in his Beretta, and the bullet tip was slightly flattened. The bullet had a thin layer of copper over its lead core. The copper coating designated the bullet to be a "Full Metal Jacket," or FMJ for short.

The bullet had a series of raised and lowered ridges on it sides called "lands and grooves" and were caused as the bullet traveled the length of the gun barrel. Bullets were designed with a slightly larger diameter than the barrel. The ridges in the barrel bite into the sides of the bullet and cause it to spiral before leaving the barrel. The tight spiral of the bullet caused its trajectory to be truer.

The ridges on the bullet were also important to the investigation for two reasons: By counting the number of ridges, their relative widths, and the direction of the twist — the list of guns that may have been used to fire it could be narrowed. Secondly, if an actual gun was located, the evidence bullet could be compared by a firearms expert against a test-fired bullet to establish it was, or was not, from that gun.

"Let's find out how much it weighs," the doctor said as he removed his latex gloves and led Jerrod and Deputy Lindsey to his private office.

His office betrayed the doctor's otherwise organized and precise personality. The small desk and various mismatched shelves were piled high with a haphazard collection of books and papers. Clear jars containing human tissue samples in formalin solution from years of autopsies were found scattered around the office.

Doctor Torosian opened a drawer and pulled out a small black electronic scale. He placed the bullet on the plate of the scale and the digital readout settled at "4.6 grams." He punched in some numbers on a calculator.

"Right about 71 grains," the doctor said. "That's a tiny bullet... and pretty rare."

Bullets are generally weighed in "grains." There are 15.43 grains in one gram. 71 grains is approximately the same weight as two US dimes.

The doctor took a pair of plastic dial calipers from his desk and measured the diameter of the bullet. "That's about a .32 caliber bullet," he said. "Probably .32 ACP."

ACP was short for "Automatic Colt Pistol."

Doctor Torosian counted the number of lands and grooves. There were six of each. He noted the twist direction — right, or clockwise.

"What type of firearm should we be looking for, Doc?" Jerrod asked.

"Just a second," he said.

He looked around his desk and shelving. He moved some piles of papers and books.

"Here it is," he said as he lifted a large book with a soft cover and placed it on his desk. He thumbed through the book filled with photographs of a variety of guns and types of ammunition. He focused on a section containing page after page of columned tables.

The doctor thought out-loud as he thumbed through the pages — ".32 FMJ." "Six." "Right."

His search slowed and he studied one final table and ran his finger down the page.

"This won't go in my report, but you are going to be looking for a pretty rare gun... these days at least."

"What is it?" Jerrod asked.

"The fatal bullet was probably fired from a Colt Model 1903 .32 ACP handgun," he said. "It's a small handgun and would be consistent with the weight, diameter, and markings on the bullet we found at autopsy. The minimal fracturing of the skull at the wound site is also consistent with the light powder charge used in the cartridges for that handgun."

"You said those guns were rare?" Jerrod asked.

"Yes," the doctor said. "The '1903' designation was actually the year that gun was introduced. A few years later, Colt introduced a newer model that fired a bigger bullet with a bigger powder charge. The .32 is not a popular round and there's just not a lot of them around anymore."

"We'll definitely have something to search for now," Jerrod said.

"If you find that gun; you may find your killer," the doctor said. "Good luck."

"Doc, I have one more question for you," Jerrod said. "Off-the-record."

"Go ahead," the doctor said.

"Hector's family asked if he had suffered, and I told them he hadn't. I need to know myself."

Doctor Torosian paused for a few moments.

"What I can tell you is this: He was obviously beaten last night, and the fractured ribs would have been plenty painful.

"As far as the gunshot wound goes, well, I'll speak in more hypothetical terms. When a bullet enters the brain and causes the damage it did, there would have been an instantaneous loss of consciousness. Depending on the portion of the brain damaged by the bullet, clinical death — the stopping of the heartbeat and respiration — may be delayed for a few seconds, minutes, or even hours in some rare cases. However, the person would typically be brain dead immediately."

Jerrod nodded.

"I can assure you, off-the-record, your friend most certainly didn't hear the shot that killed him."

CHAPTER 30

"You can take the bullet and fiber lifts now," Ted Lindsey said. "But the clothing's still wet. I'll let it air dry another day or so and then package it for you."

"That'll be great," Jerrod said.

"No problem. Sign right here."

"Can I use your phone?" Jerrod asked as he signed the evidence chain-of custody record.

"Sure. Don't use the 'dirty phone' in the autopsy room. Use the one in Doc's office."

Jerrod called Craig's desk number and got no answer. He called Willie's desk and got no answer there either. He called Pete Hanson's number, and no one picked up.

"That's odd," Jerrod said to himself.

Thinking the detectives may have gone out to follow up fresh leads, he called VVPD Dispatch to learn where they were.

"Valle Verde Police," the female dispatcher said.

"This is Jerrod." he said.

"Hey, Jerrod."

"I'm trying to get hold of any of the detectives and no one is at their desks."

"They all went home."

"Home? What the hell?"

"That's what Sergeant Hanson told me."

"Okay. Thanks."

Jerrod thought the detectives must have just taken some time off to have a meal, get some rest, and regroup to continue the investigation that night.

Jerrod telephoned Pete Hanson at his home.

"Hello."

"Hey, Sarge. This is Jerrod. I'm just leaving the morgue. We found some interesting evidence at autopsy, and we have some fibers—"

The sergeant cut him off. "Do you have any leads that have to be followed up tonight?"

Jerrod thought for a few moments. "None that *have* to be followed-up tonight, but—" He was cut-off again.

"Come back and book your evidence tonight. We'll go over everything else on Monday morning."

"You mean tomorrow morning, Sunday, right?" Jerrod asked.

"No. Monday morning. Everyone's taking tomorrow off."

Jerrod couldn't believe what he just heard. A new murder case, less than twenty-four hours old, was being shut down for a day.

"So, I have this right, we're just going to stop our investigation and wait until Monday to start again?"

"That's what I'm telling you. Finish what you're doing tonight and take tomorrow off."

Jerrod paused while he searched for the appropriate response to his supervisor's orders.

"Okay," was the only thing he could think of before hanging up.

Jerrod slammed the receiver onto its cradle a little harder than he should have. He tried in vain to think of any reasonable rationale to just stop investigating this murder, any murder, even temporarily. The decision went against every shred of training and experience he had ever received on how to work a major case.

Jerrod, completely distracted after the conversation with his sergeant, took one last look at the body of Hector Medina and silently said goodbye to his friend. He walked into the hallway toward the large exterior door.

"Want your evidence?" Ted Lindsey yelled to him from the autopsy room doorway. "You already signed for it, so you... kind of... have to take it."

Jerrod stopped, turned around, and walked back to gather the small bags of evidence.

"Thanks," Jerrod said. "Sorry, I spaced-out for a minute. No sleep."

"No problem. Get some rest. I'll call you in a couple days about the other stuff."

"Okay. Thank you."

It was five-twenty when Jerrod stepped outside the morgue doorway. The day was bright, and the skies were pale blue and cloudless. The air was comfortably warm, especially nice for a fall afternoon so near the coast. But he noticed none of those things.

He drove south on the freeway from Mesa back to Valle Verde. His mind raced uncontrollably, no doubt assisted by a lack of sleep, as he desperately tried to make some sense about the events of the day: The early morning call-out, the shocking discovery Hector had been killed, the heart-wrenching death notification to the Medina family, the emotional response from Natalie, the "street-silence" about the killing, the graphic realness of the autopsy, the cold-blooded nature of Hector's execution, and then the unexplainable suspension of the case.

There was an unfortunate reality all detectives knew very well: Having a major case does not prevent new cases from coming in. Monday morning would bring another batch of reports from Patrol, more investigations would be added to the ones already assigned, and the next major case was just around the corner.

Hector Medina's murder was neither high profile nor politically sensitive. He wasn't the son of a politician, physician, or lawyer. Hector was a street kid whose life had just met a sudden and tragic end. An end some would argue had been predictable.

Without immediate attention or a lucky break, the sad fact was the investigation would slowly fade into the background, take on less priority, become just another unsolved homicide, and eventually sink to the lowly status of "cold case" through a lack of interest.

Marko Otero was at the large table eating some fast-food take-out when Jerrod walked inside via the squad room door.

"Hey, Jerrod," Marko said as he stood up and extended his hand. "I heard about Hector. That's messed up."

Jerrod shook his hand and said, "Thanks, man. It's been a long day."

"I bet. Let me know if there's anything I can do."

"I will. Thanks, buddy."

Jerrod repackaged the small fibers collected from Hector Medina's pants and the bullet removed from his brain under the VVPD case number and secured the items in a property room locker.

He sat down at his desk in the detective bureau. As the weight eased from his feet, he let out a sigh and realized he had not stopped moving since his phone rang at home early that morning.

He also hadn't talked to Natalie since their sad encounter that morning. He punched in her home number.

"Hello," Natalie said.

"It's Jerrod. How are you doing?"

"Okay. My mom's having a rough time. It's so sad. She liked Hector so much."

"Are you going to stay with her tonight?"

"I think so. My sister had to go home, and my mom wants to go to Saturday mass at Saint Daniel's to light a candle for Hector. I don't want her to go alone."

“You’re a good daughter. I'm exhausted and wouldn't be very good company tonight anyway.”

“I love you, Jerrod.

“I love you too.

After he hung up the receiver, he looked around the cramped office space he had once only dreamed of being a part of. There was no coffee brewing, no radio playing, no phones ringing, and no detectives following the few leads they had. No one was plotting the next move they would make. No one was gathering the tiny shreds of information that would build into the evidence that would take them to whoever was responsible for the execution murder of Hector Medina.

None of those things would happen that Saturday night.

Jerrod drove home in the early darkness with the sad knowledge Natalie would not be there to greet him. His long workday ended at around seven o’clock when he parked the city-issued car and walked into the darkened house.

He collapsed on the sofa and kicked his shoes off in the middle of the living room. He was physically and mentally exhausted and just wanted to sleep. As he sat, he realized he had not eaten a single morsel of food since the dinner and wine he shared with Natalie on Friday evening.

Forcing himself from the sofa, he searched the refrigerator and was pleased to find a small piece of steak and a few tastes of rice left over from the night before. As his meal heated in the microwave, he popped the top on a Heineken. The beer was gone before the food was warmed and he grabbed a second one as he waited.

He turned on the TV and ate his meager meal. He felt the alcohol buzz and placed the empty plate on the floor.

His feet when up on the sofa and his eyes closed.

CHAPTER 31

Sunday

Jerrod Gold awoke at dawn from the very deep sleep he had on the sofa. He felt refreshed and was shocked to see he had been out for over ten hours. No dreams, good or bad, had disturbed his sleep.

The TV had been on all night, and he watched a portion of *Meet The Press,* but soon lost focus. He stepped on the empty plate on the carpet when he got off the sofa.

Outside the front door, his socks got wet with chilly morning dew when he went to the stoop to get the local morning newspaper.

He popped the rubber band on the Valle Verde *Sun* and two front page headlines caught his attention.

As a pot of coffee brewed, he laid the *Sun* on the kitchen table and read the headline:

POLICE INVESTIGATE SUSPICIOUS DEATH

The article went on to embellish the generic information Craig had written in the press release the day before. The article identified the victim of the "suspicious death" as "Hector Chavez Medina, an eighteen-year-old former Valle Verde High School student." The article said, "the cause of death was under investigation" and listed Craig's desk phone number and the VVPD Dispatch number for anyone with information to call.

The article had been written by crime beat reporter Bruce Witt, a daily fixture at the PD. He came to the lobby every morning to take notes from the Dispatch Center "press board" which contained copies of routine crime reports and an occasional press release. He took notes into a spiral bound four-inch by eight-inch reporter's notebook.

Witt would generally summarize the crime reports into little blurbs for the residents of Valle Verde to get a feel of the crimes being reported: a "residential burglary occurred...," "a shoplifter was arrested...," or "two cars collided...."

Witt was jovial and friendly to talk to. He was quick with a handshake and loved to chat. He constantly fished for any tidbit of information above what he could glean from the press board to spice his articles.

Jerrod chuckled at the thought of the reaction the ruddy-faced and pudgy reporter would have if he learned Hector Medina had been executed with a shot to the head on Friday night and the detectives working the case were taking Sunday off.

He thought Witt would mess his pants if he got that call and it would be the biggest scoop of his reporting life.

The second article was also written by Witt and its headline read:

HEROIN OVERDOSES ON THE RISE

The article accurately documented the two suspected OD deaths just outside Valle Verde, the stinker in the hotel room, and the near OD death of "an unidentified woman who was revived by EMTs."

A Mesa County Sheriff-Coroner sergeant spoke about the deaths and Captain Andrew Wheaton was quoted regarding the VVPD response to "the serious problem."

In the article, Captain Wheaton assured the public that the danger was only to intravenous drug users and "the Valle Verde Police are actively investigating all leads to determine the source of the high-potency heroin."

Jerrod shook his head and laughed at that comment as well. The detectives "actively investigating all leads" were "actively" at home, sitting on their asses drinking coffee, and were doing absolutely nothing "to determine the source" of anything.

He smiled as he visualized Witt double-shitting himself if he got a call about the reality of the OD investigation in addition to the details of Hector Medina's death.

Jerrod thumbed through the rest of the newspaper and, other than learning the Giants lost to the "Bums" in extra innings on Saturday, there was no other news that caught his eye.

CHAPTER 32

Armando Mendoza had just returned from the early Sunday mass at Saint Daniel's as he sat at the kitchen table of his 5000 square-foot Spanish-style estate. He enjoyed a cup of *cafe de olla* — a traditional Mexican brew made with bold coffee, sugar, cinnamon, and cloves — in a large brightly painted mug.

The forty-five-year-old businessman, property owner, and the father of two grown daughters, read the front-page articles of the Valle Verde *Sun*.

He read the vague information about the suspicious death of the eighteen-year-old and the heroin overdose cases that were being investigated by the local police. He moved on to the national news and business sections, but skipped the sports section, He folded the paper neatly and placing it on the table.

He finished his cup of *cafe de olla,* rinsed and dried the mug, and placed it in a cabinet. He walked to a telephone hanging on a kitchen wall and punched in a number he had memorized.

"Yes," the male voice on the other end of the line answered.

"Oso. Come to my house."

CHAPTER 33

Jerrod didn't notice his fingers fidgeting the rubber band from the paper or his left foot unconsciously bouncing from the vinyl floor as he sat at the kitchen table contemplating his unwelcomed Sunday off.

He knew that unlike a sporting event with timed periods of play, the "clock" on Hector Medina's murder investigation started the moment his body was found. The clock didn't stop for time-outs, half-time entertainment, or rest periods while investigative leads were viable, witness memories were fresh, and physical evidence was available. As the seconds ticked off one by one, the chances of proving who was responsible for Hector's death ticked off with them.

Instead, that morning, the biggest decision he had was whether to go for a run before, or after, he mowed the lawns. The lawns won.

He enjoyed maintaining the deep-green and weed-free front lawns he had installed himself from rolled sod a few months earlier. He neatly trimmed the edges and used an old-style reel mower to make a diagonal pattern just like the outfield grass at Candlestick Park. He took in the deep smell of freshly mowed grass and felt a simple sense of satisfaction for the small piece of nature he had created.

Pushing the mower was a good work-out, but he needed more activity to occupy his mind and body. He took a run on his usual five-mile course but ran the opposite direction to change it up.

It occurred to him during the run he hadn't talked to his mother since the previous weekend, and he should give her a call or pay her a visit.

He sprinted the last half-mile just to push himself as hard as he could. He finished his run and walked down the driveway to the back yard. He bent at the waist and put his hands on his knees as he caught his breath.

"Good morning, Jerrod," Charles Horvat said as he puffed a cigarette in his backyard.

"Good... morning... Colonel," he said.

"Been working on that young man's death I read about in the paper? I noticed your work car was gone all day yesterday."

"Yes... sir. It was... very sad."

"Figured so much. Got the day off?"

"Yes... sir."

"Get some rest. Come join me for a drink later."

"Sounds... good. Thank you."

He went into the house and thought about how he had just spoken to the colonel. He wanted to be respectful but had to be careful about any information he shared with the public that could jeopardize the investigation later. He was certain the colonel could keep a secret — the incident behind his receipt of The Bronze Star being at least one of them — but he could casually mention something shared with him to the wrong person and compromise the investigation.

He telephoned Natalie's home. It rang several times without an answer, and he suspected she may be back at Saint Daniel's with her mother.

Mama Segura had a strong Catholic faith and had been a very loyal member of the parish the entire time she lived in Valle Verde. She attended mass there at least twice a week and was not the type who ran to the church only on holidays or during a personal crisis.

She was a believer in the truest sense.

He hoped she found some comfort as she dealt with Hector's death.

"Hello," his mother, Laura Renaud, answered.

"Hi, Mom."

"I was worried about you. What have you been up to?"

"Just working a lot."

"Why don't you come over for lunch. Don will love to see you and we can catch up then. Come by about noon."

"Sounds good. See you about noon."

His mother had been as good a parent as two boys could expect after she divorced Jerry Gold. She provided the necessities for her sons while she started a new career in real estate sales. She began dating again after the separation and eventually started seeing a senior partner in a realty firm — Donald Renaud. They were engaged after six-months and were married a few months later.

Don Renaud, a mouse of a man who was twenty-years her senior, was a good enough husband to his mother. Beyond that, he had little use for the man.

Property values had soared in California during late 1970s and early 1980s. The real estate firm the Renauds worked with had been continually active and all of the partners had done well in the wild market.

His mother and Don were secure financially and they enjoyed the lavish lifestyle their income allowed.

Jerrod got cleaned up and sauntered the half-mile between his home and the Renaud residence. He enjoyed the quiet neighborhood and liked to walk through it from time-to-time to see the changes and improvements the racially mixed residents had made to their homes. He noticed fresh paint on one and a new redwood fence on another.

His neighborhood consisted mostly of working-class people and the houses tended to be older homes on small lots.

By contrast, his mother and Don lived just seven blocks away in a huge house on a huge lot in a mostly white neighborhood. Many of the professionals in Valle Verde lived in this particular section of the east side which was informally named after the curving street that passed through its center — Rochester Avenue.

The area was known as "The Rochester."

The Renaud's big California ranch-style house sat on a lot fifteen feet above the roadway in front of it. The gleaming ten-foot-tall windows of the living room gave the single-story house a visual effect of being much taller than it actually was. It had a pale green painted clapboard exterior and a new cedar shake roof. The heavy landscape was lush, and the front lawn was perfectly manicured, all done by skilled gardeners, none of whom were named "Don."

Freshly planted pink flowers lined the flagstone walkway leading to the massive bright-red Feng Shui-inspired front door. His mother stood in the doorway waiting for him.

"Jerrod, come in," Laura said.

"Hello, Mom," he said as they hugged.

"Don's in the kitchen. Come, come."

He followed her from the foyer and through the formal dining room with its massive dark walnut table and eight oversized chairs. Place mats and chargers were situated perfectly for the next dinner party.

"Hello, Don," he said to his stepfather while intentionally waving instead greeting him with a handshake.

"Welcome, Jerrod," Don said. "Please sit. Something to drink?"

"A soda would great. Thank you."

Don went into a walk-in pantry where he kept a ready supply of sodas, beer, wine, and cocktail mixers for the groups of higher-ups who often gathered there.

"How have you been?" his mother asked as he sat at a tall barstool at the kitchen counter.

"Good, Mom. Busy at work, you know."

Don came back into the kitchen with a Coke and a tall glass filled with ice.

"Here you go," Don said.

"Thank you."

"Are you working on the death case we read about in the *Sun* this morning?" his mother asked.

"Yeah. I was out all day yesterday. That kid's death was very tragic."

"Was he murdered?" Don asked.

"We're looking into that," he said. "I can't really get into specifics about the case right now."

"How about those overdoses?" his mother asked. "The newspaper said you detectives are working on that too."

"Well," he said as he took a drink of soda, "I'm sitting here at your counter *instead* of 'working on that too.'"

"Sounds to me like those overdoses aren't such a terrible thing," Don said. "Maybe it should happen more often. If you ask me."

Nobody fucking asked you, Don. Jerrod shouted... in his mind.

He knew better than to take the bait. Don had an ultra-conservative mentality and agenda. In fact, President Ronald Reagan was not quite "right" enough for him. Don liked social strata and had no issues with the "I've got mine; you're on your own" mentality prevalent in his particular circle.

"Just makes more work for us," Jerrod said, hoping to end the topic.

"How's the house, Jerrod?" his mother said as she correctly sensed the tension brewing between him and Don.

"The house is fine, Mom. The new front lawns look great, and I think I'll replace the back lawn next."

"That was a fine starter house," Don said. "It's cozy and has a lot of character."

Now he was really trying to bait.

'Starter house.' piss-off, Don. I might live there for twenty-years, he screamed... in his head again.

"Cozy" and "a lot of character" were realtor-speak euphemisms for "small" and "old and needs repair."

"How's Natalie doing?" his mother asked while changing the subject yet again.

"She's doing good. She's still working in Admissions, but she's interested in going to nursing school."

Jerrod had no intention of mentioning the connection between Natalie and Hector or how difficult Hector's death had been for her. He knew if he did, Don would go off on some rant about minorities and the opportunities available to them and how they needed to pull themselves up. He had heard it all before and had no interest in hearing in again.

"What are you making for lunch?" he asked his mother. He could see it involved a salad of some sort and he seized the opportunity to change the subject again.

"I thought we'd have a nice chopped grilled chicken salad with avocado," she said. "I know how much you like avocado."

"Sounds great, Mom. Can I use your phone?"

"Use the one in the living room," she said.

Jerrod walked back through the dining room and foyer to the massive living room. It had a huge floor-to-ceiling rock covered fireplace on the far wall and large over-stuffed sofas and chairs arranged carefully to insure a comfortable setting for their frequent guests. The tall front windows allowed a spectacular view of the landscape and neighborhood.

He punched in Natalie's home phone number.

"Hello," Natalie said.

"Hi, Nat. How you doing?"

"Okay, I guess. My mom's doing better. We went to church three times since I saw you yesterday. I think she'll be okay."

"I'm over at my mom's. She's making lunch."

"I thought you would be working today."

"So did I. Long story."

"I miss you." she said.

"I miss you too. I want to see you. Come over tonight."

"I will."

Jerrod enjoyed the grilled chicken salad his mother had prepared. A truce had apparently been called between him and Don. He suspected his mother had said something to Don while he was on the phone.

"That was great, mom," Jerrod said as he wiped the corners of his mouth with one of her white linen napkins.

"Yes. Thank you, dear," Don said. "That was excellent."

"You're both very welcome," she said as she gathered the plates.

"Your mother and I are leaving for Los Angeles tomorrow morning," Don said.

"What's happening in Los Angeles?" Jerrod asked.

"A real estate conference of some sort," his mother said. "We're also going to visit your grandmother in Pasadena. We'll be back Sunday night."

"Have a great trip," Jerrod said.

"What are you doing with the rest of your day-off?" his mother asked.

"I'll probably just relax," he said. "I may go over to the neighbor's house to watch the Giants play the Dodgers on TV this afternoon. I don't know."

"I prefer watching golf on TV, myself," Don said.

Jerrod glared at him.

"I should be going. Thank you, both, very much for lunch."

He hugged his mother and shook hands with Don before leaving through the big red front door. He noticed Don Renaud had a remarkably firm handshake for such a little shit of a man.

CHAPTER 34

Jerrod stopped at the front step of his mother's house to look at all the other homes on the block. They were an eclectic collection with one thing in common — all were big.

He decided to walk home on a different route to check out more of the neighborhood. He walked north along Rochester Avenue and crossed the street. He walked on the sidewalk to a meandering side street named Sherwood Drive.

He didn't care too much for the pale yellow with bright white trim Cape Cod-style house across the street but did like the large two-story earth-tone Spanish-style house he was approaching. The house was secured behind a four-foot adobe wall with an intricate two-foot high and spear-tipped wrought-iron fence above it. As he got closer, he studied the beautiful full landscaping and the majestic cobblestone driveway.

At the end of the driveway near a triple-wide garage was a car which seemed out of place. He could see from its side it was an older medium-blue sedan. He walked along the sidewalk and got a better view of the rear of the car until he could see it was an Oldsmobile Delta 88 and could read the license plate: 339FAS. There was no one around the car.

It was the car belonging to Efrain Hernandez he had seen Oso get out of at Garcia's on Friday.

He continued walking past the house but made a mental note of the street address number — 676 — from a pillar near the closed driveway gate.

What the hell was that car doing at that house? Jerrod asked himself.

He tried to explain to himself why Efrain Hernandez' car was behind the closed gate of the expensive home.

What was the connection between the car, Efrain Hernandez, Oso, Maggie, and Nopales with that high-end home and its occupant? There had to be an explanation. Just who lived at that massive house and why would *that* car be parked there?

Jerrod jogged back to his house via the shortest route he could think of, went to the garage, got in his Toyota truck, and drove back to Sherwood Drive.

He cruised by and saw the Oldsmobile still in the driveway. He parked at the curb about a half-block from the house so he could watch the street from his rear-view mirror.

Nearly a half-hour later, the blue Oldsmobile pulled out of the driveway and turned left onto Sherwood Drive — away from his Toyota.

He saw the silhouettes of two people in the car as it drove away. He shifted the Toyota into gear and drove around the block onto Rochester Avenue in the hopes of following the Oldsmobile wherever it may lead.

He pushed the engine in the small truck as he zipped past his mother's house at double the safe speed, around a curve, and over a short rise. At the crest of the rise, he pulled his foot from the accelerator.

The Oldsmobile was gone.

He looked down some side streets hoping to get a glimpse of the car, but it had vanished.

“Son-of-a-bitch.”

CHAPTER 35

Jerrod drove home and put the truck into the garage. He was disappointed with himself for losing the Oldsmobile and the chance he had of learning more about Efrain Hernandez and Oso.

He walked from the garage and saw the colonel outside having a cigarette.

"The Giants' game is on," the colonel said, "Come over and watch it with me."

"Deal," he said. "Want a beer?"

"Sure."

He went to the refrigerator and took out two bottles of Heineken. He walked over to the colonel's back door and let himself in.

"The game's already in the second inning," the colonel said as he opened both bottles and they clanked the necks.

"Cheers," the two men said simultaneously.

"Damn," Jerrod said as he sat down. "The Giants are a run down already."

The men chatted and enjoyed the beer as they watched a rather boring pitchers' duel develop. The Giants gave up another run in the top of the sixth inning and failed to score themselves. No more runs were scored by either team through the top of the ninth inning.

In the bottom of the ninth, the Giants had just three outs to score two runs to tie the game or three to win it.

The TV cameras followed some of the crowd at the game leaving the stands to get a head-start on traffic.

The first Giants batter got a clean line-drive single into left field. The second batter hit a shot past the pitcher and into center field for another single.

It was runners on first and second with no outs.

The third batter placed a perfect bunt down the third base line. The third baseman charged the ball, picked it up cleanly with his bare hand, and made a solid throw to first base. The throw was too late, and the speedy runner was safe.

Bases loaded with no outs.

The fourth batter popped up weakly to the first baseman in foul territory.

One out and bases still loaded.

The fifth batter smashed a sharp ground ball between the third baseman and the shortstop. The shortstop snagged the ball in his glove and made a leaping throw to second base for a possible double play which would end the game. The ball soared over the second baseman's head and into right field. Two runs scored.

Game tied with runners on first and third.

“Those people who left the stands early are kicking themselves now,” the colonel said.

Jerrod could only laugh. Both men were on their feet cheering for their team to beat The Bums.

The next Giants batter poked a soft fly ball into middle right field. As the ball was caught, the runner at third base tagged-up and sprinted to the plate. The strong throw came to the catcher on one-hop. The runner made a long hook-slide. The play was remarkably close.

The umpire delayed a second before signaling.

Safe.

The Giants players stormed onto the field and hugged each other at home plate. The fans who stayed in the stands went crazy with emotion.

Jerrod and the colonel shook hands to celebrate the greatest baseball come-from-behind win neither could remember.

“Small-Ball,” the colonel said. “Our Giants played brilliant ‘Small-Ball.’ They didn't give up like those silly fans did, they played smart, they got on base, and no one was swinging for the home run. They just wanted to make contact with the ball, they were willing to sacrifice themselves for the team, and they got a big break when they needed it. They played like a team and won like a team.”

“Small-Ball?” Jerrod said to himself. He had heard the term before, but never had it explained quite that way.

Feeling jubilant from the Giants' win and the brief distraction it had provided, Jerrod walked across the backyards and into his house through the laundry room door. He could hear the TV but couldn't remember having turned it on earlier.

He slowed his step as he entered the living room and saw a familiar brown leather purse sitting on the dining room table.

“Who has dared invade my palace?” Jerrod said in the deepest Barry White voice he could muster.

“I called, but there was no answer,” Natalie said. “So, I just came over.”

She was seated with her legs up on the sofa.

“I'm glad you did,” he said as he knelt on both knees in front of the sofa and hugged her. “I missed you.”

"I missed you, too."

He sat down with her and said, "I see you helped yourself to the wine."

"And I took the very last drop."

"How are you doing?"

"Okay. It's still rough."

"How about your mom?"

"She's okay too. My aunt is staying with her for a couple days."

"Sounds good."

He got a Heineken and sat back on the sofa.

"My sister's such a bitch," she said.

"What did she do?"

"We were talking about Hector," she said. "We were remembering the silly things he did, you know, like 'break-dancing' when it came out."

"I remember that," he said. "Hector came to the PD with a big piece of vinyl and did some dance moves right on the sidewalk. The chief came out of his office to watch."

"Well, my sister is a bitch because when your name came up, she said you could have done more to protect Hector."

Jerrod was rarely speechless, but the wiring in his brain shorted when he tried to process the words he had just heard.

"What did Terri say?" he asked while hoping he misunderstood what he had just heard.

"She said you could have done more to protect Hector," she repeated.

He could not believe what she just said.

"What the hell was I supposed to do," he said as his emotions went from sadness to defensive to angry. "I really liked Hector, but he wasn't *my* kid."

"He looked up to you," she said. "You were his friend. He idolized you. She thinks you let him down."

"I can't believe this," he said. "According to your idiot sister, Hector's death is somehow my fault. Bullshit."

"I'm sorry," she said. "I don't think she's blaming you. I know you were good to Hector."

Jerrod was looking right at her but seemed lost in thought and apparently didn't hear her words.

"I'm sorry," she said.

His eyes focused on hers and he said simply, "Okay."

“I know you and Hector were friends,” she said. “It wasn't your fault.”

There was no lovemaking in his bed that night.

Jerrod laid awake and asked himself if Natalie's sister was right. Had there been more he could have done to help Hector out and somehow prevent his death? Who knew?

Hector wasn't his child, but he had been his friend. Maybe he *could* have kept him alive.

CHAPTER 36

Monday

Allison Jenkins worked five nightshifts a week in the rain, the fog, and on frigidly cold nights. She had Wednesdays and Thursdays off and averaged four to five hours of restless daytime sleep.

And she couldn't possibly have been happier.

Allison, who everyone called “AJ,” was the first and only female to ever be sworn as a Valle Verde police officer.

She stood nearly six-foot tall, was athletically built, and kept her blond shoulder-length hair in a ponytail.

She was raised in Southern California and was a stand-out swimmer and water polo player at her hometown high school. She received a full-ride scholarship to the University of California where she had been a star water polo player and led the team in scoring for three years. She earned a bachelor’s degree in Public Administration but had no real career goal in mind beyond college.

Soon after she graduated, AJ and a number of friends drove up the coast to enjoy a short vacation at the beaches in Mesa County. She was pleased with the mild climate and laid-back attitude she felt on the Central Coast. She realized how manic her life had been in Southern California when she compared it to the peacefulness she felt in the Mesa area.

AJ was reading the local newspaper one morning during the trip and saw an announcement from the City of Valle Verde recruiting entry-level police officer trainees. Although she had no experience or real exposure to law enforcement before, she decided at that moment to become a police officer.

She persuaded her friends to detour through Valle Verde on the way home. They drove around the city, and she liked everything she saw. As she cruised through downtown on Main Street, she saw the City Hall building and pulled quickly into the parking lot. She ran inside, found the personnel office, and asked for a police officer application.

She completed the application at home and mailed it back to the city a day later.

A week passed before she received a letter inviting her to the police officer testing process to be held two weeks later. The letter described the “pass/fail” physical agility test and the written test that would narrow the list of candidates.

AJ returned to Valle Verde and successfully passed the physical testing portion — which involved an obstacle course, scaling a six-foot wall, and dragging a 125-pound dummy — without difficulty.

Several male candidates horribly failed the test.

The written portion of the testing was equally easy for the college educated and confident twenty-two-year-old.

She was invited to return for the final portion of the testing process, the oral interview, where she faced a panel of three male police sergeants from other agencies. Despite her lack of experience, the panel was so impressed with her demeanor, confidence, and ability to answer the questions clearly and concisely that they placed her name at the very top of the candidate list for two open police officer positions.

A few days later, AJ was telephoned by Captain Andrew Wheaton and was offered one of the open positions. She accepted and was sworn-in a few weeks later. She attended a sixteen-week police academy and placed near the top of her class in nearly every category.

She returned to the VVPD and received some uncomfortable media attention for being the first female to break into the traditional and male-dominated department. After sailing through her field-training, she was assigned to her own beat as a solo officer.

That had been the proudest day of her life.

AJ had been a patrol officer for a little over three years and loved every minute of it. Some of the senior officers were distant and suspicious of her at first, but she soon earned their respect with her abilities and disarming personality.

She was assigned to Patrol the "graveyard" shift which worked from eleven to seven in the morning. She worked a solo car and was assigned to the east side section of Valle Verde which was mostly a residential area with some small strip malls and shopping centers mixed in.

She watched and listened as she crept her patrol car through a neighborhood of slumping older houses. The faux-fur collar of her black duty jacket was pulled up to protect her neck from the brutally chilly night and a piercing wind that poured through the open driver's window.

The bitter cold had kept people indoors and her shift had been extremely quiet. She had earlier handled a few routine service calls and covered another officer, Dave Yamamoto, on a downtown alarm call, but otherwise the police radio was silent.

The term cops used was: "The night was dead."

The quiet on the police radio was interrupted by the voice of a male dispatcher: "Any unit in position. Multiple calls of a woman screaming in the front yard. 526 Bixby Street. Unit to cover."

Bixby Street was a one-block dead-end street off May Avenue and was squarely in AJ's beat. She grabbed the Motorola microphone from its dashboard holder and radioed she was enroute. Dave Yamamoto radioed he would cover AJ.

AJ flipped on the overhead red and blue lights of the patrol car but didn't activate the siren as she sped to the scene. As she turned onto May Avenue, she shutdown the overhead lights and slowed her car as she approached Bixby Street.

Dave Yamamoto pulled his black-and-white in behind.

She turned right at the corner of Bixby Street and could hear voices yelling in both English and Spanish.

The officers parked in the middle of the street and walked toward the sound of the commotion. In the bluish tint of the mercury-vapor streetlights, they could see the silhouettes of a man and a woman on the sidewalk in front of a single-story house. A second, large framed, man lumbered up the front steps and into the house as the officers approached.

The officers walked closer and found the first man facing the woman and telling her to calm down. The woman held a bundle close to her chest with both arms.

AJ shined her flashlight on the couple.

"What's the problem here?" AJ asked.

"No problem," the man said. "Just a little family disagreement."

AJ could see the woman was breathing heavy and her face streaked with tears. The bundle at her chest was a swaddled baby.

"Ma'am," AJ said to the woman. "Would you please come with me."

"She's my wife—" the man said.

"I'll talk to you here, sir," Dave interrupted and established how their conversation was going to be conducted. "Can I see some ID please?"

AJ walked with the woman on the sidewalk toward May Avenue and out of earshot of Dave and the man he was talking to.

"What's your name?" AJ asked.

"Martha. Martha Figueroa," she answered.

"How old is your baby?"

"He's about thirteen months old."

"It's a little chilly to be taking your baby out. Are you sure you're okay?"

Martha started to cry. Through her sobs she said, "My boyfriend... he's such an asshole... I just need to go to my friend's house for the night."

On her portable police radio, she heard Dave request a warrants check for "Efrain Gomez Hernandez." The name had no significance to her.

"What's going on with your boyfriend tonight?" AJ asked.

"He's a fucking asshole," Martha said.

"We've established he's an asshole, but what happened tonight?"

"He came home drunk from work again with his stupid friend. He got mad because there wasn't any food he wanted in the refrigerator."

"How did you end up outside?" AJ asked. "It's crazy cold tonight."

"I took the baby and just wanted to walk to my friend's house for the night," Martha said. "Efrain's nice when he sobers up. I don't want to get him in trouble again."

Martha's story piqued AJ interest when she said, "in trouble *again*."

"What happened last time, Martha?"

"He beat the shit out of me," Martha said. "I was in the hospital for a few days and almost lost the baby."

"Did he get arrested?"

"He went to jail, but they dropped the charges because I wouldn't go to court."

"Did he hurt you tonight?"

"No. He just yelled at me and called me names. I hate him like that."

"What's his friend's name?"

I don't know his real name," Martha said. "Everyone just calls him 'Oso.' That pig is a bigger asshole than Efrain."

"Oso" also meant nothing to AJ.

"Those two are always together," Martha said. "Oso doesn't drive a car, so Efrain drives him everywhere. He eats our food and sleeps on our couch all the time."

"Did Efrain threaten you in any way?" AJ asked.

"No threats," Martha said as she lifted the baby higher and tighter to her chest. "He just talked mean to me."

The dispatcher's voice radioed that Efrain Hernandez had no outstanding warrants.

"I can give you a ride to your friend's house," AJ said. "Where does she live?"

“I don't know the number,” Martha said. “It's on Walnut Street. I can show you.”

“Okay,” AJ said. “Wait here and I'll be right back.”

“Okay,” Martha said.

AJ walked over to Dave and Efrain Hernandez.

“Mr. Hernandez, there's generally no crime when you argue with your girlfriend,” AJ said. “Except in public at one-thirty in the morning.”

Efrain nodded.

“I'm going to give Martha and the baby a ride to a friend's house,” AJ said. “Do you have a problem with that?”

“No,” Efrain said.

“You're free to go,” Dave said. “We hope you can work things out tomorrow.”

“Okay,” Efrain said as he walked toward the front steps of the house. The porch light illuminated his face as he placed his hand on the doorknob and paused before going inside. He shot a menacing glare at Martha and walked inside.

The officers walked back to their idling patrol cars. AJ escorted Martha to her car and held the rear door open as she climbed in.

AJ closed the door and talked with Dave.

“No crime committed that I can tell,” AJ said. “I'll cut an incident report just to cover-my-ass in case something bad happens later.”

“Good idea,” Dave said.

“Thanks for the back-up.”

“Anytime.”

AJ backed the patrol car to May Avenue. She started driving toward Walnut Street and initiated some small talk.

“What's your babies name?” AJ asked.

“Efrain,” Martha said. “Just like his asshole father.”

“Have you always lived in Valle Verde?”

“No. My family is in Turlock. Over by Modesto. I moved here with my boyfriend when I got pregnant.”

“Is Efrain good with the baby?”

“He loves the baby and plays with him all the time,” Martha said. “But he won't feed or change him.”

“Do you work, Martha?”

“Not anymore. I had a good job in Turlock, but I don't work at all here.”

AJ made a right turn.

"Do you have kids?" Martha asked.

"Not yet," AJ said. "I want kids eventually, but not right away. I'll find the right guy and start a family someday."

The car was quiet again as AJ pulled onto Walnut Street.

"Which house, Martha?"

"The gray house on the right. The one with the white pickup in front."

AJ pulled the patrol car to the curb behind the truck. She walked around the car and opened the car door for Martha. Martha didn't move to get out of the car immediately.

"Here you are," AJ said. "I'm sorry we had to meet under these circumstances, but I'm glad we got to meet. Is there anything else you would like to talk about?"

Martha looked down at her baby boy, adjusted the blanket, and kissed the baby on the forehead. She looked up at AJ and then back to the baby.

After about ten seconds, Martha said simply: "No."

Sensing Martha had something else she wanted to talk about, AJ took out a business card and handed it to her.

"Call me anytime if you need help. Or just to talk. Okay?"

"I will," Martha said. "Thank you for the ride."

AJ helped Martha out of the car and watched her climb the front steps of the house. She knocked on the door, a light came on, and a woman opened the door.

Martha looked back over her shoulder toward AJ for a moment before walking inside.

AJ was unsettled by the encounter that morning. She had a feeling, a cop's hunch, there was something else going on between Martha Figueroa and Efrain Hernandez that may be important later.

CHAPTER 37

Jerrod Gold arrived for work, Monday morning, at five minutes before eight. Craig Wallace and Willie Sanchez were at their desks.

"You're early today," Craig said. "But not early enough to make the coffee."

"Big day today," Jerrod said. "Where's Hanson?"

"Meeting with the captain," Willie said.

"Good," Jerrod said. "What the hell happened on Saturday? I was ready to work twenty hours a day until we solved this thing."

"Hanson got here at about three o'clock Saturday afternoon," Craig said. "He was pissed at having to cut his trip short. We told him what we had so far on the case, which wasn't much, to be honest. He met with the captain and just sent us home until today. No explanation. No nothing."

"Interesting," Jerrod said. "I called him from the morgue, and he didn't want to hear about anything we found. He told me to just book my evidence and go home too."

"I'm sure we'll get an explanation this morning from him," Willie said. "He's a pretty straight-shooter and I'm sure there was some reason to shut the case down for the day."

The detectives started the morning routine and waited for their sergeant to come in to set the agenda for the day.

Willie said to the other two detectives, "You guys hear about the messed-up thing that happened to Rusty Browne and his wife at church yesterday?"

Both detectives shook their heads.

"Well, you're not going to believe it," Willie said.

"I've got to hear this," Jerrod said.

"Okay," Willie said. "Here's what Rusty told me: They've been going to the Mission Community Church on the north side for a couple years. He was at the service yesterday with his wife, Katy, and their son, Jimmy.

"Katy, 'the nicest woman in the world,' Browne?" Craig asked.

"Yeah, that Katy," Willie said. "Anyway, Jimmy was acting up a little during the service. Rusty took him outside and then Katy took him out, but he was still being fussy."

"Rusty told me they were dealing with some behavioral issue with him," Jerrod said.

"Yeah, they have," Willie said. "Stop interrupting. After the service, the pastor's wife came over to them all smiley-face and said it might be a good idea to not bring Jimmy to the services anymore."

"What's the big deal about that?" Craig asked.

"It gets better, well, worse," Willie said. "Rusty apologized and told her Jimmy was just having a rough day. Then the pastor's wife said, kind of under her breath, 'You must have done something terrible in your lives for the Lord to burden you with that child.'"

"No way?" Jerrod said.

"Yes way," Willie said.

"What did they do?" Craig asked.

"They left," Willie said. "And they're never going back."

"That is messed-up," Jerrod said.

"I'm glad I'm Catholic," Willie said. "My church may make us feel guilty about everything we do; but they don't damn us when our kids squirm in the pews a little."

CHAPTER 38

Sergeant Pete Hanson came into the room and slumped into the chair at his desk.

"Morning, Sarge," Jerrod said.

"Good morning," the sergeant said. "Let's get going while all four of us are here. Let's brief each other on what we know about the homicide and where the case needs to go from here. Craig, you first."

Each detective, in turn, recounted their involvement in the case, the slim leads developed, and the issues that still needed to be resolved:

Craig described the crime scene.

Willie talked about the Medina family notification, the blue car, and the lack of information coming from the neighborhood.

Jerrod talked about his conversation with the westside lumpers and the evidence gathered from the autopsy.

"Okay," the sergeant said. "I think we have a good understanding of the situation. We have two priorities this morning: First, the Hector Medina homicide is going to stay with Craig. Craig, you can ask for help from Willie and Jerrod, as necessary. Second, Jerrod is going to keep following up on the OD cases from last week."

"I'd like to stay on the Hector case, Sarge," Jerrod said. "I knew the kid and—"

"Craig has the case," the sergeant interrupted. "You may be *too* close to the victim."

"Hang on a second," Jerrod said.

"Careful," Craig whispered to Jerrod, warning his young partner to not take on their supervisor.

"Those are the assignments," the sergeant said. His annoyance with the young detective was obvious.

He spoke next to the three detectives, but stared directly at Jerrod, "Get to work."

Jerrod seethed at his desk for a few minutes while opening and closing various case folders, but not seeing a single word in any of them. He could barely contain his anger and was about to explode.

Craig watched his young partner and could see the eruption about to happen.

"Hey, Jerrod," Craig said. "Let's go have a cigarette."

"I have things to do," Jerrod said without looking up from his cluttered desk.

"I need a cigarette... *now*," Craig said.

Jerrod looked across the desks at Craig and caught his glower.

"Okay. Shit."

The two detectives walked through the squad room and to the back parking lot. Craig lit a cigarette before speaking.

"Hey, dipshit, you want to get sent back to Patrol?" Craig asked facetiously. "You're not going to win a battle with Hanson."

"Screw Hanson," Jerrod said. "I thought he was on our side. Even Andy and Barney in fucking Mayberry know you don't take a day off in the middle of a major case and let it go stale. That's bullshit."

"I agree, but there's no *our* side," Craig said. "Hanson runs the bureau. Not you. He makes those decisions. Not you."

"Maybe Patrol wouldn't be such a bad place right now," Jerrod said.

"Lot of help you'll be there," Craig said. "Writing tickets and taking chickenshit reports aren't going to help us find Hector's killer."

"I don't care anymore," Jerrod said.

"Then tell me why I should care?" Craig asked.

Jerrod didn't answer.

"Just play the game Hanson wants you to play," Craig said. "Handle the cases you have. I'll keep you in the loop on the Hector case and you'll be right there with me when something breaks."

Jerrod knew Craig was right... again.

"Okay," Jerrod said. "His game. His rules. Got it."

Jerrod stayed outside and took some deep breaths before going back to his desk. He knew he was pushing the bounds of insubordination and was going to lose big-time if he crossed that line. He was frustrated he wasn't going to have a bigger role in the homicide case and felt he was more than ready to handle the responsibility.

He tried to calm himself and think rationally. He asked himself if he was *too close* to the case to be effective.

He decided to just back off and do as he was directed... for the time being.

CHAPTER 39

Jerrod went back to his desk and looked through his reports on the homicide.

"I've got some follow-up on the bullet recovered at autopsy," Jerrod told the sergeant. "I'd like to run by MLD Guns and talk to Marv about it. Then everything I have can go to Craig."

"Go ahead," the sergeant said – clearly surprised at the attitude turnaround.

He was still fuming about being pulled away from the murder investigation and struggled to understand his sergeant's reasoning behind the decision. He was glad to get out of the office for a while. He needed to clear his head and get a grip on how *he* was going to find Hector Medina's killer through Craig.

Jerrod drove to an east side strip-mall and parked in front of a small shop with a modest sign reading: MLD GUNS and AMMO. A used bookstore was situated to the left of the gun shop. A small breakfast and lunch diner was located to its right. The fourth business, to the right of the diner, was a hair and nail salon.

The gun shop was easy to find as it was the only business in the mall with bars over the windows and a front door that looked like it came off a jail cell.

He walked into the store and was greeted by the owner, Marvin L. Denny, the "MLD" in the store name.

"Hello, Jerrod," Marv said. "Here on business or pleasure today."

"Hello, Marv. Business today. I need some technical advice."

"I hope you came to the right place. How can I help?"

Marv Denny, a US Army veteran from the Vietnam War, was the most knowledgeable firearms expert and skilled gunsmith in the area. He stood behind a glass display case containing numerous handguns and gun accessories. The wall behind him was lined with a variety of rifles and shotguns.

"It's related to a homicide victim we found Saturday morning," Jerrod said.

"The kid on the westside? I read about it in the paper yesterday."

"Yeah. The kid was shot in the head with a small-caliber handgun. The bullet recovered at autopsy was a 71-grain FMJ. Possibly a .32 ACP. Doctor Torosian did some research and suggested the bullet may have been fired from a Colt Model 1903."

"What's your question?"

"Well, how common are those guns? And have you ever sold one or the ammo that goes with it?"

"I'm familiar with the handgun. There were probably over half-million of them manufactured. Those handguns are still around, but I don't see many of them in the shop and no one has ever come in looking to buy one. I happen to have a Model 1903 in my safe."

"Can I see it?"

"Sure. I'll be right back."

Marv walked to a backroom and returned a few minutes later with a small handgun. He pulled the slide back to assure it was unloaded and locked the slide with a catch he activated with his right thumb. He put a black pad on the glass countertop and laid the handgun on it.

"May I?" Jerrod asked.

"Go ahead," Marv said.

Jerrod picked up the handgun and checked himself to make sure it was unloaded. He found the handgun to be heavier than it looked. The pistol had a blued finish on the metal and brown checked walnut grips. There was no exposed hammer, unlike many semi-automatic pistols he had seen before.

"No hammer?"

"It's called 'hammerless' on purpose," Marv said. "It was designed with an internal hammer because it was made to be carried in a coat pocket. An exposed hammer would snag on the material. That gun was popular with the gangsters in the 1930s. Capone. Dillinger. Bonnie and Clyde."

The handgun operated like any standard auto-pistol: a metal magazine containing live cartridges was inserted into the base of the grip. The slide was racked back, and a cartridge was stripped from the magazine into the firing chamber as the slide went forward. When fired, the bullet traveled down the barrel and exited the muzzle of the pistol. At the same time, the slide traveled back, and the empty cartridge case was ejected through an opening on the right side of the slide and a fresh cartridge was chambered as the slide traveled forward again. The process repeated each time the trigger was pulled until the magazine was empty.

"Have you ever had one of these guns here for service, that you recall?" Jerrod asked.

"Not that I can remember," Marv said. "I see a lot of guns. I might have had a customer come in with a question about one of those pistols, but I can't remember who or when."

“Can I look at just the barrel?” Jerrod asked as he placed the Colt back on the pad.

“Sure,” Marv said as he picked up the handgun, pulled the slide back slightly, twisted the barrel at the muzzle and pulled the slide forward off the frame. He lifted the barrel from the frame and put the disassembled handgun on the pad.

Jerrod raised the barrel so he could look through it at a ceiling light. In the barrel, he counted six ridges with a slight twist that would cause a bullet to rotate clockwise, or right, as it traveled the length of the barrel.

“Thank you,” Jerrod said as he handed it to Marv.

Marv wiped down the barrel with a special oil cloth and reassembled the handgun.

“Have you sold any .32 ACP ammo here?” Jerrod asked.

“It's not a very popular round, to be honest. I think I've ordered only two or three boxes of .32 ACP, or .32 Automatic, as it’s sometimes called, since I opened the shop and maybe sold one of them five or six years ago.”

He looked into a cabinet under the glass display case and said, “There's one left.” He brought out a white cardboard box and placed it on the counter.

The box was printed with: WINCHESTER 32 Auto 71 GR. FMJ. The box contained fifty .32 caliber FMJ cartridges.

Jerrod picked one cartridge from the box and examined it closely. It was less than an inch long and about one-quarter inch in diameter. It had a shining copper-colored bullet in a bright brass case. The head-stamp on the base of the cartridge read: WIN 32 AUTO.

“Do you have any records of the one box of these rounds you sold?” Jerrod asked.

“If I had sold the actual handgun, I could look in my records and get the buyer information to you by the end of the day. But I don't keep any records for ammunition sales. It’s not required. Sorry.”

“If you think of anything, please call me,” Jerrod said. “Thank you for your help.”

“Anytime,” Marv said.

Jerrod left the gun store confident he knew the type of handgun and ammunition used to kill Hector Medina.

Finding the actual pistol would prove to be not as easy.

CHAPTER 40

Jerrod left the gun store and drove toward "The Rochester" portion of the city. He cruised by the Spanish-style estate at 676 Sherwood Drive where he had seen the Oldsmobile the day before. There were no vehicles or people in front of the house.

He drove back downtown and parked at the City Hall. At the service window at the Building Department. A male clerk with short brown hair and a slim build came to the window to greet him.

"You look familiar," Jerrod said. "Aren't you with the Fire Department?"

"I'm a volunteer there," the clerk said. "This is my full-time gig."

"I'm Jerrod Gold," he said. "I'm with the PD. What's your name?"

"I know who you are," the clerk said. "I'm Doug Fuller."

"Nice to meet you, Doug," Jerrod said as he extended his right hand.

"How can I help?" Doug asked after shaking hands.

"I'm trying to find the ownership of a house on the east side. Am I at the correct office?"

"Well, the actual ownership and property tax records are with the Mesa County Assessor's Office," Doug said. "But I can get that information here. It may take a few minutes."

"Sure. The address is: 676 Sherwood Drive."

"Sherwood Drive? Nice neighborhood. I'll be right back."

Jerrod waited at the window for about three minutes while he watched the clerk look through some card files and then onto a microfiche machine. He wrote on a pad of paper and returned to the window.

"The owner of record on the Sherwood Drive property is: 'Armando Mendoza.'"

"Armando Mendoza?" Jerrod said.

"Mr. Mendoza's name is connected to several other properties in the city," Doug said. "Beside the Sherwood Drive property, there are two commercial buildings downtown, one more commercial property and two residential properties on the east side, and some west side farmland. I wrote down those addresses for you."

"Wow, thank you. You've been a great help. I owe you one."

"Come by anytime. I can find *anything* in the files here."

Armando Mendoza was a name Jerrod should have been familiar with but could not place. He became determined to find out more about him.

CHAPTER 41

Jerrod drove back to the PD and found only Willie at his desk when he walked into the bureau.

"Did you read the morning reports yet, Jerrod?" Willie asked.

"Not yet."

"AJ wrote an incident report from last night that mentions your guys. Efrain and Oso. I left the report on your desk."

"You've got to be kidding me," Jerrod said as he read the details of AJ's conversation with Martha Figueroa. His eyes widened as he read Martha had been dropped off at a friend's house for the night.

"I have to talk to this woman. Right now," Jerrod said as he grabbed his jacket and headed back out of the office.

He drove directly to the Walnut Street address. He had previously found that the victims of abusive relationships were very forthcoming with information about their abusers while they were still angry. However, the flow of information quickly shut down after they made-up and got back together. The cycle of violence would then reset to the "honeymoon phase" until the next escalation and blow-up of the relationship.

He found the Walnut Street address and rang the doorbell.

"*Hola*," said the middle-aged woman who answered the door.

"Is Martha Figueroa here?" he asked. "I'd like to speak with her."

In broken English, the woman said, "Martha went home this morning."

Jerrod thanked her and walked back to his car.

He slapped the steering wheel when he acknowledged he had missed his opportunity to interview Martha before she returned to her abuser.

AJ's incident report listed Martha's home as being on Bixby Street. He drove to May Avenue and slowed as he passed its intersection with Bixby Street.

"Hell yes," he said when he saw the blue Oldsmobile parked at the curb in front of the tan single-story house. He was pleased to know where Efrain Hernandez lived and where the Oldsmobile could be located.

He still wanted to interview Martha but decided the smart thing to do was to wait until the Oldsmobile was gone and it was safer to approach her.

CHAPTER 42

Jerrod pulled out the sheet of paper Doug Fuller had prepared containing the list of properties owned by Armando Mendoza.

He located the first one of the east side residential addresses. It was a modest ranch-style house on an average-sized lot in a newer neighborhood. The stucco exterior was tan and the landscape tidy. There were no cars in the driveway or parked in front of the house.

The second address was another modest light blue stucco house in the same neighborhood and about two blocks from the first. A new bright red BMW 525i coupe was parked in the driveway. The personalized license plate number was easy to remember — it read, "CATSBMR."

The east side commercial property listed on the sheet of paper was on a main Valle Verde thoroughfare. As Jerrod got closer to the address, he found it to be in the same strip mall MLD Guns and Ammo was located.

The suite number was for the beauty salon — Final Touches Hair and Nails.

While still on the east side, he drove by the Sherwood Drive address again and found a vehicle parked on the cobblestone driveway near the front door. It was a black, early 1980's Chevrolet Suburban. He noted the license plate number and jotted it down on the sheet of paper.

Jerrod drove downtown to check the two other commercial properties owned by Armando Mendoza.

The first address was a bar on Main Street. The bar, El Ocotillo Club, was located in what cops referred to as "South Main" or the first three blocks of Main Street between the Valle Verde River bridge and the City Plaza. The area was a mix of grocery stores, retail shops, restaurants, a theater, and a few bars which catered specifically to the Latino community.

He had been in the El Ocotillo Club many times during his time in Patrol and was familiar with the layout of the bar.

The second downtown commercial address was in the "North Main" area between the City Plaza and the "Y" intersection with Independence and Constitution Avenues. As he ticked off the ascending street numbers of a bank, a gas station, and a stationery store, he found the address to be the restaurant he had visited the previous Thursday night — Nopales.

"I'll be goddamned," Jerrod said.

The final property on the list owned by Armando Mendoza was a ten-acre parcel of flat land on the west side and just inside the city limits. The land had perfectly straight rows of manicured strawberries plants grown in raised mounds of rich dark soil. A weather-worn and faded white clapboard-sided barn sat in the middle of the parcel. A narrow, rutted dirt road led to the barn from the paved roadway.

His mind went into full gear making the various connections: *Armando Mendoza owned all of the properties. The business on one of the properties was run by Maggie Mendoza. Was Armando Mendoza a relative? Her father or an uncle? That would explain the Efrain Hernandez and Oso connection to the restaurant and the Sherwood Drive estate.*

The ownership of the other two businesses still needed to be determined. The two residences on the east side were owned by Armando Mendoza. But who actually lived there?

Much more about those connections needed to be explored.

Jerrod drove back to City Hall and hoped Doug Fuller was at his desk. He walked to the Building Department where an overweight female clerk forced herself from her desk and waddled to the window.

"May I help you?" the clerk said.

"Is Doug in, by chance?" he asked.

"No, he went to lunch," the clerk said. He should be back in about twenty minutes. Can I help you?"

"I'll check back in later. Thank you."

He walked out of City Hall and could smell the aroma of hotdogs and chili wafting through the air from The Corner.

"If Doug gets lunch," he said to himself. "I might as well, too."

Jerrod left his car in the City Hall lot and walked the half block to The Corner where he found a line of teenagers from the high school crowding the order window.

There were two VVPD patrol cars in the parking lot. Officers Kevin Arneta and Kevin Holcomb, "The Kevins," were busy munching chili dogs and cold drinks in Coke cups.

"Enjoying lunch, guys," Jerrod said.

"Hey, Jerrod," Big Kevin said through a mouth full of hotdog, bun, mustard, chili, and onions.

Tall Kevin kept his mouth closed and just gave a "man-nod" — a simple raise of the chin.

"Are detectives taking foot-patrol beats downtown now, or what?" Big Kevin asked after his mouth now cleared of debris.

"Just at City Hall getting some info."

"Anything happening on the homicide from the other night," Tall Kevin asked.

"Not really," Jerrod said. "Craig has the lead on that one. I'm working on the OD cases."

"We knew that kid, Hector," Big Kevin said. "We know you guys already asked around his neighborhood—"

"But we talked to a few 'friendlies' anyway," Tall Kevin interrupted. "No one is talking about Hector or about the killing. Period. Everyone is scared shitless over this thing."

"Thanks," Jerrod said.

"We'll call in if we hear anything," Big Kevin said.

"Maybe you guys would know?" Jerrod asked. "Do you know who owns the hair and nail shop on the east side near Marv's gun store?"

Both officers shook their heads.

"How about the El Ocotillo Club downtown?" Jerrod asked.

"We know the owner," Tall Kevin said. "We grew up with him in Plumdale. His name is Joaquin Cervantes, but we just called him 'Chimo.'" He's married to Maggie Cervantes. She owns Nopales restaurant up Main Street. We were both at the wedding. Big church deal. Awesome party."

"Maggie Cervantes, okay," Jerrod said. "I knew her as Maggie Mendoza."

"That's her," Big Kevin said.

"Do you know who her father is?" Jerrod asked.

"Sure, he's Armando Mendoza," Tall Kevin said, "Met him at the wedding. Super nice guy. Real proud dad. Big smile the whole time. Shook everyone's hand. He spared no expense — good food, awesome music, and lots of booze. You name it."

"Do you guys happen to remember when the wedding was?" Jerrod asked.

"Easy," Big Kevin said. "The wedding was the very next day, the Saturday, after we graduated from the police academy. June 18, 1982. We partied pretty hard."

"The newspaper did a big write-up about the wedding the next week," Tall Kevin added.

"Does Armando Mendoza have any other kids?" Jerrod asked the two officers.

"Maggie has a younger sister," Big Kevin said. "I don't remember her name. She's probably twenty-two or twenty-three now. She was one wild chick. Got drunk off her ass and danced all night. Remember her, Kevin?"

"Silver dress?" Tall Kevin asked as he grinned.

"Yep," Big Kevin said with a snicker. "She was a 'TPU.'"

"What's a 'TPU?'" Jerrod asked.

The Kevins looked at each other and said simultaneously: "Tight Professional Unit."

The high school kids around the order window hadn't thinned, so Jerrod walked to the opposite corner of the intersection and into the Valle Verde Public Library.

He went to an area near the librarian stand where editions of the Valle Verde *Sun* newspaper, dating from the turn of the century, were stored on microfilm. He found the canister of film which included June 1982 and threaded it into the reader-printer.

He spun the hand reel of film as full-page images of newspaper headlines, articles, announcement, public notices, and editorials sped across the reader screen. He stopped occasionally to find a date. June 2, June 10, June 17. The slowed the pace of the images and eased through the grainy grayscale pages of the Tuesday, June 22, 1982, edition.

On the social page, the big church wedding of Magdalena and Joaquin Cervantes was documented in great detail. A photograph of the smiling new bride and groom on the front steps of Saint Daniel's showed Maggie holding a bouquet and glowing in her elaborate white dress. A very handsome Joaquin, tall and fit looking, wore a dark tuxedo as he grinned and waved.

The article read, in part: "The bride was given away by her father, Armando Mendoza."

"Maria Mendoza" was named as the mother of the bride and "Catalina Mendoza" was one of the bridesmaids.

Jerrod pushed the "print" button and a piece of glossy acid-smelling paper with the wedding article dropped into a tray.

The kids had dissipated from The Corner as they headed back to campus. Jerrod ordered "two without" and a Coke.

As he waited, he couldn't believe his good fortune in running into The Kevins at The Corner.

The information was starting to come together: *Armando Mendoza was Maggie's father. Maggie's husband, "Chimo," ran El Ocotillo, and there was a younger daughter, Catalina, involved somehow.*

He took the first bite of a chili dog and a lifetime of memories and celebrations flashed through his mind.

"Only good things happen at The Corner."

Jerrod walked back to the Building Department and was glad to see Doug at his desk.

"Back already?" Doug said as he walked to the window.

"Just a few follow-up questions," Jerrod said.

"Sure. Fire away."

"Can I get the business ownership records for the three commercial addresses you gave me earlier?"

"Yeah. No problem. That information is in the Clerk's Office. But I can get it. Give me a couple minutes."

"Could I also get the water bills for the three residences, please?"

"That's easy. I'll be right back."

While he waited for Doug to return. Jerrod created a rough flow chart on a pad of paper:

He started at the top left of the page with an oval and wrote in "Nopales" and "Maggie."

In the top right corner, he drew an oval and wrote "Ocotillo" and "Chimo" inside it.

Below the "Maggie" oval, he drew two smaller ovals with "Efrain" in one and "Oso" in the other.

In the left side middle of the page, he drew an oval and wrote "Hair/Nails."

In the right-side middle, he drew another oval with "Farm" in it.

In the bottom left corner, the oval read, "Blue house" and "BMW."

In the bottom right corner, he wrote in the oval "Tan House."

In the very center of the page, he drew a larger oval and wrote "Armando" and "Sherwood" inside it.

He drew arrow-pointed lines to and from the "Maggie" and "Chimo" ovals. He drew a line between "Nopales/Maggie" and "Oso." He drew a line between "Efrain" and "Armando/Sherwood."

He drew lines between "Hair/Nails," "Farm," "Blue Stucco" and "Tan Stucco," "Nopales/Maggie" and "Ocotillo/Chimo" with their one common denominator, the biggest oval in the center, "Armando/Sherwood."

Doug returned to the window. He pushed a piece of paper across the counter and said, "Is this what you were looking for?"

Jerrod gave a faint smile as he read the information written on the paper:

Nopales: Owner — Magdalena Cervantes.

El Ocotillo Club: Owner — Joaquin Cervantes.

Final Touches Hair and Nails: Owner — Catalina Mendoza.

Sherwood Drive: Billed to — Armando Mendoza

Tan Stucco House: Billed to — Joaquin and Magdalena Cervantes

Blue Stucco House: Billed to — Catalina Mendoza.

"Thank you very much," Jerrod said.

At the PD, Jerrod went right to the Dispatch Center and Al Kees saw him coming.

"I know that look," Al said. "I'm busy."

"Come on, pal. Just a couple license numbers."

"Go away."

"I'll just go out to my car and call 'em in on the radio," Jerrod warned.

"Give them to me."

"Two license plates and driver's license info on the owners, please."

"No beer this time?" Al asked.

"I think you still owe me," Jerrod said as he gave him the license numbers and Al wrote them down on his steno pad.

Jerrod walked to the bureau and found only Pete Hanson in the office. He decided to take Craig's advice and just "play the game."

"Hey, Sarge," Jerrod said with a feigned light-hearted tone.

"Hello... Jerrod," the sergeant said as he looked back to him with some surprise at his drastic change of attitude from earlier that morning. "Any luck with Marv?"

"He was great," Jerrod said. "He pretty much confirmed we are looking for the Colt Model 1903 as the murder weapon. I'll write it up and give my report to Craig."

"Oh, okay. Anything else going on?"

"Nope," Jerrod answered.

Jerrod was typing his report on the interview with Marv Denny when his desk phone rang. It was Al.

"I've got your DMV stuff," he said. "Come and get it."

He walked to Dispatch, and Al handed him the printouts.

"Thank you very much," Jerrod said. "Now we're even for sure."

Jerrod read the DMV printouts: The black Chevy Suburban was a 1983 model and was unsurprisingly registered to Armando Mendoza at the Sherwood Drive address.

The red BMW, CATSBMR, was a 1985 model registered to "Catalina R. Mendoza" at the address of the blue stucco house.

The driver's license printouts listed Armando Mendoza's birth date as being in 1940 and his residence as the Sherwood Drive address. He had no violations or accidents listed.

Catalina Mendoza was a completely different story. She had been born in 1963 and had several violations noted — all for excessive speed — and two traffic accidents. He was surprised to see her license was still valid.

"'One wild chick,' indeed," Jerrod said to himself, repeating how The Kevins had described her.

The detectives had a collection of Valle Verde High School yearbooks going back to the 1950s. The high school yearbook faculty advisers routinely had one extra copy of each yearbook printed specifically for the VVPD.

If Catalina Mendoza had also gone to VVHS, he estimated she had graduated in 1981. He found the 1981 yearbook and flipped through the senior class photographs. Right where it should be under "M," was a photo he was looking for.

Catalina Mendoza was an attractive young lady with a huge smile and clear light-toned skin. She had highlighted shoulder-length crimped hair that had been very much in style at that time.

Jerrod went back to his desk and pulled out the flow chart he had started earlier. In the "Armando/Sherwood" oval he wrote "Suburban." In the "Hair/Nails" oval, he wrote "Catalina." In the "Blue Stucco/BMW" oval he also wrote "Catalina."

The addition of Catalina Mendoza to the chart changed little. Nearly all of the lines on the chart still pointed to, or from, the middle oval — that of Armando Mendoza.

CHAPTER 43

Jerrod finished typing his report and tossed the pages onto Craig's desk.

He grabbed a few manila folders off his desk. They were thefts or burglaries or vandalisms or forgery cases — he paid no attention.

"Got some follow-up on these, Sarge," he said to Pete Hanson holding out the case files. "Probably finish the shift in-the-field. Okay?"

"Sure," the sergeant said. "See you tomorrow."

Jerrod threw the case files on the passenger seat of his car and drove straight to Bixby Street. He slowed at its intersection with May Avenue and looked down Bixby Street. The blue Oldsmobile was gone. That was his chance.

He parked several doors down from the address listed on AJ's report.

A boy about ten years old was playing with a volleyball in a yard across the street. The boy watched him as he stepped onto the sidewalk and walked to the house. The "soft" clothing and unmarked four-door American-made car didn't fool even a little kid. No one on that street needed to see a badge to know who he was.

"Might as well have rolled up in a patrol car," Jerrod said to himself.

He knocked on the front door. He heard a door being closed and someone moving around inside. A woman answered the door and opened it a few inches.

"Martha?" he asked.

"Yes."

"I need to talk to you about the problem here last night. I'm with the police department."

"The baby's asleep. I can't—"

"I'll be very quiet," he interrupted.

"My boyfriend will be home soon."

"May I come in," he said in a less polite and more official tone.

"Okay."

She opened the door and he walked into the living room. The house was simply furnished, but tidy and clean. A door to a bathroom stood open and another door, perhaps to a bedroom, was closed.

"Is the baby in there?" he asked in a hushed tone and pointing to the closed door.

"Yes," she said.

A dining table with three chairs was situated in an opposite corner of the living room.

"May we sit?" he said in a softer-toned voice and motioning his hand to the table.

"Sure," she said.

They sat at the table, and he moved his chair, so he was facing her directly from about two feet away. She placed her elbows on the table and cradled her chin in her hands. She was most obviously uncomfortable talking with him.

"You came back here from your friend's house this morning," he said. "So, you must feel safe being here."

"I'm fine," she said. "We just had a misunderstanding."

"I saw the report from the incident last year," he said. "You got pretty messed up."

"I went to the hospital," she said. "It wasn't that bad. He promised to never hit me again... and he hasn't."

"Where is Efrain today?" he asked.

"I don't know," she said. "Running errands, I guess."

"Where does he work?" he asked.

"I'm not sure. I mean I don't know," she said. "He just works... odd jobs."

"Do you work?"

"No."

"You have a beautiful house," he said. "You must have some type of regular income to afford this place?"

"Efrain always makes enough to pay for the bills and buy food," she said.

"Who's Oso?" he asked. "Do you know his full name?"

"Oso is Efrain's friend," she said. "He comes over all the time. Everyone just calls him 'Oso.' He's a big man. I don't know his real name or anything else about him."

"Do you know Magdalena, or Maggie, Cervantes?" he asked.

"Yes," she said. "She owns Nopales."

"Ever eat there?"

"Efrain brings... no I haven't been there," she said with a grimace when she realized the slip she had made. She glanced at the bedroom door.

In his mind, Jerrod added a new line on his chart between Efrain Hernandez and the "Nopales/Maggie" ovals.

“Do you know Maggie's husband, Joaquin Cervantes? he asked. “Everyone calls him ‘Chimo.’”

“No,” she said.

“How about her sister, Catalina? Or her father, Armando Mendoza?”

“No,” she said. “I don't know them either.”

She was lying. There was no doubt about it. Her body language was easy to read. It shouted out she had much more information and she wanted, in the worst way, to answer every question he had. But that was not going to be the time to push her. Martha Figueroa was in a bad situation, and she was deathly afraid.

“Thank you for your time,” he said. “That’s all the questions I have. I'm glad you and your baby are safe back here at home.”

“Thank you,” she said as she stood up from the table.

“Here's my card with my desk phone number on it,” he said. “You can call me anytime.”

She looked at the card and read, “‘Jerrod Gold, Detective.’”

“That's me,” he said. “Call anytime.”

She nodded but made no sound.

“Thank you,” he said. “I'll let myself out.”

He opened the door and stepped outside. She stood in the doorway as he walked down the steps.

“Goodbye,” she said softly.

She averted her eyes when he turned to respond and walked back into the house.

CHAPTER 44

Martha went into the house, closed the door, and leaned her back against it for a few moments. She read the name on the business card again and the telephone number on it.

A huge, bearded man opened the bedroom door and lumbered into the living room.

"Give me that," Oso said as he snatched the card from her hand. "You almost fucked up, *chica*. You're lucky you didn't say any more than you did."

"I didn't know what to do," she said. "I didn't want him to get suspicious. He knew so much. He knew everybody's name."

"He didn't know shit," Oso said. "He was just fishing. Screw that punk-ass cop. Don't talk to him again."

Martha said nothing as she shuffled into the bedroom to check her sleeping baby. She softly closed the door behind her.

The cheap sofa moaned as Oso flopped his mass onto the cushions. He lifted the receiver to a black telephone on the coffee table and punched in seven numbers.

"Armando," Oso said quietly into the receiver while looking at the business card in his hand. "We have a problem."

CHAPTER 45

Jerrod's car radio was playing Michael Jackson's “Beat It” as he drove away on May Avenue. He could feel the Bixby Street neighborhood let out a quiet sigh as if it had held its breath while he had been there.

It was only four o'clock, so he decided to actually follow-up on one or two of his “real” cases. He pulled over near the high school and looked at a couple of the random files he had taken. He selected one he could work on when the continuous police radio chatter was interrupted.

“David-15, David-15. Call Dispatch,” the voice of Al Kees said.

“David-15” was his radio call-sign. “David” being the police phonetic for “D” as in Detective and 15 being his badge number based on his seniority with the VVPD.

“David-15, copy,” he said into the microphone.

He threw the case file back on the passenger seat with the others and drove to a pay phone at a nearby Beacon gas station.

“Valle Verde Police,” Al said.

“It's Jerrod. What's up?”

“There's a woman here in the lobby who says she has to talk to you right away.” he said. “She's says she'll only talk with you.”

“What's her name?”

“She wouldn't give her name.”

“Describe her.”

“Bright red hair—”

“I'll be there in five minutes. Don't let her leave.”

Jerrod drove to the PD as fast as the late afternoon traffic would allow. He parked at the curb in front of the lobby doors and bound up the stairs.

Stella Leiter had been sitting in a lobby chair and jumped to her feet when he walked in.

“I really need to talk to you,” she said. “It's about Val.”

“Come with me,” he said.

Al buzzed the door between the lobby and Dispatch Center. Jerrod escorted Stella inside and waved a thank you to Al.

They went directly to the bureau where he found only Craig at his desk.

“What's up?” Craig asked.

“She needs to tell us something about Val,” he said.

“Hello Stella. Have a seat and relax,” Craig said.

Stella sat down in a chair facing the side of the two detectives' desks. Craig caught her glance at his pack of Salem 100s.

“Want a smoke,” Craig said.

“Sure,” she said.

She leaned back in the chair after the first long puff of the cigarette. It had a visible calming effect on her.

“Are you okay?” Jerrod asked her.

“I still haven't used junk since I OD's last week,” she said. “I'm feeling a lot better now.”

“What's up with Val?” Jerrod asked.

“I went to visit him at the county jail today and leave some money for his canteen fund,” she said. “He told me he doesn't want to go back to prison and is willing to make a deal.”

“What kind of deal?” Craig asked.

“He's willing to work with you guys and give up the source of the new heroin in town in exchange for a release on parole in some other area.”

Jerrod nodded.

“He said he'll tell you everything about the operation. But he said he needs the deal in writing before he'll talk.”

“That's tempting,” Jerrod said. “But I'm not sure CDC will go along with the vague information you're giving us.”

“Tell us what you know about the heroin supply, and we can go from there,” Craig said.

Stella sat back in the chair and smoked the cigarette down to the filter before speaking again.

“Okay,” she said. “I don't know much, but I'll tell you what I do know.”

“Go ahead,” Jerrod said.

“Here's what Val told me: He met a guy in prison who hooked him up with some people who bring heroin in from Mexico and distribute all through the state. It gets smuggled into the country in small packages. Less than a pound. But it's super-high quality. A group of US citizens get paid to walk across the border and act like tourists. The ‘tourists’ may buy a bottle of tequila or some trinkets, but they pick up the dope and walk it right back across the border past the Border Patrol and Customs agents. No one has ever been searched and they don't have any drug dogs there.”

“What border crossing would that be?” Craig asked.

“The US side is near Yuma, Arizona,” she said. I don’t know what the Mexico side is.

“Go on,” Craig said.

“The smugglers distribute this strong dope all through California. Val had been going to Bakersfield to get the dope. He would take a bag full of cash — until he got ripped-off.”

“Do know the names of any people involved in the smuggling?” Jerrod asked.

Stella didn’t answer.

“No deal,” Craig said. “Screw Val. This is all a bunch of crap.”

“Thanks for coming in, Stella,” Jerrod said as he stood up. “Have a great life.”

“One of the guys is named ‘Efrain’,” she said.

Jerrod looked at Craig and smiled as he sat back down.

“You know Efrain?” she said.

“I know *of* Efrain,” Jerrod said. “I've been looking at him for something else.”

“Val told me Efrain and another guy drive to Bakersfield now and bring back the dope with them,” she said.

“Who's the other guy?” Craig asked.

“He's a big guy,” she said. “Everyone calls him ‘Oso.’”

Jerrod looked at Craig and shook his head.

“Who's receiving the dope here in Valle Verde?” Craig asked.

“I don't really know,” she said. “Val told me the heroin gets processed somewhere right here in Valle Verde and then goes out on the street. They've got the dosage right, finally, and they can barely keep up with demand. They're making huge profits.”

“There's no way Efrain and Oso can be running this operation,” Jerrod said. “Who's actually in charge?”

Stella thought for a moment. “Can I have another cigarette?” she asked.

“Sure,” Craig said. He shook out a cigarette, but quickly pulled the pack back when she reached for it.

“Who's in charge?” Craig demanded.

“I swear to God. I really don't know their names,” she said.

“Bullshit,” Jerrod said.

“All I know is it's a family deal,” she said. “The dad owns property all over the area and the kids run legitimate businesses to launder all the cash they're raking in.”

Craig tossed the entire pack of cigarettes to Stella.

"Thank you," she said.

"Anything else you'd like to share, Stella," Jerrod asked.

Stella leaned forward and grabbed Craig's Zippo lighter. She lit a cigarette and put the lighter back on the desk. She tilted her head back and blew a large smoke cloud straight into the air.

"One more thing," she said. "It's about the dead kid from the other night. Hector... right?"

"Yes, his name was Hector," Jerrod said.

"Val told me he was working for Efrain and Oso."

CHAPTER 46

Sergeant Pete Hanson was more than annoyed when he arrived at the detective bureau at five-thirty.

"This better be good," he said. "I have dinner plans with my wife tonight."

Craig briefed the sergeant on the information Stella Leiter had given them and the deal Val Reyes wanted to make.

Jerrod outlined the connections he had linked between Efrain Hernandez, Oso, and the Mendoza family.

"So, I have this straight," the sergeant said. "All Reyes wants is his parole hold dropped and to be relocated somewhere other than Valle Verde to help take down an international heroin smuggling operation?"

"That's what she told us," Craig said.

"And somehow Hector Medina was involved?" the sergeant asked.

"That's right," Jerrod said.

"I find it hard to believe, honestly," the sergeant said.

"This could be huge, Sarge," Craig said. "Val Reyes may be able to give us the whole thing."

"I need to run this situation by the captain before we go any further," the sergeant said.

"The captain told us to get to the bottom of these OD cases and we did," Jerrod said. "I'm sure he'll sign-off on it."

"This may be the break we needed on the Hector Medina case," Craig said.

"We'll see," the sergeant said. "Everything is on hold until tomorrow morning."

CHAPTER 47

"Fucking put on hold again," Jerrod screamed at the top of his voice as he slammed his fist down on the dashboard in the privacy of his unmarked car.

Mocking his sergeant, he yelled out loud: "We need to get permission. We'll pick it up tomorrow. Don't want to miss dinner with my wife. Bullshit."

He grew more disgusted with the situation as he drove home. "'Play the game,' my ass. There's no game to play. That bastard makes the rules *and* keeps the score."

It was nearly dark when Jerrod got home. He was actually pleased the house was vacant when he stepped inside. He needed to calm down and relax before having any company.

He changed out of his suit and placed his gear in the dresser drawer.

He opened a Heineken, turned on the TV, and plopped on the sofa. The local news was on, and the anchors droned on and on about the events of the day.

He heard none of it.

He was deep in thought trying to figure how to convince his bosses Armando Mendoza was running a dope operation. Even if they decided the case was too big for the VVPD to handle and they brought in state or federal agents to take it, that would be okay with him.

But nothing was going to happen that night and there wasn't a damn thing he could do about it.

CHAPTER 48

Tuesday

Jerrod Gold uncharacteristically arrived for work at seven o'clock. He made coffee, turned on KHJB, and started preparing for the day.

He had had a fitful night sleep with disturbing dreams as his mind would not shut down. He finally gave up and got out of bed just before dawn.

He redrew the rough relationship chart should Captain Wheaton need a visual aid to help make his decision. He added another oval to the chart with "Hector Medina" in it and connected it to the "Efrain" and "Oso."

Craig Wallace arrived and was surprised to see Jerrod at his desk.

"I thought we had left the bureau door open last night," Craig said. "This is weird seeing you here this early."

"Big day."

"Maybe. I hope so," Craig said.

Sergeant Pete Hanson and Willie Sanchez walked into the bureau together at seven-fifty.

"Did you talk to the captain?" Craig asked.

"Called him last night," the sergeant said. "I'm meeting with him at eight."

"Did I miss something?" Willie said.

"We got a break on the ODs and the Hector Medina murder," Jerrod said. "We'll get you caught up while Sarge is talking to the captain about it."

"Is there anything else I should know before going to his office?" the sergeant asked.

"Good-to-go," Craig said.

Jerrod handed him the chart.

After the sergeant left the bureau, Jerrod and Craig got Willie up to date on the cases.

"That's awesome," Willie said. "I can't wait."

At eight-ten, Craig's desk phone rang, and he picked up the receiver.

"Jerrod, it's Ted Lindsey from the Coroner's Office for you," he said. "I'll transfer."

"Hey, Ted," Jerrod said into his phone receiver.

"I've got the clothing from the Hector Medina case all dried and packaged for you," the deputy said. "I was just leaving the morgue for Valle Verde to pick up a CHP crash victim from the hospital. I can drop the clothing off when I'm done there, or you can meet me at the hospital."

"And save me a trip to Mesa," Jerrod said. "I'd appreciate that, pal. Whatever you'd like is fine with me."

"How about at the hospital. It's been a long shift already. We worked all night on an in-custody death at the jail. Suicide... maybe. Looks like an inmate jumped over the second-tier railing at lights-out. It squashed his head like a grape on impact with the concrete floor. Our detectives are looking into it, but nobody is saying it was anything other than a suicide."

Jerrod felt his stomach tightening. "Who was the inmate?" he asked cautiously.

"His name was, hang-on a second...," the deputy said. "Valdemar Reyes."

Jerrod sat in silence for a few seconds after he hung up the phone.

"You're not going to believe this," he said.

"What?" Craig asked.

"Val Reyes is dead. Fell off a second deck at the jail and splattered his head on the floor."

"Did he get tossed off?" Willie asked.

"He said they're looking at it as a suicide," Jerrod said. "The Mesa SO detectives are investigating. I don't know."

"Come in," Captain Andrew Wheaton said to the knock on his office door.

"We have a situation," Jerrod said to the captain and Pete Hanson as he walked into the office. "Valdemar Reyes is at the morgue. He died at the jail last night. Suicide... they think."

The room was quiet for a few moments as Jerrod sat down.

"Devastating news," the captain said. "He could have helped us break these cases wide open."

More quiet.

"Can the girlfriend help us any more than just repeating what Reyes told her?" the sergeant asked.

"Not really," Jerrod said. "She said she got all the information straight from Reyes. There's nothing she knows firsthand we could use to make even a weak case."

"We were so close," the captain said. "There must be another angle."

"Let's get the Feds involved," Jerrod suggested. "If this is an international smuggling thing as she described, I suspect the DEA would be very interested in taking it on. Then we can focus our attention back on the Hector Medina case."

Silence. Very uncomfortable silence followed.

"Let's not jump-the-gun and get the federal government involved just yet," the captain said. "I don't think it would be wise to drag them in on this now based on the secondhand word of a heroin-addict hooker."

Pete Hanson glanced at Jerrod.

"We'll see what else we can come up with, captain," the sergeant said as he stood up. "Thank you, sir."

Jerrod didn't stand.

"How about just a phone call—" Jerrod said.

"We're done here," the sergeant interrupted. "Let's go."

"So let me get this straight," Jerrod said. "No one else in this room cares that there were three OD deaths and a young man executed in the last week. And now we're just going to 'see what we can come up with.' I can't believe this bullshit."

There was absolute silence. Jerrod had crossed a line and he instantly wished he could pull his words back.

"Hang on a second, Sergeant," the captain said. "Please have a seat."

Jerrod didn't look at the sergeant as he slowly sat back down. He tried to contain his delight that the captain was considering his suggestion and was ready to listen to reason. Pete Hanson would have no choice but to go along with the captain's decision.

The captain quietly studied the chart Jerrod had prepared.

"How, exactly, did Armando Mendoza's name get pulled into this investigation?" the captain asked both investigators. "Did this girlfriend-hooker-informant give you his name or is this just some type of speculation on your part?"

Pete Hanson hesitated as he tried to carefully form an answer.

"She said she didn't know the names of the people involved... other than Efrain and Oso," Jerrod said. "I came up with Armando Mendoza's name as part of the OD investigation. He and his family just fit the description of the heroin operation she gave us. I honestly don't know, right now, whether he's involved or not."

The sergeant started to speak and was cut-off when the captain lifted his left hand from his desk and pushed his palm toward him.

"Well, I happen to know Armando Mendoza," the captain said. "We're not close friends, but we know each other from Saint Daniel's. I see him at a couple masses each week. He's a good family man and he helps the church anytime they ask. He's a valued member of this community."

"That may be true, sir, but—," Jerrod said.

"'But' nothing," the captain said as he lifted his left hand again. His face got red, and his mouth slightly twisted. "I suggest you take your investigation in another direction. The Armando Mendoza I know is most certainly not involved in any type of heroin smuggling ring. You're wasting valuable time and resources looking into his activities."

The captain crumpled the chart in his hand. He leaned forward in his chair and placed his palms flat on the desk. He looked first at Pete Hanson and then Jerrod. His glare was intense as he spoke.

"I personally vouch for him."

CHAPTER 49

"I quit," Jerrod said to Craig as he drove away from the PD. "I've had it with this fucking job."

"Relax... and grow up a little while you're at it," Craig said. "You can't just quit. Besides, you don't know how to do anything else."

Jerrod didn't respond.

"Did anyone tell you this job was going to be easy when you started?" Craig asked. "If it was easy, anyone could do it. This job is like jumping on a roller-coaster. You take the ups and downs, and you may even scream a little, but eventually you finish the ride. It's not personal. Wheaton and Hanson aren't obstructing you. You're obstructing you."

"How do you figure?"

"You have this ridiculous idealistic vision of the job. You think everything should happen, you know, 'A then B then C' and you get bent-out-of-shape when it doesn't. The real-world works, 'K, or maybe F, then C, then T.' You have to adapt. Not the other way around. There's no formula or recipe to follow."

Jerrod didn't comment.

"I know what you're thinking," Craig said.

"You can read my mind now?"

"You're thinking you'll just go over the captain's head to the Chief, Sheriff, DA, Attorney General's Office, or the Feds. Anybody you think is going to see the situation just like you do."

"Then what do you suggest I do?" Jerrod asked.

"There's an old saying my dad used all the time," Craig said. "Especially when he had a decision to make that involved some risk. It was all about weighing the benefits of the result he wanted against the effort and cost needed to make it happen. It's in the form of a simple question."

Jerrod glanced at his partner. "Yeah, so what's the question?"

"Was the juice worth the squeeze?"

CHAPTER 50

Jerrod and Craig found Stella Leiter in the cheap hotel room they had left her the day before. She answered the door with her hair wilder than ever and a face that looked like she had just woken up. She was wearing a thin t-shirt that was four sizes too big for her.

"We need to talk to you," Jerrod said.

"Well, then, come on in," she said with an exaggerated sweep of her right arm as she opened the door for the detectives. The large bruise on her inner arm had faded to a greenish-yellow hue.

"Have a seat," Craig said.

"Okay," she said as she walked across the filthy carpet and creaked the springs when she flopped her skinny rump on the crumpled bed.

"Is Val getting his parole?" she asked.

"Val died in jail last night," Jerrod said.

"Come again?" she said.

"Val took a fall off a second-tier railing and was killed. In jail. Last night," Craig said.

"Someone killed him?" she said as tears filled her eyes.

"The Sheriff's Office is handling it as a suicide," Jerrod said.

"He didn't commit suicide," Stella said. "There's no way. I just talked to him. He wasn't suicidal. He just didn't want to go back to prison."

"How are you so sure?" Jerrod asked.

"He didn't kill himself. They killed him."

CHAPTER 51

"What the hell happened in Wheaton's Office?" Willie asked before the two other detectives had a chance to sit at their desks. "Hanson stormed out of here like the place was on fire."

"Believe me," Jerrod said. "You don't want to know what happened in Wheaton's office."

"Anyway, glad your back," Willie said. "I just got a very interesting phone call."

"Let's hear it," Craig said.

"I got a call from a young man," Willie said, "a maybe thirteen or fourteen-year-old I met Saturday morning in Hector Medina's neighborhood. He didn't say anything then but had plenty to talk about today."

"What does he know?" Jerrod asked.

"He told me he was Hector's cousin," Willie said. "He said Hector was working for some older guys and had been running dope and cash between various drug dealers around town. He said Hector got into trouble for something he did and took a beating the other night from those older guys."

"He got jumped alright," Craig said. "And Hector knew exactly who did it."

"The kid told me his homeboys are scared shitless and were just acting tough about avenging Hector's death when I talked to them. They know those older guys were involved in the murder somehow, but they're afraid to say or do anything about it."

"Did he know the names of the 'older guys?'" Craig asked.

"Just one," Willie said.

"Well?" Jerrod asked.

"'Efrain.'"

"None of this information is usable," Craig said. "It's all interesting background, but Stella and Hector's cousin are just telling us things they heard from someone else. We can't use any of that — it's all hearsay. There's nothing we can do with any of it right now. This is going to be a very tough nut."

"I recently heard someone say, 'If it was easy...,'" Jerrod said.

"Very funny," Craig said.

"Seriously," Jerrod said. "We may not be able to convince Wheaton, or even Hanson, we're on the right track. So, unless I hear a better idea, we can quietly follow this path as far as it goes."

"Agreed," Willie said as he shook his watch.
"I'm in," Craig said.
"One other thing," Jerrod said. "Let's keep this in-house for now."

CHAPTER 52

The door of a heavy black wall safe stood open as Joaquin “Chimo” Cervantes sat at the desk inside the private office of the El Ocotillo Club.

On the desk were five three-quarter inch tall stacks of used United States currency separated by denomination. The bills had been delivered to him in a plain brown paper bag by his father-in-law, Armando Mendoza.

The five stacks, containing exactly one hundred each of one-, five-, ten- and twenty-dollar bills, were held with thick blue rubber bands known as “broccoli bands” used in the local produce business.

He prepared a bank cash deposit slip to the club’s checking account for "$3,837" – well under the ten-thousand-dollar cash limit that would trigger a currency transaction report under the Federal Bank Secrecy Act.

He placed the slip with the bundles of cash in a zippered canvas bag for his daily trip to the merchant window at a Main Street bank.

CHAPTER 53

Jerrod got back to his desk after a fast-food lunch and poked through the mound of cases he had assigned to him.

One of those cases involved a series of stolen payroll checks from a Mesa fish processing plant, RJB Seafood, that had been cashed in a variety of Valle Verde businesses.

The checks were authentic, the date and payee information were neatly typed, and a Paymaster machine had been used to imprint a random check amount consistent with a typical week's pay.

Various victim businesses had unsuspectingly cashed the checks and deposited them in their bank accounts. The accounts were later debited the amount of the check when they were returned by the bank as forged.

A new crime report had come in from Patrol after a woman attempted to cash a RJB Seafood check at a grocery store. The clerk had asked for identification from the woman passing the check. The woman fumbled through her purse and said she couldn't find any. When the clerk told her he couldn't cash the check without ID, the woman picked up the check, tore it in half, and ran out of the store.

The patrol officer had collected the torn check and booked it as evidence.

Jerrod visualized how the woman would have torn the check: She would have had to hold the check in both of her hands between her thumbs and forefingers as she twisted the paper to tear it.

He suspected there should be at least two thumbprints on the of the check — one on each side of the tear.

He went to Property and signed for the two torn portions of the forged check. He took the check outside the squad room, held the halves by a corner with his bare fingers while he sprayed the check surfaces with a chemical from an aerosol can.

The chemical, Ninhydrin, was used on porous surfaces such as paper to develop fingerprints. The chemical reacted with the amino acids left by anyone who had touched the paper. As the chemical dried, a previously "latent," or invisible, fingerprint would become "patent," or plainly visible. The ridge patterns of the developed fingerprints would contrast with the paper in vivid purple.

As he had suspected, two identifiable fingerprints developed on the face of the check on either side of the tear.

He had over-sprayed some of the Ninhydrin onto his left thumb and the skin around the nail developed a purple stain. He scrubbed the stain on his thumb with soap and water, but it would not come off.

CHAPTER 54

Jerrod saw Marko Otero and Rusty Browne in the PD hallway as they were heading out on patrol following the three o'clock roll call.

"Meet me in the lot at the high school gym at four," he told the two officers.

Efrain Hernandez and Oso walked out of the Bixby Street house and into the bright afternoon sunshine. Oso maneuvered into the front passenger seat of the Oldsmobile and Efrain Hernandez got behind the steering wheel.

Efrain made a three-point turn in a neighbor's driveway and coasted the Oldsmobile past the stop sign as he made a right turn at the Bixby Street intersection with May Avenue.

Oso started to say something when his words were cut off by the blaring siren of a black-and-white with rotating overhead lights that had pulled in behind them.

"Pull to the curb," Marko's deep voice ordered over the public address speaker.

The Oldsmobile pulled sharply to the curb.

"Turn the ignition off," the booming PA voice directed.

The neighborhood kids stopped their play and were drawn to the commotion like the jingle of an ice cream truck passing by.

"Why did you stop me, officer?" Efrain asked.

"Driver's license and vehicle registration, please," Marko demanded through the open driver's window.

Oso looked into the passenger side mirror and saw another officer, Rusty Browne, at the right rear fender. The officer's hand rested on the grip of his revolver.

"I pulled you over for failing to stop for a posted stop sign back there, sir," Marko said. "I'll be right back. Please stay in the car."

Marko filled out a citation for the driving infraction and returned to the driver's window.

"Please sign here," Marko directed Efrain. "This is not an admission of guilt—"

"You're giving me a bullshit ticket," Efrain interrupted.

"It's called a traffic citation, sir," Marko said. "You can call it whatever you wish."

Efrain was so angry his hand shook as he scribbled his name.

Marko handed him the yellow duplicate copy of the citation, his driver's license, and registration."

"Have a wonderful day, sir," Marko said.

Efrain mumbled something inaudible under his breath.

"Oh, before I forget," Marko said. "Detective Gold sends his regards. He's right over there."

Marko pointed to the maroon car parked down the block and across May Avenue. A suit-sleeved arm of the young detective waved to them from the driver's window.

"Motherfucker," Oso said just loud enough for Marko to hear.

CHAPTER 55

Catalina Mendoza locked the front door of the Final Touches Hair and Nail Salon after escorting the last customer of the day out. She went to her office and kicked her black designer-brand high heels off near the door.

The office was a collection of contemporary tones and hard-corners — thick carpeting, bright primary colors, and square furnishings — she had selected and coordinated herself.

She dialed the combination to a small floor safe and removed four stacks of cash secured with thick blue rubber-bands. She removed the bands and counted out one thousand dollars using a combination of bills. She folded the bills and tucked the skimmed cash into her purse.

She counted her cash receipts from the shop for the day — $453 — and separated the bills by denomination. She prepared a deposit slip to her business checking account in the amount of $3,453 and placed the remaining cash into a deposit bag she would drop off at her bank on her way to the shop the following day.

She had repeated this task at the end of every business day for the last two years — just as her sister and brother-in-law had also done at their businesses.

CHAPTER 56

It was after sundown when Jerrod got home.

Natalie had gotten there before him and had changed into her favorite pair of shorts and white tank top.

He changed out of his suit and put on the green hospital scrub pants with his white t-shirt. His police gear went into the dresser drawer.

They enjoyed some takeout she had picked up at a Chinese restaurant as they discussed the events of the day.

After dinner, they moved into the living room. She sat on the sofa, and he walked to the large plate-glass window. He grabbed the panels of the off-white draperies and saw his reflection in the glass. He paused and studied his face. It looked strained and tired.

“Come over here,” Natalie said softly as he glanced to the reflection of her stretching out onto the sofa.

He looked back at the reflection of his face again and a smirk emerged.

He pulled the heavily lined drapery panels tight to ensure their privacy and nestled next to her on the sofa.

A popular sitcom, *Who's The Boss?* played, unwatched, on the TV.

Jerrod smelled her hair and kissed her neck. Their mouths met in a deep kiss. She moved him onto his back and straddled his thighs. Her body arched as his hand moved under the tank top and along the tight skin of her belly. Their eyes locked as she untied the draw string to his scrubs. He moved his other hand under the elastic of her shorts at the small of her back as she cradled his face with her hands and bent forward to kiss him again.

CHAPTER 57

Jerrod thought a car had hit the house at first.

A booming sound. Glass shattering. Exploding plaster on the wall above the sofa.

A single gunshot. Large caliber. A shotgun.

He froze as Natalie raised above him. Her eyes, unsure and afraid, were wide and fixed on his. An open laceration had appeared on her cheek just below her left eye. The wound seemed to hesitate before red poured out onto her face and his white shirt. Small specks of the glass peppered her face, neck, and torso.

Time seemed to go into slow-motion. He pushed her up and then pulled her down off the sofa. She landed on top of him, and he rolled her to her back. Thousands of glass shards covered the floor. Blood from her face streamed to the carpet.

The heavy drapery covering the front window hung in strips as wind whipped through the opening. The unmistakable smell of gun smoke hung in the air.

He picked her up from the floor and carried her to the master bathroom. He put her down gently on the cold tile floor and grabbed one of the soft white bath towels from the rack. He pressed the towel to the wound on her face and watched bright red soak through the towel and spread under his hand. He folded the towel once, then twice, then a third time to stop the blood.

Tears streamed from her right eye, and she made no sound — the fear and confusion on her face shouted to him her emotions.

He pulled her to the heavy cast iron bathtub and shower.

"Get in the tub!" he yelled. "Hold the towel on your face. Hold it tight. I'm going to lock the door. Stay quiet and don't open the door for anyone except a police officer."

"Don't go out there, Jerrod. Don't leave me," she cried.

"I'll be back for you."

Jerrod closed the shower curtain and ran in a crouch to the doorway. He peered into the bedroom as he locked the doorknob. He low crawled into the bedroom as he pulled the door closed.

He rose to his feet and sprinted to the dresser. He pulled the Beretta 9mm from the drawer, unsnapped the leather holster, and let it fall to the floor.

All of his police tactical training kicked in at once. Countless hours at the police range and years of training scenarios placed him into a combat-ready mindset.

He crept from the bedroom — the Beretta comforting in his right hand — all of his senses on full alert.

The hallway and living room were clear. He tactically moved to the kitchen and through the laundry room to the back door. He peered outside and silently opened the door.

Jerrod stepped outside and heard sirens in the distance. He looked to his right and raised his Beretta to the silhouette of a man holding a handgun in Charles Horvat's backyard.

"Freeze right there!" Jerrod yelled at the moving dark figure as his finger put pressure on his handgun trigger.

"Jerrod, it's me," the colonel said.

"Colonel, get back inside."

"I heard a gunshot out front—"

"Get back inside your house!" Jerrod shouted.

"Okay," the colonel said as he slipped into the doorway.

Jerrod ran down the driveway to the front yard and lowered the Beretta to his side. His neighbors had come out of their houses and milled in their yards.

The shooter was long gone.

CHAPTER 58

The air around Jerrod Gold's house was thick with the exhaust from a knot of idling emergency vehicles which had converged on his neighborhood. The red and blue overhead lights whirred from two ambulances, a fire truck, and at least ten patrol cars from the VVPD, Mesa County Sheriff's Office, and the California Highway Patrol.

Natalie lay on an ambulance gurney on the front lawn. An EMT placed a stack of white gauze four-by-fours over the blood-soaked ones already covering the left side of her face and neck. Small wounds with coagulating streaks of blood dotted her left arm, torso, and legs.

Jerrod was standing on the lawn near the gurney. He held Natalie's hand with his — a hand covered with streams of blood from a bandaged laceration on his arm mixed with that of his lover. His white t-shirt and scrub pants were covered in blood. His clothing and skin were speckled with darkening patches from dozens of tiny shrapnel wounds.

"They're going to take you to the ER now, Nat," Jerrod said. "I'm going to get things secured here and come out there as soon as I can."

"I'm scared," she said.

"Me, too," he said. "You're safe now."

The EMTs rolled the gurney away and into the ambulance.

Officer Marko Otero cleared a path through the tangle of emergency vehicles to allow the ambulance to leave.

Officer Rusty Browne yelled at a rubbernecker who stopped in the street to gawk at the scene.

Officers Dave Yamamoto and Allison "AJ" Jenkins had come to work early when they heard about it. They interviewed neighbors and kept the looky-loos out of the scene.

Officers Kevin Arneta and Kevin Holcomb showed up to do whatever they could to help.

Sergeant Pete Hanson and Captain Andrew Wheaton talked quietly together on the sidewalk.

MCSO deputies and CHP officers — some who Jerrod recognized and others he didn't know — talked in small groups and glanced over at him occasionally.

Craig Wallace and Willie Sanchez stood next to Jerrod. Craig broke the silence first.

"So, what the hell happened here?" he asked.

Jerrod recounted the events of the shooting and aftermath.

"I thought she got hit with a shotgun pellet at first," Jerrod said as he checked a gauze pad covering one of his wounds.

Willie shook his watch.

"My neighbor, Colonel Horvat, was outside with his old army .45 in his hand," Jerrod said. "I nearly shot him. I went back in and yelled to Nat to come out of the shower and unlock the door. The wound on her face wouldn't stop bleeding and there was still glass in it. There was glass everywhere. She got hurt bad."

Jerrod looked around the scene for a few moments.

"I didn't see a car or who the shooter was. But I have an idea who did it."

Andrew Wheaton stayed on the sidewalk giving an interview with the Valle Verde *Sun* crime beat reporter, Bruce Witt, as Pete Hanson walked over to the three detectives.

"Sarge," Jerrod nodded.

"The captain said this case is our top priority until we find the shooter," the sergeant said.

"Thank you," Jerrod said.

"He's still pissed at you from this morning, you smart-ass. He told me he was thinking about busting you back to Patrol, minimally... until this happened."

Jerrod nodded.

"I was going to suggest you take tomorrow off," he said. "But the captain wants us both in his office at eight-thirty sharp.

"Okay," Jerrod said.

"Jerrod, do you have any idea who may have done this?" the sergeant asked.

Jerrod looked down and stretched the blood-soaked t-shirt away from the wounds on his chest. Small diamonds of glass rained down onto his well-tended lawn. He raised his bloodied hand to his head and felt more glass embedded in his hair.

He slowly looked up and met the sergeant's eyes with his before he spoke. "I have absolutely no clue, sir."

CHAPTER 59

Wednesday

Craig gave Jerrod a ride home from the ER at one-thirty.

A VVPD officer in a black-and-white was stationed in front of his house. He walked over to the patrol car and shook hands with the officer. He was nearly overcome with emotion when the officer told him every sworn officer at the VVPD, sergeants and lieutenants included, had volunteered to take shifts guarding his home.

He walked in the front door and took in the damage: His eyes were first drawn to the blood stains on the carpet where someone, with good intentions, had smeared while attempting to clean them. A sheet of plywood had neatly replaced his missing front window by a neighbor who was a construction contractor. The tattered drapery still hung from its valance.

There were blood stains on the cushions of the sofa and blood had streaked the front of it.

There were holes in the plaster wall just above the center of the sofa where nine lead buckshot pellets had been removed as evidence. The pellets would have struck the face of any person with the misfortune of having been seated upright on the sofa at that moment. Natalie had been in the exact position seconds before the window exploded.

The carpet from the living room to the bedroom was stained with blood. The blood in the bathroom tile and tub had been cleaned and the blood-soaked bath towel was removed.

Most of the glass had been vacuumed, but he could see small glimmers of light reflecting off the thousands of small shards that remained.

He showered and got into bed. His body ached each time he moved and the sheets touched his tender wounds.

He was exhausted but laid fully awake in the darkened room. He closed his eyes and relived the terror of the night.

He was thankful to all the officers that responded to his house, the neighbors who helped him, and the hospital ER staff who so competently cared for them.

He thought of the ER doctor who had used the smallest needle, the finest silk, and all of her skills to delicately suture the one-inch laceration Natalie had under her eye. Despite her earnest effort, the doctor told them the wound would leave a permanent reminder on Natalie's otherwise unblemished face.

He was thankful to Natalie's sister who took Natalie to her Mesa home where she could be safe while she healed from her injuries.

He was glad his mother was in Los Angeles for the week and wouldn't be subjected to the intense worry she would be experiencing.

He felt extreme guilt for exposing Natalie to the danger he brought home. Each time he closed his eyes, all he saw was the blood on her face and the terror in her eyes.

But, more than all else, he was enraged beyond words and wanted revenge.

CHAPTER 60

"Have a seat, gentlemen," Captain Andrew Wheaton said to Jerrod Gold and Pete Hanson after they reported to his office at eight-thirty as directed.

The captain paused while his gaze drifted to Jerrod's light blue dress shirt. Jerrod looked down and found a small spread of fresh blood had seeped through the material from one of the many wounds he had received the night before.

"First, how are you this morning?" the captain asked softly. "And your lady friend, of course?"

"We'll be okay, sir. Thank you."

"I have a bit of a dilemma," the captain said. He sighed heavily before taking on an official tone and training his eyes at Jerrod. "When you left my office yesterday morning, I was so angry at your snotty attitude and level of insubordination I prepared a document for the chief recommending disciplinary measures against you."

He picked up a typewritten single page memo from his desk and shook it in his hand as he continued.

"I recommended you be suspended without pay for one week and then be reassigned to Patrol immediately on your return. This memo would also be a permanent black-mark in your personnel file."

Neither Jerrod nor the sergeant spoke.

"I've already met with the chief this morning. He agreed with the disciplinary measures I recommended. However — considering the incident at your house last night, the injuries you and your lady-friend received, and the incredible outpouring of support you seem to have from the other personnel in this office — the chief modified the discipline down to a simple letter-of-reprimand. There will be no suspension and no reassignment at this point."

"Thank you, sir," Jerrod said.

"Don't thank me," the captain snapped back. "You're on very thin ice, son. You're a loose cannon who thinks you can do whatever you think is right with no regard for this organization, its policies, or the chain-of-command."

Jerrod knew the captain's description of him was accurate and that he held the upper hand in the situation. No response was clearly the best response.

The captain sighed and sat back in his chair. He spoke again in a fatherly tone.

"Are you a Christian, son?" he asked.

Caught off-guard, Jerrod gave a non-answer. "I was raised Christian, sir."

"Have you studied the Bible?"

"I have, sir."

"There's an oft-used verse, Proverbs 16:18. 'Pride goes before destruction, a haughty spirit before a fall.'"

"Thank you. I'll remember that, sir."

The captain's demeanor became dour. He leaned forward in his chair and his voice firmed. "You just received a second chance. There will not be a third."

Andrew Wheaton asked Pete Hanson to stay behind when Jerrod was dismissed.

Jerrod closed the door quietly and gave a big exhale as stood just outside the office. He could hear the captain's voice as he tore into the sergeant.

"You better keep an eye on that boy," the captain said. "If he isn't reeled in, he's going to cause us all our jobs."

Jerrod moved his ear closer to the door.

"My wife and I are leaving for a church retreat in Northern California this afternoon and won't be back until Sunday night," the captain said. "I do not want to be disturbed. I expect you to keep the lid on that brat detective while I'm away."

Jerrod walked away from the captain's door and Al Kees was on duty in the Dispatch Center.

"Sorry to hear about last night," he said.

"Thanks, Al," he said. "We'll be okay."

Down the hallway near Records, he heard a female voice call his name. He turned and saw Ann Rogers in the half-door.

"Are you okay?" she asked gently as her eyes darted to the blood spot on his shirt.

"I'm fine, Ann, Thank you. Everyone's been so kind."

"If there's anything I can do," she said.

He was greeted by two senior day shift patrol officers near the squad room and they each shook his hand. They wished him and Natalie a quick recovery and offered any help they could.

In the detective bureau, Craig and Willie smiled as he sat down at his desk.

"Welcome back," Craig said. "I figured you'd take a couple days off."

"I would have milked at least a few days away if my house got shot up," Willie said.

"I don't recommend it as a way to get some free time," Jerrod said.

"How did it go with the captain?" Craig asked.

"I'm getting a letter in my P-file, but no reassignment or days-at-the-beach."

"Days-at-the-beach" was a cop term for time-off on suspension without pay. The etymology of the term being when an officer received extra days off, he or she might as well make the best of it... and spend the "day-at-the-beach."

"That's not too bad," Craig said.

"The captain told me I was a loose cannon, and I wasn't going to get another chance if I screw-up again," Jerrod said. "Hanson was getting his ass reamed when I left Wheaton's office and is probably more than a little pissed at me now."

"Before the Sarge gets back," Willie said as he peeked at the doorway to make sure no one was standing there. "AJ and Dave talked to one of your neighbors last night. The neighbor didn't want to get involved or give her name, but she said she saw a blue sedan takeoff out of the neighborhood right after your house got shot up."

"Blue sedan? Really?" Jerrod said. "Shocking."

"It looks like you really pushed someone's button," Craig said.

Jerrod's desk phone rang, and he found Gary Pell, his health department inspector friend, on the line.

"Hey, Dave Yamamoto told me about the deal at your house last night," Gary said. "Are you doing okay?"

"I'm fine," he said. "But Natalie got hit on the cheek and took a few stitches."

"If I can help, let me know."

"I will, buddy. Thanks for the call."

A half hour later, Jerrod's desk phone rang again.

"This is Lucho. You talked to me the other day about Hector."

"What's up, Lucho?" he said remembering the lumper he had known from school.

"I can't talk long. I'm at a pay phone and there's people all over the place here."

"Okay."

"Here's the deal. I heard your house got shot up last night. That's fucked up, man."

"Thanks."

"Sorry about being a dick the other day. I didn't even know Hector was dead until you told me, and I couldn't talk in front of that other dude anyway. I'm going to tell you some stuff, but you have to promise you don't use my name."

"No problem. Talk to me."

"Hector stopped lumping after he got recruited to run dope. He wasn't selling the dope, but just running drugs and cash to and from dealers all over the city. Business was real good and he was making some pretty nice money."

"How do you know that?"

"Hector told me himself, man. I talked to him a few days before he got killed."

"Did he tell you who he was working for?"

"He didn't tell me. But I found out from someone else."

"Who was that?" Jerrod asked.

"Hang on a second," Lucho said.

He heard Lucho yell at someone to get away from the phone booth until he was done.

"I got picked up on some bullshit warrants Saturday night. And I just got out of county jail this morning. I was housed with a guy named Val Reyes. He said he knew you."

"I knew Val."

"Well, Val told me all about a heroin operation in Valle Verde. He told me about a guy named Efrain and another guy, a big mean motherfucker named Oso, who ran a whole network of runners like Hector. He said the new dope was so good they could barely keep up with the demand. They paid kids like Hector to do all the running around town."

"Why would Val tell you about that?" Jerrod asked.

"He was afraid for his life, man. He had been working for these guys too. He told me he got ripped-off for a whole bag of cash headed for Mexico. He knew he was a dead man, so he turned himself in on his parole hold. He asked me to call you if anything happened to him."

"Did Val tell you who was running the heroin operation?" Jerrod asked.

"He did. You have to promise me, man. My name can never come up on this."

"You have my word," Jerrod said.

"The guy in charge of everything is named Armando Mendoza. He apparently acts like a businessman around town but is tits-high in dope and cash."

"Are you absolutely sure about that name?"

"That's the name Val told me."

"The Sheriff's Office thinks Val killed himself," Jerrod said. "What do you think?"

"No fucking way he killed himself. He got helped over that railing."

"How do you know?"

After a pause, Lucho said in a whisper: "I just know, man."

CHAPTER 61

Jerrod told Craig and Willie the details of the conversation with Lucho.

"Wonderful," Craig said. "Another untested, second-hand informant we can't use. That's more great background, just like Stella and the kid who called Willie, so we know we're looking in the right direction. But an Assistant DA or a judge would just laugh at us if we went to them with a warrant affidavit based on only those three chunks of information. We could have a hundred people tell us the same thing, but if none of them can testify about what they know first-hand, there's no case to make."

"What else can we do? Legally, that is," Jerrod asked.

"Legally, I don't know," Craig said. "I don't want to get into the things we could do illegally. There's just way too much risk."

"The 'Juice-Squeeze' factor?" Jerrod asked.

"Now you're getting it... Grasshopper," Craig said.

The detective's conversation was interrupted when two patrol officers walked into the bureau.

"Hey, Jerrod," Big Kevin said as he handed him a white business envelope thick with cash.

"Everyone chipped in for a new window at your house or whatever else you need it for," Tall Kevin said. "There's nearly five hundred dollars in there. Everybody at the PD donated. Even the SO, CHP, and Fire guys at the scene last night threw in some cash."

"If you need anything, buddy, call us," Big Kevin said.

"Call any of us," Tall Kevin added.

"Thanks, guys. I don't know what to say."

Craig watched his young partner for a few moments without speaking.

"Me and Willie are going over to The Corner for a cup," he said as he grabbed his pack and lighter from the desk. "Go see Natalie. Take the rest of the day off. I'll cover it with Hanson."

"Thanks," he said.

Craig and Willie left the bureau and closed the door.

Jerrod leaned forward with his elbows on his desk and held his face in his hands. He looked at the envelope and the symbol of support it represented.

He shook his head as he thought about the crazy events of the last week and could no longer contain his emotions.

Jerrod took Craig's advice and drove to Mesa to see Natalie. Her sister, Terri, answered his soft knock on the front door.

"She's been awake off and on," she said. "But she didn't get much sleep last night and is real sore. She's in the back bedroom."

"Thank you," he said.

"I want to talk to you before you leave."

"Okay."

The hinges on the bedroom door creaked when he slowly pushed it open. Natalie was propped up in a bed by a pile of pillows. She was wearing a loose dark pajama top.

"Hello," he said in a whisper.

She turned her head slightly toward the door and her eyelids opened slowly. The left side of her face was bruised and swollen. The tiny dark ends of the six delicately set sutures poked from the laceration on her cheek. Her bare left arm and leg had dozens of small, reddened shrapnel wounds caused by the exploding glass.

"You're bleeding," she said as she strained her neck to look at the blood on his shirt that had grown from one to three spots.

"I'm fine," he said. "But I'm worried about you. How are you doing?"

"Not much to look at right now, I'm afraid," she said as she winced in pain while attempting a smile.

"You're beautiful. You'll heal quick and be as good as new in no time."

"With a delightful story to tell people about the big scar on my face, right."

Tears rolled from the corners of her eyes and she wiped them away.

"I am so, so sorry this happened. I would have never intentionally put you in any kind of danger. I hope you know that?"

"I do. I don't blame you. I was so afraid last night. That was the most scared I've ever been in my life."

"You'll be safe here while you get better."

She made a weak smile. He watched her eyelids slowly droop as sleep took her over.

"Get some rest," he said gently to his sleeping lover as he kissed her on the forehead.

"She's sleeping," he told Terri. "Thank you for bringing her here. She looks as comfortable as she possibly could be."

"She's on some pretty strong medication. She just needs some rest."

"I should get back to work."

“You mean, get back to getting someone else you know shot, or worse?” she said as she placed one hand on her hip.

“Come on, Terri. I would have never placed her in any danger. She was in the wrong place at the right time.”

“I'm just saying you're dangerous to be around. People around you are getting hurt.”

“Are you talking about Hector now too?”

“Yes, Hector too. You could have helped him more before he was killed... instead of afterward. Now my sister is just another victim left in your wake.”

“Are you serious?”

“Does it look like I'm joking?”

CHAPTER 62

Willie was at his desk and his phone rang.

"There's a man on the phone for you," Al Kees said. He said his name was 'Humberto.'"

"Send it back. Thanks."

Jerrod's drive back to Valle Verde from Mesa took one-half hour and Jerrod remembered none of it. His thoughts became confused by the wild series of events from the previous days.

Terri's words echoed in his ears. *Could she be right?*

He thought about Hector. Dead. He thought about Val Reyes. Dead. He thought about Natalie. Wounded and scarred both physically and mentally. *Who was going to be the next victim?*

He thought about how disillusioned he had become at choosing law enforcement as a career. He feared Andrew Wheaton's warnings and understood the perilous position he had placed himself in. There was no doubt in his mind another incident would be his last act as a detective or even as a police officer.

His anger grew as he got closer to Valle Verde — the only place he had ever called home. The place where his family lived. The place where he wanted to a raise his own family someday. The place he swore to protect — even if it cost him his life.

Jerrod drove off the freeway and the length of Independence Avenue. His anger continued to grow as he stopped for a traffic signal at the "Y" intersection with Constitution Avenue and Main Street.

He stared at Saint Daniel's Church. He felt a pang of envy for all the faithful, like Mama Segura, who found comfort and strength and forgiveness with the church. He wished the church could somehow give him relief from the anger and guilt he felt that very moment.

As he drove down Main Street back toward the PD, he passed a black Chevrolet Suburban parked at the curb in front of El Ocotillo Club. He recognized the oversized truck as being the same one he had seen parked inside the protective gate of the Sherwood Drive estate of Armando Mendoza.

He wondered if Armando Mendoza was inside the club at that moment. He tapped the brakes to stop but thought better of it and changed his mind. He made a right turn at the next intersection and pulled to the curb. He turned off the car ignition and took several deep breaths to calm himself. He envisioned confronting Armando Mendoza.

Face-to-face. Telling him all he knew about his operation. The dope. The cash. The money laundering. His family involvement. And the murders.

He sat in the car for five minutes contemplating the next move he would make. He weighed the options and calculated the risks. He was certain his career would be on the line. But was he willing to risk it?

He started his car and circled the block until he again drove south on Main Street. He slowed in the traffic lane near the large black truck in front of El Ocotillo Club and made his decision at that moment.

Willie's desk phone rang.

"This is Andrew Wheaton," said the voice on the other end of the line.

"What's up, Captain?" Willie asked.

"Who was the man who called the office earlier today to talk to you? 'Humberto,' I believe his name was."

"He was a witness in a burglary case I'm working on, sir. He decided he didn't remember anything and isn't going to help the case at all."

"Okay. Thank you, Detective."

"What was that call about?" Craig asked Willie.

Willie nodded. "I think I know who the office snitch is."

CHAPTER 63

Jerrod drove past the Suburban and went straight to the PD. Craig and Willie were at their desks when he walked into the bureau.

"How's Natalie?" Willie asked.

"Okay, I guess. She got pretty banged up and needs some rest."

"How are *you* doing?" Craig asked.

"I'm fine," he said. He then thought about his answer. "Terrible, actually."

"Talk to me," Craig said.

"My head is just messed up right now. I've got way too many thoughts and emotions going in every direction. I can't seem to focus and feel like I'm only moving backward. That thing at my house last night was scary as hell. If the shooter had held the muzzle of that shotgun just a couple inches lower, both me and Nat would have taken a direct hit from the buckshot. You saw what it did to the wall. We were lucky to only get hit with glass. Wheaton and Hanson are on my ass and watching every move I make. And, on top of it all, Nat's sister said something today that's really bothering me."

"Maybe you should take the day off," Craig said.

"Maybe so," Jerrod said. "Maybe so."

There was no black-and-white parked in front of his house when Jerrod arrived home at two o'clock. Natalie's VW blocked the driveway.

He parked at the curb and stood on the sidewalk for a moment. He looked at the plywood reminder of a peaceful and tender evening that had been violently interrupted. He thought about the absolute terror he and Natalie had experienced after the window exploded. And he thought of the scar on Natalie's face that would forever remind them of that night.

Once inside the house, he walked straight to the bedroom and ignored the damage inside the house. He shed his blood-spotted clothing and examined the multiple shrapnel wounds on his bare skin. He felt a tender spot on his right leg and pulled a small piece of glass out of his skin with his fingernails. He put on a dark blue t-shirt and jeans and started to walk out of the bedroom barefoot before remembering the glass the carpet would still contain.

Jerrod moved Natalie's car to his backyard and saw Charles Horvat behind his house having a cigarette.

"You're home early," the colonel said.

"Took the rest of the day off. I'm beat."

"Come in for a 'snap.'"

The colonel made two tall Fat-Burners and the two men walked to the living room with their drinks. The colonel turned off the TV before sitting in his recliner.

"How's Natalie doing?"

"She's going to be sore for a while, I'm afraid. She's staying with her sister for a few days."

"That was some deal last night. I thought I was back in a war zone. I was ready for battle."

"It was pretty scary, sir."

"The shooting last night reminded me of a situation in Korea — the incident behind that Bronze Star you've asked me about a few times."

"Yes, sir."

"Other than with some of my Army buddies and my wife. I have never told that story to anyone. Would you like to hear it?"

"Yes, sir. Very much so."

"Where to begin?" the colonel said. "It was October in 1951. I was a captain at the time and was commanding an intelligence detachment in a small village about fifty miles south of Pyongyang."

He took a sip of his drink.

"There was one sergeant and three privates with me. We also had a civilian interpreter, a South Korean fellow, assigned to our unit. There were a few South Korean soldiers and a small police force in that village.

"We were living in a house in the village but had built some defensive shelters and worked out a plan in case we got attacked."

The colonel leaned forward in his chair and took another sip.

"Before dawn one morning, we were awakened by small arms fire somewhere around the village. We implemented our plan, grabbed all our weapons and ammo, ran to the defensive shelters we had built, and prepared to be attacked.

"We had no communications outside of the village. We all knew we didn't have any support beyond ourselves and the gear we had with us.

"In the available light, we could see a band of men — maybe twenty or more — creeping slowly towards our shelter. We didn't know if they were friendly or enemy. We decided to stay still and wait to see what the band of men did next. We watched them shoot into some other potential hiding areas as they continued to approach us."

He scratched his beard, took a deep breath, and another sip of his drink.

"I decided to have the interpreter call to the approaching men to determine if they were friendly or not. He yelled something to them in Korean and they started shooting toward our shelter. We fired back and a few of them went down. None of my men were hit. The rest of the other group scattered, but they called to us in both Korean and in broken English. They said, 'come out' and 'we won't hurt you.'"

He shook his head and took another sip.

"Around dawn, they took the gas cans from our Jeeps, lit burning fuses to them, and threw them at our shelter. Fortunately, the fuel burned out before it got us. They then threw a hand grenade at the opening of the shelter. It exploded, but only caused a minor injury to the sergeant.

"We stayed quiet in the shelter, but it was apparent the enemy wasn't going to leave us alone and it was just a matter of time before they got organized and staged an attack."

The colonel sat back in his chair.

"I made... we made a plan to charge out the front of the shelter, to yell and shoot at anything in our way, to run toward a particular building and through a rice paddy to a wooded area in some foothills. We gathered and checked our weapons. The interpreter wanted to go with us, and we gave him a sidearm as well.

"On a signal, we ran from the entrance of the shelter and shot at every threat we saw. They were completely unprepared for our offensive assault. I shot at least two more enemy soldiers. We ran and shot and ran and shot until we got out of the village and into the woods. None of our people got hit, although we later found a bullet hole through one of the private's uniform blouse.

"We kept running through the woods until we found some friendly troops and knew we were safe."

The colonel had told the entire story in a monotone fashion without a single hint of emotion.

Jerrod fought the tears welling in his eyes.

"Once we got to safety," the colonel said. One of the privates came up to me and saluted. I saluted back and he said: 'Captain Horvat, I'm sure glad you were with us.'"

And the colonel started to cry. Big tears. Like it had happened just the day before instead of thirty-four years earlier.

Tears streaked down Jerrod's face.

The colonel composed himself, took another sip, and said: "Sometimes all you have are the people you can trust. No one else is going to help you. You have to make a plan and take the assault to the enemy. I had to kill people that morning and I'm not proud of that. But that's what happens in war. Kill or be killed. It was a risk we had to take to survive. I had to get my men out alive."

He took a long drink. They sat quietly for a few moments.

"Just like our Giants did the other night and we did in Korea, it was all 'Small-Ball'," the colonel said. "You don't get to give up. You don't get to leave early. You can't sit back and wait for something to come to you. You become the aggressor. You make the assault. You take the personnel and weapons you have, and you make it happen."

The two men quietly finished their drinks.

"Thanks for telling me about Korea, sir."

"You were going to hear it eventually."

"I really appreciate it, sir."

The colonel leaned forward in his chair, looked Jerrod directly in the eyes, and said: "Did I ever tell you about the two Australian girls I met on R&R during World War II?"

CHAPTER 64

Jerrod walked back to his house and flopped onto the sofa. He was feeling a buzz from the Fat-Burner and was still emotional from the combat story he had just been privileged to hear.

The TV was on, as it usually was, and a nature program caught his attention: It involved a group of men in Texas hunting snakes for an annual Rattlesnake Round-Up. The snake hunters ventured into the brush and used a method in which they sprayed gasoline vapors into potential rattlesnake dens to force the snakes out into the open for easy capture.

The technique the snake hunters used was barbaric, but also incredibly simple and effective: They made the hiding place so uncomfortable the snake chose to expose itself to capture in order to escape the discomfort they had created.

Jerrod stared at the shredded draperies and the sheet of raw plywood covering the opening that once was his plate glass window. He stared at the pellet holes in his wall and the stains from his lover's blood on the sofa and carpet.

He felt absolute responsibility for the terror and pain Natalie had suffered. He desperately needed to find Hector Medina and Val Reyes' killers. He needed to personally place the handcuffs on Armando Mendoza's wrists and watch him and his stooges go off to jail. He was fed up with the interference from his superiors. He was tired of waiting for something to happen. He needed to make it happen.

He leaned back on the sofa and closed his eyes for a few moments. A jumble of thoughts went through his mind. The Giants' baseball victory over their rivals. The colonel's emotional war story. Catching rattlesnakes for a round-up.

Play Small-Ball. Use the resources you have. Take the attack to the enemy. Force the snake out of its den and into the open for capture.

His eyes shot wide open when he realized what he needed to do.

Craig was right. He had been getting in his own way.

The stakes were huge... and he was going to need some help.

CHAPTER 65

Thursday

Jerrod Gold arrived at work at one minute to eight. Pete Hanson, Craig Wallace, and Willie Sanchez were at their desks.

"Fine morning, gentlemen," Jerrod said.

"I thought you might take the day off," the sergeant said.

"All nice and rested, sir. Ready for a new day."

"Well, okay," the sergeant said. "Welcome back."

Jerrod sat at his desk. He looked over at Craig and around him to Willie. Their facial expressions told him they knew he was up to something.

And they were correct.

The detectives did their morning routine. The coffee was bitter, but strong. KHJB pumped out rock hit after hit. Springsteen. Benatar. Sting. Prince.

The sergeant announced he was heading out for a community meeting and would be back after lunch.

After he was sure the sergeant was gone, Craig asked Jerrod, "What the hell are you up to?"

"I have a plan," Jerrod said in a hushed voice. "But we can't talk about it here. Let's get lunch. My treat."

"Okay," Craig said.

"Free lunch," Willie said. "I'm in."

CHAPTER 66

Jerrod walked past the big black Chevrolet Suburban parked on Main Street and through the front door of the El Ocotillo Club. He wore a suit jacket over his police equipment but knew he would stand out in that bar.

The dark interior setting of the club hadn't changed a bit since he first entered it as a patrol officer over five years earlier. It was a long and narrow room with a vinyl-padded bar and well-worn wooden stools occupying the entire right side. Eight small tables with steel chairs were scattered along the left side. The walls were covered with posters and lighted signs. Coors. Tecate. Dos Equis. Corona.

Small lights danced on a silent jukebox along the left side wall. The club had a smell of Pine Sol mixed with cigarette smoke and urine.

In the very back of the room, six men sat around a worn round green-felt poker table. The table was well lit by a hanging rectangular stained-glass Miller Lite Beer lamp more suited for a pool table.

The only other person in the club sat on a stool at the bar. The man stood and placed himself between the detective and the poker players.

Jerrod recognized the man as being Joaquin "Chimo" Cervantes, the owner of the bar, from the grainy newspaper wedding photo he had seen at the library. He had grown a light beard and had gained a few pounds since his wedding day.

"I'd like to speak with Armando Mendoza," Jerrod said with a tone that was far more weighted toward demand than request.

"He's busy right now," Chimo said. "Come back some other time."

"I'll wait right here until he's *not* busy." Jerrod pulled out a stool from the bar and sat down. "May I have a Coke, please."

"You have to leave," Chimo said.

"I said I'd wait until he's available." Jerrod stood back up. "Unless you want to make me leave."

Chimo froze and appeared unsure of what to do next. He outweighed the detective by thirty pounds but was hesitant to place hands on the plainclothes officer. He looked back over his right shoulder to the men at the poker table. A player in the seat farthest from the bar nodded his head subtly back to Chimo. Chimo turned back around.

"Wait here," he said.

The man at the poker table said something to the other players in Spanish and stood up. He walked around the table and along the bar until he was shoulder to shoulder with Chimo.

Armando Mendoza was tall and lean. He had a handsome face with dark features that somewhat resembled the late movie actor Clark Gable. He had a neatly trimmed thin mustache and goatee. He wore an open collar dress shirt. Custom-made black cowboy boots extended from the boot-cut legs of his creased jeans. A modest silver watch was on his left wrist. There was no wedding ring.

"Detective Jerrod Gold," Mendoza said. "It's a pleasure to finally meet you. I've been hearing so much about you."

Neither man initiated an effort to shake hands.

"Is there someplace we can talk privately?" Jerrod asked.

"Sure, come into my office," Mendoza said as he spun smartly on the undercut heels of his expensive boots and walked toward a wooden door just past the bar.

Jerrod kept his eyes locked on Chimo as Chimo watched his father-in-law walk away. As he walked past Chimo, he ran his shoulder into him and caused Chimo to lose his balance. Chimo stumbled backward and had to catch the bar with his hands to prevent himself from falling.

One of the poker players laughed at the sight.

"Excuse Me," Jerrod said in the same tone and cadence one would say "Fuck You."

The office was a great contrast from the motif of the bar itself. The walls were painted off-white and the room was well lit. The furnishings were spartan, but clean and tidy. An uncluttered average-size wooden desk was in the middle of the room in front of a brown high-back desk chair.

A black leather-bound Bible sat open on a small table near the desk. A bookcase near the door contained labeled binders, books, family photos, and nick-knacks.

Mendoza walked around the desk and sat in the big leather chair. He leaned back and clasped his hands behind his head in a gesture of power and confidence.

Jerrod sat in the single wooden chair in front of the desk.

"What brings you to my establishment, Detective?" he said softly.

"I just wanted you to be aware that I know about your entire drug operation. And I plan on doing everything I can to take it down."

Mendoza laughed. He moved his hands to his belly and rocked back in his chair as he laughed harder.

"Detective, you are young and foolish," he said through his laughter. "I don't know where you get your information, but you are gravely mistaken. I am just a simple businessman. I am just trying to be a good American citizen. I have no knowledge of the drug trade you talk of."

"I'm making a case that will take your entire operation down," Jerrod said as he leaned forward in his chair. "And everyone you love will go down with you."

Mendoza stopped laughing. His coal-black eyes narrowed as he placed his hands on the desk.

"I read in the paper that your house was shot into the other night. Is that right?"

"Yes, it was."

"Do you think someone was trying to get your attention or actually wanted to harm you... and your lady friend?"

"I have no idea. In either case, it didn't seem to work. Did it?"

Mendoza's demeanor changed to defiance. "Are you implying I have something to do with the shooting?"

"I don't know if you were involved or not—"

"You don't know much of anything, do you?" he interrupted.

Mendoza lifted his hands from the desk and pushed them forward with the wrists held together.

"You're way out of your depth, Detective. But if you have some evidence against me, take me to jail right now."

"In due time, sir. In due time."

Mendoza clasped his hands in his lap. His demeanor became calm. He spoke in nearly a whisper as he leaned back in the chair.

"The sermon I heard in church this Sunday spoke about pride, arrogance, and hubris," he said as he reached for the Bible and placed it on the desk. "You could benefit from the wonderful sermons at my church."

He thumbed through the pages before saying, "I particularly like this one passage. Here it is. Proverbs 18:12. 'Before destruction the heart of man is proud, but before honor is humility.'"

"That's the second time this week someone has quoted scripture to me," Jerrod said. "I'm honestly not feeling at all enlightened by it."

"Our conversation is over," Mendoza said.

"Very well. I'm certain we will meet again under different circumstances."

Jerrod stood up and walked to the door. He placed his hand on the knob and paused. He looked back to Mendoza and said, "While you've got your Bible open, look up a verse I particularly like. Job 40:12. Just for fun."

Jerrod left the office and closed the door quietly.

CHAPTER 67

Armando Mendoza sat at his desk and shook his head at the boldness of the young detective. He was sure the brazen visit was no more than a futile scare tactic from a stubborn investigator unable to make a case otherwise.

But then. *What did he know?*

He closed the Bible and went to put it back on the small table. He stopped as he recalled the passage the young detective had mentioned. Job 40:12.

He opened the Bible and thumbed the pages until he found the verse and violently slammed the Bible shut after reading it.

The verse read: "Look at everyone who is proud and humble him. Crush the wicked in their place."

CHAPTER 68

"I talked to Armando Mendoza this morning," Jerrod said as he took a bite out of his cheeseburger.

"You did what?" Craig said as he nearly spit out the chunk of BLT he had just taken. He swallowed hard and wiped his face with a napkin.

"Wheaton was right, dude," Willie said. "You really are a loose cannon."

"No, not at all," Jerrod said. "You should have seen Mendoza when I sat down in his office. He was smug and superior and confident when we first started talking. But he was pissed when I left. Now he thinks we may have more info than we really do. He may even think someone in his group has turned informant. He'll be watching all of his people awfully close."

Craig pushed his eyeglasses higher on his nose. "Is that part of the 'plan' you alluded to earlier?" he asked.

"Yep. Here's the plan. There's a lot of moving parts and we're going to need help."

The two detectives nodded.

"I heard Wheaton say he would be out-of-town until Sunday night," Jerrod said. "So, it all has to go-down before he gets back."

"I'm in," Willie said.

"Okay," Craig said. "What's the plan?"

Jerrod glanced around the restaurant and leaned across the tabletop before speaking in a hushed voice.

"Do you know how they catch rattlesnakes in Texas?"

CHAPTER 69

Stella Leiter was dressed, had her make-up on, and her red rat's-nest hair tamed when she answered the knock on her motel room door.

She pulled her head back in surprise when she saw Jerrod and Willie standing outside the door.

"Who died this time?" she said as she invited them in and sat down on the bed.

"No one's dead," Willie said.

"Are you still 'clean?'" Jerrod asked.

"I haven't used since the OD. No bullshit. Check me if you want."

"Stella." Jerrod said. "We have something we need you to do. It has some risk to it. Here's how it's going to work."

The detectives drove back to the PD and Jerrod went straight to the half-door at Records.

"Hello, Ann."

"Hello, right back, Jerrod," Ann Rogers said as she got up from her desk and glided to the window.

"Can I ask you for a favor? I need something done. Quietly."

"Sure. Anything."

Stella washed off her make-up and mussed her hair. She locked her motel room door and walked through the motel parking lot to the adjoining street. She held her purse close to her as it contained the three hundred dollars in cash Jerrod had handed her earlier.

She was unsure exactly where to begin, so she started walking toward Main Street. She hadn't walked more than a block when a middle-aged man in a yellow taxi stopped at a traffic light and honked his horn. She looked at the man and didn't recognize him. He waved for her to come over to the taxi.

"Need a ride, pretty lady?" the man said as she walked up to the passenger window.

"Sure. Downtown. And a few other places."

"Mesa County Health Department, this is Dave Pell," the voice on the phone answered.

"Dave, it's Jerrod."

"Hey, buddy. How are you doing?"

"Good. Can you be available in Valle Verde tomorrow?"

"Yeah, sure," he said. "Why?"

"Here's what's going to happen."

Ann closed Records at four o'clock and enjoyed a walk past the busy downtown businesses on Main Street. She stopped and looked at some new shoes in the window of a department store and could smell the pleasant aromas coming from a Croatian family restaurant as they prepared the dinner menu.

She walked another block and into Main Street Printers.

"Hello. How can I help you?" the young male clerk behind the counter said as he straightened his posture and smoothed the front of his shirt.

"Hello," Ann said. "I'd like one hundred of these printed, please."

She admired the handiwork of the sample flier she had designed before handing it to the clerk.

"When will you need these?" he asked.

"By tomorrow at noon," she said. "Print them on pink paper, please."

"The fliers will be thirty cents each and I'll have to charge ten dollars extra because it's a 'rush' job," he said. "That will come to forty dollars plus tax."

Ann counted out fifty dollars onto the counter from the cash Jerrod had given her.

"Keep the change for yourself," she said.

At five-twenty, Al Kees had just gotten home from work and changed out of his dispatcher uniform.

He was looking in the refrigerator of his one-bedroom rented duplex for something to eat when he heard his doorbell ring. He opened the door and was surprised to see two detectives — Jerrod and Willie — at his front step.

"Al, we need to talk," Jerrod said.

"He's up my ass all day long," Al complained. "The captain listens to every minute of radio traffic and asks me about nearly every call that comes in. He takes notes off my notepad, for Christ's sake. I think he's afraid he's going to miss something that's going on."

"Did you tell Wheaton about the call from 'Humberto' yesterday?" Jerrod asked. "Other than Willie, you were the only other person who knew he called."

"No... yes... no, I guess," Al said as he glanced over at Willie. "He came out of his office and asked who had just called for you. I gave him the name I had. He does that all day... everyday."

"Did you tell him about the game Patrol was playing, Grommet Wars, last week," Willie asked. "And don't lie to me."

"Well, yeah," Al said. "I had seen the guys doing the thing with the batons and they told me how the game was played. I thought it was hilarious. Wheaton asked me what I knew about it, and he said it was in my best interest to tell him the truth." He swallowed hard. "So, I did."

"Nobody likes a snitch around the office, Al," Jerrod said. "We need your help with something. Can we count on you?"

At five-forty-five, Jerrod and Willie pulled up next to two black-and-whites in the parking lot of The Corner.

"You called this meeting," Marko Otero said.

"What's going on?" Rusty Browne asked.

"Have you guys ever heard the baseball term: 'Small-Ball.'"

At six o'clock, Stella Leiter walked through the parking lot toward her motel room. She slowed and then stopped when she saw two men get out of a dark four-door sedan.

"I should have worn more comfortable shoes," she said.

"Let's talk in your room," Jerrod said.

She sat down on the bed and took off her high-heeled strapped shoes.

"How many places?" Willie asked.

"Eleven," she said. "Look."

Stella lifted her purse and opened it upside down over the bed. Cash, a scrap of yellow paper, a pen, and thirteen cellophane bindles containing small pieces of black tar heroin fell out onto the blankets.

"How much did you spend?" Jerrod asked.

"I don't know," she said. "I paid a taxi guy fifty to drive me around. There's some left. Count it."

Jerrod counted the cash and found sixty dollars left.

"Stella, look up at me and close your eyes," Willie directed.

Stella closed her eyes for ten seconds.

"Open them," Willie said.

She opened her eyes and her pupils contracted to a normal size as they adjusted to the light.

"I told you I stopped using," she said.

Willie nodded.

"Are those the addresses?" Jerrod asked as he pointed to the piece of yellow paper.

"Yes," she said. "They're all there."

"You have dinner yet?" Jerrod asked.

"Not yet," she said. "I didn't eat all day."

Jerrod reached to his inside suit pocket and pulled out the white envelope. He took three twenty-dollar bills and combined it with the other sixty before handing it to her.

"Treat yourself to someplace nice. Thank you."

At six-forty-five, Oswaldo "Ozzie" Suarez walked into the El Ocotillo Club and sat down on one of the wooden stools at the bar. Five men were seated at the bar. Six others played cards at the poker table.

An attractive female bartender with a dark complexion – perhaps Cuban, rather than Mexican – was in deep conversation with one of the men at the bar. She rolled her eyes as she walked over to greet the new customer.

"What do you want?" she asked in not-so-polite Spanish.

"Budweiser, *por favor,*" he said.

The bartender trudged away toward a cooler on the other end of the bar to get the beer.

A sign hanging on the back bar wall read:

NO PERSONS UNDER 21 ALLOWED TO PURCHASE ALCOHOL

The bartender returned with the open bottle of Bud.

"Two dollars," she insisted in Spanish.

Ozzie pulled three crumpled dollar bills from his pants pocket and placed them on the bar. The bartender grabbed the bills, walked past the cash register, and placed all three bills in her pants pocket before rejoining her conversation.

Ozzie held the beer in his hand and glanced toward the front door, as did all of the other patrons, when two uniformed VVPD officers walked in. The officers looked around the room and approached Ozzie at the bar.

"May we see some identification, sir?" Marko Otero asked.

"Sure," the man said as he got out his wallet and pulled out a California driver's license.

“Oswaldo Suarez,” Marko said as he read the information on the license. “Your birthday was in November 1965. That makes you only twenty — if my math is correct.”

“Yes, sir,” Ozzie said.

“Who sold you the beer?” Marko asked.

“Her, right there,” Ozzie said pointing to the woman behind the bar who unsuccessfully tried to make herself as small as possible.

One of the men from the poker table folded his hand of cards and rushed along the bar to meet the officers.

“I own this bar, officers,” Chimo Cervantes said with a smile to Rusty Browne. “Is there a problem?”

“I'm afraid this man is underage and was served an alcoholic beverage in your establishment,” Rusty said.

“I'm sure there's been a mistake,” Chimo said.

“Afraid not, sir,” Marko said. “This minor will be placed under arrest, and we'll be issuing you a citation for the alcohol violation.”

“Why me?” Chimo asked. “I didn't serve him.”

“You're the licensee, sir,” Rusty said. “So, you're responsible for everything that happens here. May I see some ID, please.”

Marko handcuffed Ozzie's hands behind his back as Rusty issued the misdemeanor citation to Chimo.

“Have a pleasant evening, sir,” Marko said as the officer led the young man through the club front door and into the backseat of a black-and-white.

Chimo followed the officers out to the sidewalk still holding his ID and the yellow copy of the citation in his hand. He stood silently as he watched the officers drive away.

The two patrol cars pulled behind the PD and Ozzie was helped out of the backseat. Marko removed the handcuffs, and the young man rubbed his wrists.

“How did it go, Ozzie?”

“That was fun, Uncle Willie,” he said.

“Don't tell your mom what we did tonight, okay?” Willie said.

“Let's do it again,” Ozzie said.

“Some other night, Ozzie,” Jerrod said with a smile. “Here's twenty bucks for your help. Thanks.”

"You're not going to believe what just happened," Chimo Cervantes grumbled into the telephone receiver before Armando Mendoza could say hello.

"Slow down. What happened?"

"The cops were just at the club, and they gave me a ticket for serving a minor at the bar."

"Why did you do that?"

"I didn't. That stupid bartender did. But I got the ticket. They arrested the minor and took him away in handcuffs."

"Was that smart-ass detective involved?"

"No, just two uniform guys."

"Okay. Don't worry about it."

The dinner crowd at Nopales was exceptionally large for a Thursday night and the bar did an equally good business. It was just after midnight when the last customer left, and Maggie Cervantes could finally lock the doors.

Oso and Efrain Hernandez waited in the bar while she tabulated the receipts for the night. She smiled when she realized the restaurant had netted nearly sixteen hundred dollars for their efforts.

She unlocked her safe and placed the receipts inside until her next bank deposit on Monday. The deposit would be combined with five or six of the fifteen bundles of bills with blue broccoli bands her father had given her.

Officer Dave Yamamoto turned his portable police radio down so he could barely hear it. He stood across Main Street in the landscape of a medical office and watched the activities at Nopales. He held his right hand over the gold badge pinned to his left chest to prevent any glare from shining off it. He had parked his black-and-white behind the office.

He watched a tall man he recognized as being Efrain Hernandez and a large, bearded man leave the restaurant through the front door. The men stood together in the parking lot while the last of the restaurant interior lights went dark. A nicely dressed woman came out through the door and locked it behind her.

The woman got into the driver's seat of a newer white Cadillac Seville. The men got into a blue Oldsmobile. Efrain got in the driver's door and the large man in the passenger side. The Cadillac's headlights came on and he watched it pull out of the lot and drive east away from the restaurant. The Oldsmobile followed close behind. He watched the taillights of the two cars disappear around a corner.

He waited for five minutes and saw no other activity at the restaurant.

Dave walked across Main Street, through the parking lot, and along the east side of the building which housed the Nopales restaurant. He found the unlocked electrical service panel and opened the cover. He clasped his hand over the beam of his large black flashlight so only a sliver of light came out. He scanned down the labels of the individual breakers and found the one he wanted. With the flip of his finger, he switched the breaker from ON to OFF.

He would return just before the end of his shift at seven o'clock to switch the breaker back to ON.

CHAPTER 70

Friday

Maggie and Chimo Cervantes were sound asleep at eight-thirty when their home phone rang.

"Maggie, Maggie, come to the restaurant right away," the frantic male voice of her morning prep cook on the phone said in Spanish.

"What the hell's going on?" she said as she tried to clear her head.

"The inspector. He's here now. We have trouble," the cook said.

"I'll be right there."

Officers Kevin Arneta and Kevin Holcomb typically had Fridays off. But not that Friday. They wore jeans and loose button-up shirts to conceal the badges and pistols fastened to their belts.

They sat together in Big Kevin's personal car, a brown Honda Accord, and watched the first of the eleven addresses Jerrod had given them.

"I'm afraid to tell you all of that food in the walk-in will have to be discarded, Maggie," Gary Pell said. "I'm sorry."

"Gary," Maggie said. "We've known each other a long time. Is there anything we can do?"

"Not really. The temperatures in both the refrigerator and freezer are at least ten degrees higher than the health code allows. The food in there might be fine, but it could also be spoiled and contain a whole variety of bacteria. I just can't take the chance and endanger the public by allowing any of it to be served."

"You realize there's hundreds of dollars worth of meat and produce in there. I can't just throw it out. It's Friday and I was stocked for the weekend."

"I'm afraid you'll have to, Maggie. Perhaps your supplier can get a rush delivery to you today."

"That'll cost me a fortune."

"I wish there were more I could do. Again, I'm sorry, but I'll have to supervise the disposal."

At nine-thirty, The Kevins watched a handsome young man they estimated to be around sixteen walk to the front door of the first house. The boy was carrying a brown paper sack.

He knocked and another child, a girl no more than seven, opened the door and the boy went inside.

Less than a minute later, the boy came back out and bounded down the steps onto the sidewalk. He was carrying a white paper bag in his left hand.

The Kevins watched the boy walk toward them and waited for the precise moment to jump out of the Honda and trap the boy between them. The boy tried to run, but Tall Kevin caught him by the arm and the boy wasn't able to take another step.

"Police. Stop struggling. We're not going to hurt you." Big Kevin told him with an official tone.

"What's your name?" Big Kevin asked.

"George," the frightened boy said as he looked down at Tall Kevin's huge hand clamped to his arm.

"Where do you live?"

"478 Third Street. With my mom and dad."

"What's in the bag, George?" Tall Kevin asked.

"I don't know," the kid said.

"Mind if we look?" Big Kevin asked.

"Uh, sure, I guess," George said as he held out the bag to him.

Big Kevin took the crumpled bag and weighed it in his hand. He opened the bag and found loose stacks of cash in all denominations. He thumbed through the stacks and estimated there was seven or eight hundred dollars.

"You can leave," Tall Kevin said to George as he released his arm.

"What do I tell... the guy... who I'm supposed to give the bag to."

"Tell him he can claim his dope money at the police department," Big Kevin said. "And remind him to bring some ID so we're sure who he is when he comes in."

"Don't let us catch you with another bag, *George who lives at 478 Third Street with his mom and dad*," Tall Kevin said.

"Remember," Big Kevin said as he wagged his finger. "'Just Say No to Drugs' and now get the hell out of here."

Maggie's stomach felt like the coffee she had been drinking for the last hour was battery acid.

She had called all of her kitchen crew and some of the wait staff in early to empty the walk-in refrigerator and freezer. She stood with Gary and watched them throw away at least a thousand dollars worth of food — food she had already paid for — into a city dumpster.

She had been on the phone since then with her suppliers trying to get a rush order of meat, vegetables, fruit, and bakery goods to operate the restaurant for the weekend.

Some suppliers said they could help, for a premium price, and others weren't able to accommodate her.

She cried when she realized she would have to close for the Friday lunch and shop at retail grocery stores for enough supplies to open the doors to dinner customers.

At ten-thirty, Allison "AJ" Jenkins was thoroughly enjoying the articles in the most recent edition of *Cosmopolitan* magazine while her feet soaked in a warm and swirling bath of mineral salts.

She was accustomed to filing her own fingernails and applying a clear finish, so she didn't conflict with VVPD grooming standards but had never had a pedicure. She soon understood the attraction that women — and surely some men — got from the attention and pampering received during the "spa experience."

The staff at the Final Touches Hair and Nails Salon were friendly and professional. The adorable young woman who introduced herself as "Cat" was charming as she offered her "coffee, tea, or something a little stronger" while she soaked. She accepted the coffee and savored the strong blend served to her in a white china cup — with a saucer.

After her feet had soaked, they were dried in an ultra-soft towel and massaged with a silky lotion by a smiling and attentive nail technician. She settled for a deep violet nail color called "Midnight at the Casbah" and was amazed at the gentle skill of the technician as she trimmed and pushed the cuticles and shaped the toenails one by one. Several layers of polish were expertly applied to her nails to create a deep and elegant shine.

When the process was over, AJ stood and carefully slipped her feet into her flip-flop sandals. She smiled as she wiggled her toes and admired her fresh look.

"How much do I owe you?" AJ asked the friendly technician who was looking down and approving her own work.

"Eighteen dollars, ma'am," the technician said.

AJ removed a twenty and a ten-dollar bill from the fifty dollars Jerrod had given her and handed it to the technician.

"Keep it," AJ said.

"A twelve-dollar tip?" the technician said. "Thank you very much. You come back and ask for me. Okay?"

"Okay. Thank you very much," AJ said.

AJ walked back over to the table near the foot bath and placed the *Cosmopolitan* back with the other magazines. She paused for a moment near the foot bath and glanced at the technicians to assure she wasn't being watched. She raised her right foot and appeared to adjust the cuff on her jeans.

"Thank you again," AJ said as she waived to "Cat" and the technician and went to the door to leave.

She held the door open for a middle-aged woman with huge hips and a sour face who brushed past her without an acknowledgment.

"You're welcome, bitch," AJ said to herself as she walked out of the salon.

The Kevins watched the second and third houses on the list for a half-hour each but saw no runner coming or going from either address. However, at the fourth, sixth, eighth, ninth, and eleventh houses they confronted five more young men and boys leaving the houses with bags full of cash.

One of the boys wet his pants as Tall Kevin grabbed him because he thought he was being robbed and was about to be shot.

They were all told to let their boss know who had the money and to come right into the PD lobby to claim it.

The sour-faced woman at Final Touches Hair and Nails was a Friday regular. She was always in a hurry, was rude to the staff, was unreasonably critical of the quality of the pedicures and, on top of that, was a bad tipper.

The two technicians in the salon pointed to each other when the woman walked in. The technician who had just received the twelve-dollar tip from AJ giggled and whispered in Spanish, "Your turn."

The other tech put on her best fake smile and approached the woman who was looking at the toenail finishes available.

"This pink," the woman said pointing to the color board. "Square nail, not rounded like you did last time. And I'm in a hurry."

"Yes, ma'am," the second technician said. "I'll have you soak now."

"I want a fresh mineral bath," the woman demanded. "Did you change the water after the last customer?"

"Of course, ma'am," the tech said.

Ann Rogers closed Records for lunch. She walked downtown and straight to Main Street Printers where she found the same clerk behind the counter.

"Good afternoon," the young clerk said. "I have the fliers right here." He pulled a cardboard box out from under the counter and opened it.

Ann pulled one of the fliers on pink paper and examined every detail.

"Perfect."

Jerrod Gold met with The Kevins at The Corner a little after noon.

As they munched on chili dogs and drank Cokes, Jerrod peeked into the large brown grocery bag the smaller white bags of dope money had been dumped into.

"How much is in there?" Jerrod asked.

"A little over thirty-five hundred," Tall Kevin said.

"Wow," Big Kevin said. "We're in the wrong business."

"What are we going to do with the cash, Jerrod?" Tall Kevin asked.

"It'll be going to a noble cause," Jerrod said before finishing the last bite of his second 'dog.

The men stopped talking, and eating, as they watched Ann approach them. She walked with the effortless grace of a professional dancer.

Tall Kevin stood a little taller. Big Kevin swept his tongue over his teeth to make sure there was no visible debris.

"Good afternoon, gentlemen," she said as she handed Jerrod the box of fliers.

"How did they come out?" Jerrod asked.

"They should do the trick."

"Thank you very much."

"Anytime," she said before gliding back to the PD.

AJ pulled her car into the lot of The Corner and stopped near the three men. Her radio was blasting the Eurythmics playing "Would I lie to you?"

"Is it done?" Jerrod asked.

"It's done," she said. "I love my new nails. Thanks. I could make that a regular thing... but at a different salon.

The men all laughed.

"Here's the extra twenty I didn't need," she said as she reached out and handed it to him.

Jerrod took the twenty-dollar bill and put it in the grocery bag with the dope money.

Jerrod handed the box of fliers to Big Kevin and said to the three off-duty officers:

"If you don't mind, just one more thing to do."

The second nail tech's eyes grew wide, and she let out a huge gasp when the sour-faced woman pulled her right foot out of the warm mineral bath.

"What's wrong?" the woman said as she lowered the magazine she was reading.

The tech held the ultra-soft towel ready in her hands but was paralyzed.

"Catalina," the tech yelled as loud as she could.

Catalina Mendoza ran from her office and stopped abruptly in the middle of the salon and covered her mouth with her hand when she saw it.

The sour-faced woman started screaming hysterically as her left foot emerged from the water.

Her feet and ankles were both a vivid purple color. They were so purple, it looked like she was wearing a pair of socks.

"What the hell?" Catalina screamed as panic set in. "Rinse it off. Rinse it off."

They tried every soap, shampoo, and lotion in the salon, but were only able to lighten the purple stained feet to a medium violet color.

"I'm going to sue you," were the last words the woman said as she stormed from the salon in tears and headed for her car.

Armando Mendoza thought he was living out an episode of *The Twilight Zone*.

He had just gotten off the telephone with Catalina, who was sobbing about "someone with purple feet" at the salon.

He was still dealing with Maggie's call about the health inspection and her having to throw out all the spoiled food. And that was after Chimo's call from the night before about the alcohol violation.

He thought there was no way the series of incidents could be a simple coincidence.

The phone rang again, and he found Oso on the other end.

"Armando," Oso said. "Two cops caught six of our runners this morning and took all of our money from them."

"Cops? In uniform?" Armando asked.

"The kids told me two guys had guns and badges but were in regular clothes."

"They couldn't be real cops? Could they?" Armando said. "Do you think those kids are stealing from us?"

"No, I don't think so," Oso said. "They all came to the house alone but told us the exact same story."

"Did you or Efrain take the money, Oso?"

"No, Armando. Of course not. We would never steal—"

"Shut-up, Oso. And get *my* money back."

Gary Pell had just gotten back to his office in Mesa when his desk phone rang.

"Mesa County Health—," he said before being interrupted by a nearly incoherent woman's voice.

He could make out only certain words: "feet," "soak," "purple," and "lawsuit" were the ones he heard clearly.

A man's voice came onto the telephone. "Is this the Health Department?"

"Yes, sir. I'm one of the inspectors," he said. "How can I help you?"

"My wife, well, she gets her nails done at a salon here in Valle Verde every Friday," the man said. "She just got home, and her feet are purple."

"Purple, sir?" Gary asked.

"Yes, purple," the man said. "And it won't come off."

"What's her name, sir?"

"Margaret. Margaret Smith."

"And your name, sir?"

"Franklin Smith. Pastor Franklin Smith."

"I'm leaving right now. Can you meet me at the salon in half an hour?"

"Yes, I can," Pastor Smith said.

Gary hung up the phone and froze with his hand on the receiver for a second when he realized he had forgotten to ask the pastor which salon in Valle Verde the incident involving his wife occurred.

He already knew where he would be going.

Jerrod walked back to the PD from The Corner to make a few telephone calls. Craig Wallace and Willie Sanchez were at their desks.

"Everything's going according to plan... so far," Jerrod said. "Anyone want to go on a quick road-trip."

The three detectives got into Jerrod's car, and he pulled out of the PD lot. He turned right on Fremont Street and drove its length south until it ended at River Drive and the Valle Verde River levee. He turned right and then right again onto the first block of Main Street.

As they cruised north on Main Street, Willie saw the first one and Craig the second. Seconds later they saw nearly every car on Main Street with a pink flier under the driver's side wiper blade.

Gary Pell arrived at the Final Touches Hair and Nails salon at about three o'clock and parked next to a bright red BMW 535i.

He correctly assumed the big-bellied and red-faced man leaning against a silver Lincoln Town Car was Franklin Smith.

"Pastor Smith?" Gary asked.

"I am," he said. "This is the salon. They've locked the doors and won't let me in."

"They'll let me in," Gary said. "Please wait here."

He walked to the salon door and caught the attention of Catalina. He pressed his County credentials against the glass of the door and she unlocked it.

"I understand there was an incident here this morning," he said. "May I come in?"

Catalina explained what had happened and assured Gary they always change the mineral solution between each client.

"Is that the same solution in the bath now?" he asked.

"Yes, it is." Catalina said.

"What ingredients do you use in the solution?" Gary asked.

"Just Epsom salts and distilled water," she said. "That's all. We mix it here."

"I'll need to take a sample for analysis, okay," Gary said. "And then we can pour the rest out."

"Okay," Catalina said.

"And you'll have to close the salon until we find out what caused the skin... complication... on Mrs. Smith's feet.

"I took a sample of the water used in the foot bath, sir," Gary said to Pastor Smith. "I've ordered the salon closed until we have the water tested and that will take a few business days. We should know by Wednesday or Thursday of next week."

"What about my wife's feet... now?" the pastor asked. "She's afraid to go outside and we have a special service this Sunday."

"I'm afraid I can't help you there, sir."

Jerrod pulled his car to the curb in front of the home of Carmen and Yvonne Medina.

"Oh, hello," Yvonne said when she answered the knock on her door.

"How are you doing?" Jerrod asked as he was invited into the house.

"We're doing okay, I guess. Hector's funeral is going to be on Monday. Can you be there?"

"I'll be there," he said. "I need to tell you something."

They sat at the kitchen table. Carmen came into the room and sat down with them.

"I don't know how to put this," Jerrod said. "Hector was involved with a group of drug dealers. He ran dope and money between the supplier and the houses around town that sold the drugs."

Yvonne nodded as he spoke. Her facial expressions signaled acceptance rather than disbelief as he explained what the investigation had uncovered. She translated his words into Spanish for Carmen. Carmen nodded and seemed to also accept it as the truth.

"We're not surprised, Jerrod," Yvonne said. "We suspected he wasn't loading trucks. Especially when he bought those damn shoes."

"I've got something for you" he said as he handed her the brown grocery bag. "We did a little collection at the office. We hope it helps a little with expenses and things."

"Thank you," she said without opening the bag. "It's been pretty tight money-wise here."

"I just wanted you to know we haven't forgot about Hector and your family," he said. "I'll see you on Monday."

Yvonne walked Jerrod to the door and thanked him again. She returned to the kitchen and opened the paper bag. Carmen nearly fainted when Yvonne poured $3,643 in cash onto the table.

"What was the name of that chemical, Jerrod?" Gary Pell asked from a pay phone near the Final Touches Hair and Nail Salon.

"Ninhydrin," he said while looking at the purple skin around his own left thumbnail.

"I took a sample of the bath water, but I'll send something else to the lab. I'll drag the results out for a week and then let them re-open the salon."

"Thanks, buddy. Who got the purple feet?"

"A woman named Margaret Smith. Wife of Pastor Franklin Smith of the Mission Community Church."

"Okay. Thanks for everything today."

Jerrod hung up his desk phone and looked around Craig to Willie at his desk.

"Hey, Willie. What was the name of the church Rusty and Katy Browne stopped going to last week?"

"Mission Community Church. Why?"

"You're not going to believe this."

Maggie was able to restock her walk-in with a combination of supplier goods and grocery store purchases that cost her over three thousand dollars.

A refrigeration service technician had checked the mechanical workings of the walk-in and had told her there was nothing wrong with it. That cost her another one hundred fifty.

Nopales closed for lunch, which gave her kitchen crew a chance to prepare for the most popular dishes a Friday night dinner crowd would likely order.

She had been able to run home, take a relaxing bath, and get herself ready to reopen the restaurant.

Maggie arrived back at Nopales shortly before four o'clock and was pleased to see a small crowd already at the front door waiting to be let in.

She went into the restaurant via the kitchen entrance and made sure they were ready for customers.

"Go ahead and unlock the door," Maggie told one of the servers.

"Hello," Terri said when she answered the telephone call from Jerrod.

"Hello, Terri. How's Natalie doing?"

"She's doing better. She's up if you want to talk to her."

"Sure."

Natalie got on the line.

"Hello, Jerrod. Thought you had forgotten about me already. You know, 'When the cat's away....'"

"That's hardly the case. How are you?"

"Better. The swelling on my face has gone down quite a bit. I'm feeling pretty good. How about you?"

"I'm fine. I heal quick, too."

"Have you heard anything about Hector's funeral?"

"In fact, I have. I talked to his sister and the service will be on Monday. I'll come get you if you want to go."

"We'll see. I'm not much for being in public right now... stitches in my face and all."

"I understand. We'll see how you feel then."

"Okay."

"Hey, I got the window at the house replaced today. I ran home and let the glass guys in. They knew about the shooting and gave me a real fair price. I already patched the wall over the sofa, but I still need to paint it."

"That's nice..." she said as her voice trailed off.

"What's wrong?"

"Jerrod, I don't know if I can go back to that house. I'm sure I'll get over it at some point, but I'm still scared."

"I'm doing everything I can to make sure nothing like that ever happens again."

The police radio call came out as "an angry crowd" outside Nopales restaurant on Main Street. Marko and Rusty radioed they would handle the incident.

They found nearly fifty agitated people in the parking lot. Some people in the crowd were holding pieces of paper in their hands. Pink paper.

The officers waded through the crowd and to the locked front door.

"Someone called us," Marko said to Maggie when she cracked the door open and invited them in. Male and female voices shouted at her from the crowd and Maggie locked the door behind them.

"Look at this," Maggie said as she handed a pink page to the officers.

The officers read the artfully prepared and professionally printed flier:

NOPALES RESTAURANT ON MAIN STREET
ALL ENTREES--HALF PRICE
ALL BEER, WINE AND COCKTAILS--HALF PRICE
FRIDAY NIGHT ONLY

"So, what's the problem?" Marko asked.

"Sounds like a clever way to get a nice big crowd in your restaurant," Rusty said.

"But I didn't have this flier made," Maggie said. "Someone else did this. It's not fair."

The officers were quiet for a few moments.

"I see two options," Marko said. "Either we can all walk out to that angry crowd, and *you* can announce to them there has been some terrible mistake made—"

"We won't let anything bad happen to you," Rusty interjected.

"Or," Marko continued. "You can honor the advertisement, authentic or otherwise, and keep those customers happy."

"Your choice," Rusty said. "We're here to help you with whatever you decide."

The variety of expressions on Maggie's face told the story as she weighed her options.

"I can't believe this is happening," she said. "Screw it. Let 'em in."

Dave Yamamoto noticed the new color on AJ's toenails as she prepared for their eleven o'clock roll-call.

"Nice toes," he said.

"Thanks. Jerrod bought them for me. I wish I could wear flip-flops on duty tonight."

"Sergeant Murray may have an issue. I'm not sure. Try it. I dare you," he said as they both laughed.

She wiggled her toes one more time before banishing them to a pair of highly shined ankle-covering black boots.

"I sure hope it stays quiet tonight," he said.

"I know. We have one more thing to do for Jerrod and we have to time it exactly right."

"What the hell is taking her so long?" Oso said to Efrain as he took a swig from his second beer in fifteen minutes.

They sat at the bar at Nopales after the doors had been locked and the last customer had been, literally, pushed out.

"I can't believe the crowd tonight. Holy shit. This place was packed," Efrain said as he worked on his fourth beer. "Look at all those empty liquor bottles."

"Maggie said she didn't make that flier," Oso said. "But it sure brought in a lot of people."

The Nopales restaurant had never seen so many customers in one night. Every chair of every table and at the bar were occupied. The wait staff had to get surly with customers who wanted to sit and have conversations after their meals.

The kitchen had run out of food and the two bartenders worked so hard they had to take a break before finishing their clean-up duties.

"It's almost two now," Efrain said. "We have to leave for Bakersfield no later than ten to make it back here for the dinner crowd."

"We'll leave at ten," Oso said.

"What a crazy day," Maggie said to herself in the privacy of her office. She was exhausted from the longest day she had ever had and was having trouble focusing on her daily tabulations. The second full glass of red wine she had just finished was not helping her either.

At one point during the overwhelming dinner rush, it had occurred to her the half-price flier hadn't been such a bad idea. But she had changed her mind after her staff had become exhausted and they started running out of supplies.

She pressed the "equals" button on her calculator and discovered the restaurant had a net loss of nearly four hundred dollars for the day -- not including the food that got thrown away and the retail groceries she would have to buy for Saturday and Sunday.

She screamed "Fuuuuccckk," so loud Oso and Efrain got off their bar stools and headed to her office door to see what the problem was.

"Let's get the hell out of here," she said as she slammed the door.

She turned off the lights and followed the two men out the front door. She got into her Cadillac while Efrain and Oso got into the Oldsmobile.

AJ and Dave stood in the medical office landscape across Main Street with their hands covering their badges and their portable radios on low volume.

"Here they come," she said.

"Let's do this," he said.

The two officers drove their black-and-whites from behind the office with the headlights off. Predictably, the Cadillac and Oldsmobile turned east as they were driven away from the restaurant and south at the first intersection.

“What the hell,” Oso said as the red and blue overhead lights and a bright spotlight shined through the rear window of the Oldsmobile.

Efrain saw the brake lights on the Cadillac flash on for an instant, but the car then sped away.

The street was lined at both curbs with dew covered cars and trucks belonging to the residents there, so Efrain stopped his car in the traffic lane.

“Driver’s license and registration, please,” Dave demanded at his open driver’s window.

“Why am I being stopped... this time?”

“You drove over the center yellow line back there, sir. Have you been drinking tonight?”

Efrain’s hands were cuffed behind him, and he sat in the caged backseat of Dave’s patrol car. He had failed a series of field sobriety tests and was deemed to be too intoxicated to drive.

“Do you have a driver’s license, sir?” AJ asked Oso after he struggled to lift himself from the passenger seat.

“No license. No ID,” he said.

“I would let you drive the car away if you had a license,” she said. “But since you don’t, we’ll have to impound the car. It’s blocking the traffic lane, you see.”

“Just park it somewhere,” he said as he looked around in a futile effort to find a parking spot at the crowded curb.

“I’m afraid departmental policy prohibits us from operating a private motor vehicle in this situation,” she said. “It will have to be towed.”

“This is bullshit,” Oso said. “When can we get the car back?” Oso moved a step toward AJ and narrowed his eyes on hers.

AJ stepped toward him and matched his glare.

“I’m afraid you’ll have to wait until at least Monday, sir,” AJ said with no hint of fear on her face or in her voice.

“Fuck you,” Oso said.

“That, sir, is never going to happen,” she said.

Dave walked over to AJ, and they watched Oso waddle away down the sidewalk.

“Scary guy,” he said.

“Not so scary.”

"When did we get a policy that says we can't drive someone's car out of a roadway?"

"Oops, my mistake. Sorry."

Jerrod was having a decent night's sleep until his home phone rang at two-thirty.

"Efrain's on his way to jail," Dave said.

"How about Oso?"

"Last I saw him; he was walking away like a sad puppy."

"Was there anything in the car? A .32 auto? A shotgun? Dope? Cash?

"Nothing in the car, brother."

"Okay. Thanks for everything."

"He what?" was the first thing Armando Mendoza yelled into the telephone receiver at Oso when he answered his home phone at three-fifteen.

"And the car got towed," Oso said as he held the receiver away from his ear. "We were supposed to drive to Bakersfield. We were going to leave at ten. They're expecting us to be there by two-thirty."

"You idiots," Mendoza yelled. "Where are you now?"

"I'm at Efrain and Martha's house."

"Stay there. I'll call you back."

Armando Mendoza knew he would have trouble getting back to sleep.

He got up and put on a robe. A warm black terry robe his wife had given him. He went to the kitchen and started a pot of strong coffee.

As the coffee maker came to life, he sat, alone, at the kitchen table of his huge empty house. His elbows were on his knees. His face in his hands.

He thought about the path his life had taken to get to that point in his life. He thought about the decisions he had made — some successful and some disastrous. He pondered how his careful planning seemed to be spinning out of control.

His coffee was ready, and he poured himself a tall mug. He cradled its warmth with his hands, and it reminded him of his daughters when they were newborns.

Small and warm and comforting.

He had only wanted the best for his girls. He loved them more than anything else in the world. He wished for them to be happy and to have everything they desired.

He had no intention of bringing them into the terrible business he was involved in. But the business was so easy. The profits so great. The risk so minimal.

He lost his way when their mother, Maria, died. He had shied away from anything to do with drugs until she was gone. He knew people in *that* business and had politely avoided getting involved with them. But with her gone, there was no longer a reason to resist. He finally said yes. Little trips and little packages with little profits led to bigger trips and bigger packages with ridiculous profits. So much profit that he had no outlet for the cash he was collecting.

He approached his daughters. He financed their businesses. He charged them premium rents so he could show an income himself and was able to launder the cash away through them. No one was the wiser.

On paper, at least, they were all just successful businesspeople... but with a big secret to keep.

The events of the previous day had been beyond believe. He knew that running a business, any business — big or small — had its share of headaches, but not the magnitude of that day. Hearing his daughters cry on the phone, one after another, had broken his heart.

That brazen young detective would just not leave things alone. He would not go away. A shotgun blast through his window still wasn't enough to make him realize his life was in danger. He would have to be dealt with more severely... and soon.

He finished the first cup of coffee and poured a second. He leaned against the kitchen counter and weighed his options. He was sorry he had brought Efrain and Oso into the business. They were loyal, but stupid and expendable.

A delivery had to be picked up in Bakersfield that afternoon. His idiot driver was in jail and his car impounded. His idiot driver's partner didn't even know how to drive a car.

He created his operation so he would never be anywhere near the drugs and, if it all went bad, others would be the one's arrested — not him. He had always kept himself well insulated.

He weighed his options and decided to take personal charge of the situation before it spun completely out of control.

He already had more money than he could ever spend. He would be getting out of the business. Maybe even retire. This would be the last trip to Bakersfield. And he would make the trip himself.

Oso answered the phone before the first ring ended. "Yes, Armando."
"I'll pick you up at ten. Be ready."

CHAPTER 71

Saturday

Armando Mendoza laid back down in bed but couldn't sleep. He tossed for an hour thinking about the trip to Bakersfield. He at one point decided to cancel the trip and picked up the phone to call Oso. He changed his mind. He was in charge. Nothing could stop him. And that one trip would be very lucrative to him personally.

But it was going to be the last one.

He showered and shaved. He selected a comfortable pair of Wrangler jeans and a blue dress shirt. He put on his favorite pair of black cowboy boots over thick white cotton socks and selected a medium-weight black leather jacket.

He spun the dial to the safe bolted to both the floor and wall of his study. The safe stood five feet tall, was four feet wide, and two feet deep. He carefully turned the dial. First left. Then right. As he entered the five numbers of the combination only he knew. He turned the handle and pulled the heavy door open.

He noticed the familiar smell first. It reminded him of spoiled milk. It felt dirty to him, and he was disgusted by the thought of the many others who had touched it before him. He always washed his hands after handling it.

The interior of the safe was filled to nearly its capacity with United States currency. Neatly stacked. In packets of both one hundred- and fifty-dollar bills held together by thick blue rubber bands.

He selected twelve packets. Six containing one-hundred-dollar bills and six fifties. Ninety-thousand dollars. The amount he would need to take to Bakersfield to purchase four hundred eighty grams, or about one pound, of quality brown heroin from Mexico.

He couldn't help but doing the math in his head: He would have the brown forty-percent pure heroin "stepped-on" or diluted five times to produce roughly two thousand grams of eight-percent street-grade black tar.

Each gram of tar, the same approximate size and weight of a single almond, would sell for about five hundred dollars after being packaged in smaller plastic-covered quantities for addicts.

The two thousand grams of black tar would fetch gross sales of around one million dollars. After deducting for the Mexican heroin, processing, and distribution overhead expenses, he would pocket nearly six hundred thousand in untaxed US currency for himself.

He placed the cash in a black-and-gold Valle Verde High School gym bag. The one Efrain should have been delivering with Oso... instead of him.

He went to his bedroom closet and stretched to his toes as he reached for an old cedar *La Amenidad* Cuban cigar box on the top shelf. He laid the box on his bed and opened the cover.

The Colt Model 1903 pistol was as beautiful as any piece of art. It was in the same pristine condition it had been the day his father gave it to him just before his death in 1974. The semi-automatic had a brightly polished silver receiver and slide. Intricate hand-engraved floral designs covered the exposed gunmetal. The grips were white Mother of Pearl. Fourteen-karat gold emblems with the rearing-horse design of the "Rampant Colt" emblems adorned the grips.

He picked the handgun up. It fit his hand well and its weight felt good.

He removed the magazine and it slid out of the well with ease. He counted the .32 ACP cartridges in the magazine and found it to be one short of its capacity of eight.

A MLD Guns and Ammo price sticker was attached to a white box of Winchester ammunition housed in the cigar box. He picked one cartridge from it. The bullet was a full-metal jacket. He pressed the cartridge into the magazine and reinserted it in to the well. It snapped in securely. He pushed the safety lever on the receiver with his thumb and placed the pistol into the inside pocket of his leather jacket.

CHAPTER 72

The VVPD police radio operated on three color-coded frequencies:

"Blue" was the primary channel and the one most people would associate with police radio. All of the routine radio chatter to and from the Dispatch Center was done on Blue.

Captain Andrew Wheaton, and every local police buff with a RadioShack police scanner, listened to Blue. And all radio traffic on Blue was tape recorded.

"White" was a California-wide law enforcement channel. It was recorded as well.

"Orange" was an informal Mesa County frequency shared by all agencies but used exclusively by units in the field — both from car and portable radios. The Dispatch Center did not monitor Orange and, therefore, it was not recorded.

Jerrod Gold stood at one of the tall windows in the living room of his mother's home on Rochester Drive. His unmarked car was safely hidden from view in the garage the Renauds had graciously vacated while out of town.

His plan had worked perfectly... so far. Everything was in place. They had played Small-Ball. Everyone on the team did their part. They took the fight to the enemy. The gasoline had been sprayed. Now he just needed the snake to slither out of its den.

At nine-fifty, the "snake" appeared in the form of a black Chevrolet Suburban as Armando Mendoza drove the massive truck from Sherwood Drive onto Rochester Drive.

"On the way," Jerrod said into his portable radio on Orange channel.

Five minutes later, Craig Wallace radioed from Bixby Street, "At the house" on Orange. One minute later, he radioed, "Heading out... with a big passenger."

Three minutes later, Willie Sanchez said, "On the bridge" as the Suburban left the city limits and traveled south over the Valle Verde River Bridge on its way to Bakersfield.

"Let's meet at the high school lot near the gym," Jerrod said on Orange.

The bright sun had still not made an appearance when the detectives met at the high school. The sky was gloomy with thick overcast clouds.

"I figure it will take them four hours travel-time," Jerrod said. "Each way, to get to and from Bakersfield. Add the dope pick-up, gas stops, and maybe food too."

“I don’t think Oso would make it two hours without food,” Willie said.

“Maybe so,” Jerrod said. “They should be back between six-thirty or closer to seven. We need to be ready to go by six to play it safe. We can meet right back here.”

“Six it is,” Craig said.

“Six, okay,” Willie said. “I’ll be ready.”

“Marko and Rusty are both on-duty tonight. I’ll call them at home, so they know what’s going on,” Jerrod said.

CHAPTER 73

Six o'clock could not come fast enough for Jerrod.

The waiting was painful. The idle time filled his head with doubt. He had calculated every risk. *Or had he?* He was fully committed but wondered what he had missed.

The whole plan had been devised to force Armando Mendoza into the position where he *had to* get personally involved in the dope operation. Direct, hands-on, involved.

The part of the plan involving the harassing pranks — the conversation at El Ocotillo Club, the alcohol sales citation, the walk-in cooler failure, the dope money confiscation, the purple feet caused by Ninhydrin, and the half-price fliers — were just distractions. They all were designed to alarm Mendoza, get his attention, and make him anxious.

The most important part of the plan had been arresting Efrain Hernandez and impounding his car.

Everyone knew Oso didn't drive, so Mendoza would have to either send Chimo Cervantes to Bakersfield or, preferably, make the trip himself.

Mendoza had taken the bait.

Mendoza had to be caught with the dope on him or at least in his vehicle while it was under his control. A lot of dope. Enough dope to show he possessed it with the intention of selling it. A serious felony under both California and federal laws. A charge so big there would be no wiggle room for a plea deal. Enough to send him, Oso, and Efrain Hernandez to prison for years.

And that was just the start.

They were responsible for Hector Medina's murder, Val Reyes' murder, and three overdose deaths. They were responsible for shooting into his house and for injuring Natalie. Those charges would be harder to prove.

The dope arrests would lead to search warrants. Search warrants would lead to other evidence. Searches would turn up a .32 Colt, a shotgun, ammunition, rusty-gold-colored carpeting, heavy-gauge plastic, blood stains, telephone records, and banking records to support murder charges.

But, if he was wrong, there would be no mercy for him. He had been warned. Wheaton's threat had not been vague. Reassignment was no longer in play. Termination was inevitable and it was certain his law enforcement career would come to a sudden and tragic end.

There would be plenty of discipline to go around for everyone else involved. A letter of reprimand would be the least one could expect for just knowing what had happened. Suspensions, days-at-the-beach, were more likely for anyone involved in the plan. Termination wasn't out of the question.

After leaving Craig and Willie, he had gone home to wait. He decided to make the best of the down time. He had plenty to do at the house. The lawns needed to be mowed, the patches made to the plaster on the living room wall needed to be painted, and he still hadn't found time to wash his truck.

His mind raced. More doubts crept in. He needed to stay busy.

CHAPTER 74

The detectives met at six o'clock. Jerrod, Craig, and Willie were together at the high school gym lot. They assembled their police gear. Handguns. Extra ammo. Handcuffs. Body armor and raid jackets. Checked and rechecked.

Conversation was minimal. They knew the risks.

Marko and Rusty arrived in their black-and-whites.

"It's been crazy busy all shift," Marko said.

"Call-to-call," Rusty said.

"Here's how it going to work," Jerrod said. "We'll sit on the most likely routes back into town — the river bridge and the freeway. We'll set up to spot the Suburban as it gets into the city limits. As soon as practical after they get in the city, we'll make the stop. This all has to go down inside the city limits."

The others nodded.

"Honestly, we don't have probable cause to stop the Suburban," Jerrod said. "We have to create a pretext to make the traffic stop on it."

"I can find an equipment violation on *any* car," Marko said. "Give me a few seconds with a brand-new car and I can find at least three reasons to stop it."

The others nodded and no one doubted him.

"The only thing we don't know right now is how Mendoza and Oso will react when they know they're about to be stopped with the dope," Jerrod said. "They could run, but I've talked to that smug bastard Mendoza. I'd bet good money he'll just pull over and try to bullshit his way out."

"What happens when we get the Suburban stopped?" Willie asked.

"We'll all converge wherever the stop happens," Jerrod said. "It'll all depend on what they do."

"Any chance they have guns on board?" Rusty asked.

"We should be ready for anything."

More waiting.

Jerrod and Willie set up along River Street to watch the Valle Verde River Bridge. Craig parked at the freeway off-ramp on the west side.

The detectives stayed on Orange channel. Marko and Rusty stayed on Blue, but were able to hear any developments on Orange.

Six-thirty went by. Seven also.

It had become dark, but downtown Main Street glowed blue from the mercury vapor streetlights.

Jerrod felt a slight headache. Doubts started to creep into his brain again. What-if's: *What if "D" doesn't come after "C" and "X, Y and Z" come at them like a cannon ball. Will they be ready?*

At seven-eighteen, the black Suburban was driven over the arch of the Valle Verde River Bridge. "On the bridge," Willie radioed on Orange as he pulled from the curb and watched the Suburban drive onto the first block of Main Street.

"Copy," Craig said as he spun his rear tires in the roadside gravel and headed toward downtown.

Rusty and Marko were a block off Main Street and headed into position.

"North on Main," Jerrod radioed on Orange. "200 block. Outside lane. Two on-board."

They passed City Hall and Fremont Street. The neon sign from The Corner flashed in Jerrod's peripheral vision to his right.

A black-and-white pulled behind Jerrod in the 300 block of Main Street. The City Plaza was to the right. Marko pulled his car to the left and gunned the accelerator as he shot past Jerrod and pulled up in the inside lane next to Willie.

As they passed Nopales restaurant, Willie slowed down, and Marko punched the accelerator again to pull in behind the Suburban.

"Fresh green light on Main. 400 block," Jerrod radioed on Orange.

The brake lights of the Suburban flashed for a split second. Mendoza may have watched the patrol car move up and tapped the brake pedal out of panic.

Or maybe not.

That momentary flash of red was all Marko needed. He noticed a sliver of white light from a tiny crack in the red plastic of the left stop light lens. The lowest form of traffic infraction. Normally cause for no more than a "fix-it" ticket. And exactly what they needed.

"North on Main," Jerrod radioed on Orange. "Coming up to the 'Y.'"

The left-turn signal of the Suburban came on and it moved smoothly to the inside lane. Marko's black-and-white and the two unmarked cars changed lanes behind it.

The traffic light was red for northbound Main Street traffic at the "Y" intersection with Independence and Constitution Avenues. The Suburban slowed and stopped for the light.

"I'll make the stop on the next block of Independence," Marko said on Orange.

Rusty was in his black-and-white at the curb off Constitution Avenue. Craig had stopped off Independence Avenue.

Jerrod glanced at Saint Daniel's Church. People milled and chatted on the front steps before the Saturday night mass. They had no idea what was about to happen in front of them. He wondered: *Was Mendoza saying a prayer at that moment? Was he asking for some intervention from a higher power? And if so, was he going to get it?*

The traffic light turned green, and the Suburban started through the intersection onto Independence Avenue. Marko followed close behind with Willie and Jerrod behind him.

Rusty and Craig joined the caravan.

The rotating red and blue overhead lights on Marko's patrol car switched on. The brake lights on the Suburban glowed red as it slowed and moved right and into the outside lane without signaling.

The Suburban slowed to a near stop at the curb.

Jerrod thought: *This had been too easy. The plan had worked. The "snake" had come out of hiding and was about to be captured.*

Marko keyed his microphone on Blue and radioed he was making a traffic stop. Location. Vehicle description. License plate number.

Five seat belts in five city-issued cars were unsnapped as five officers prepared themselves for anything.

CHAPTER 75

Armando Mendoza's 1983 Chevrolet Suburban was powered by a 454 cubic-inch 230 horsepower V-8 motor. When he mashed the accelerator from a near stop, the rear wheels spun violently, and it jetted forward with a huge plume of tire smoke left in its place.

"I'm in pursuit," Marko said on Blue. "North on Independence."

"I'm with him," Rusty radioed on Blue as he sped past the unmarked cars with his overhead lights twirling and siren blaring.

The detectives followed behind and stayed off the air.

"West on Williams Boulevard," Marko radioed as the 8,600-pound Suburban blew through a red traffic light and skidded left toward the west side of the city.

"65 on Williams," Marko radioed their speed as they accelerated through the 35-mph zone.

"South on Lassen," Marko radioed as they made another skidding left.

Rusty stayed a safe distance behind Marko. The detectives stayed farther back.

"They threw something out of the passenger side," Marko radioed on Orange as he sped by a brick-sized package cartwheeling along the curb.

Willie was still behind Rusty in the line of cars. He pulled the steering wheel violently to the left, crossed the double-yellow line into the oncoming traffic lane, slammed on the brakes, and skidded to a stop. Jerrod and Craig zipped by him as Willie shifted the car into reverse and backed up. He jumped out and grabbed a silver duct-taped bundle from the roadway.

"West on Eucalyptus," Marko radioed. "70."

At the intersection of Eucalyptus and Carpenter Roads, the Suburban tried to make another left turn. It braked too late, and the weight of the massive vehicle was too much. The Suburban bounded over a curb and skidded to a stop just short of crashing into a huge, raised concrete planter.

"Suspect crashed. Eucalyptus and Carpenter," Marko radioed as he slammed on his brakes to pull directly behind the Suburban and pin it in.

The pursuit was about to end.

Marko pushed the brake pedal to the floor. Nothing. He pumped the overheated brakes to no avail. He expertly steered to the right and missed the Suburban by a few inches. The patrol car traveled another 100 feet before finally coming to a stop.

Rusty watched Marko avoid the collision and saw the back-up lights of the Suburban come on as he closed in.

The Suburban accelerated full-speed backward and the grill of the black-and-white collided with the rear of the big truck at nearly 40 mph. The hood of the patrol car crumpled in half and it careened off the roadway in a cloud of dust.

The Suburban sped away on Carpenter Road with Jerrod and Craig driving the only cars still in the pursuit.

The taillights of the Suburban had been demolished in the collision and the heavy chrome rear bumper of the massive truck hung loose on one side. A brilliant arc of sparks spewed behind the Suburban as it sped away with the bumper grating the asphalt.

"Someone help Rusty," Jerrod radioed on Orange.

"I'm with him," Willie radioed.

Red and blue flashes from Marko's car were far behind the two unmarked cars as they sped through a series of west side streets surrounding a group of frozen food plants.

Jerrod stomped on his brake pedal with both feet when the Suburban unexpectedly, but no-doubt intentionally, skidded to a stop. He yanked the steering wheel to the left and was able to scrub-off some speed as his sedan slid sideways toward the dangling rear bumper of the big truck.

His body was tossed to the right, and he was covered with shattered window glass when the passenger side of his sedan slammed into the back of the Suburban. His seatbelt kept him in his seat and his body snapped back upright when the car came to rest.

Jerrod sat dazed for a fraction of a second. He glanced out the driver's window and his eyes grew wide as he watched the headlights from Craig's car bearing down directly at his driver's door.

"Shhiiiit," Jerrod yelled as he futilely pressed his shoulders and head into his seat and braced for a second collision.

At the very last moment, Craig veered his car right to narrowly miss both Jerrod's car and the Suburban.

The Suburban turned left and sped into a loading dock area of a frozen food plant. It accelerated through a parking lot and made another sharp left.

The Suburban made more desperate turns. Left. Right. Left. Jerrod and Craig stayed close behind.

As they passed through a loading dock there was a loud explosion. The right front tire of the Suburban had had enough and let go. The huge black vehicle veered sharply to the right in an all four-tire skid until it slammed head-on into a solid concrete loading ramp. The impact was the end of the massive vehicle. Its front end was demolished, and steam erupted into the cool fall air from the mangled radiator. The chase was over.

The right side of the Suburban came to rest against a concrete wall. The only way out was from the driver's side doors.

Jerrod skidded his car to a stop and his headlights lit up the Suburban. It was the perfect scenario. They had full tactical advantage.

Jerrod jumped out of the driver's seat with the Beretta in his right hand. He crouched into a cover position behind his open driver's door. Craig had pulled his car next to him on the right and took cover behind his door as well. His revolver was out.

"Come out, Mendoza," Jerrod yelled to the Suburban.

There was no response. Maybe they were seriously injured. Good. Maybe they were dead. Better.

"Come out," he yelled again. "Keep your hands in plain sight."

Nothing. No movement. No yelling back. No negotiated surrender.

They heard a siren from a patrol car wail as it passed by them on the roadway. Marko. They were hidden from his view and he had no idea where the pursuit had ended.

More silence.

The driver's door of the Suburban opened slowly. It let out a loud creak as it was forced away from its frame. The inside of the Suburban was dark.

"Come out with your hands exposed," Jerrod yelled. "No sudden moves. Make your arrest easy. You don't want to die here."

Mendoza pushed the door open and slid out of the seat. Specks of blood dotted his face from broken glass. The headlights from the unmarked cars blinded him and he raised his left arm to shield his eyes. His right hand hung down at his side. He looked injured and appeared ready to give up.

"Oso's hurt," he yelled. "He's bleeding and may be dying. He needs help."

"That's the least of our problems right now," Craig yelled to Mendoza. "Get on the ground. Get your hands where we can see them."

Mendoza kept his right hand to his side.

"Down on the–," Craig yelled as Mendoza raised his right hand and an orange bright fireball came toward them.

One shot.

Jerrod fired a round from his Beretta. Sparks flew from the concrete behind Mendoza from the bullet impact. A miss. Mendoza ducked but didn't go down.

Mendoza was frozen for a moment. He held the pistol out in front of him, but it didn't fire again.

Jerrod thought: *Why didn't he fire? Did his pistol jam? Did it break? Did his ammunition misfire?*

"I'm hit," Craig yelled. "In the leg. Shit."

Mendoza turned to his right, lowered the pistol to his side, and started running.

Jerrod was paralyzed for a moment. He was torn between chasing Mendoza and helping Craig.

"I'm okay," Craig yelled. "Get that bastard."

Jerrod left the cover of his car door and chased after Mendoza. The dark leather jacket made Mendoza hard to see him in the limited light. He could hear running footsteps and followed the sound around a shed and stacks of wooden pallets.

The thought of Mendoza escaping was not an option. He was either going to jail or the morgue that night.

After about fifty yards, the footsteps stopped. Mendoza had quit running.

Was he setting an ambush? Jerrod thought.

Jerrod slowed his pace.

Catch your breath. Approach carefully. Be ready for anything. Use all your training.

Jerrod held his Beretta in his right hand. His left hand cupped his right. A strong combat grip. He held the pistol in front of him. Arms extended. Muzzle just below his line of sight. Low-ready combat position. He moved cautiously.

He's close. He's got to be nearby. Stay calm. Move slow. Stay in control.

Jerrod peeked around the corner of a ten-foot-high stack of wooden pallets. A single bright security light hung from a wall straight ahead of him. The light made him squint as he searched. Left and right. Up and down. He listened. Only silence.

Where was he hiding?

Jerrod crept past the first stack of pallets. There was a flash of movement in his peripheral vision. Something moving to his right.

From the darkness of a gap between the stacks of pallets, a length of two-by-four lumber was swung with immense force. It struck Jerrod on the right forearm just above the wrist. Pain shot up his arm. His hand went numb, and the Beretta clattered to the pavement. The piece of lumber tumbled next to it.

Mendoza slowly stepped from the shadows. A shining silver pistol was in his right hand. A Colt Model 1903. The slide held back with an empty cartridge case in the ejection port. A "stovepipe." A simple problem. He pulled the slide back with his left hand and the case fell to the ground. The slide snapped back in-battery. A live round chambered. There was nothing wrong with the pistol.

Mendoza's eyes narrowed as he walked forward. He looked like a viper prepared to strike. Not out of fear or defense, but as a predator. He smiled as he spoke.

"You said we'd meet again."

CHAPTER 76

Jerrod had been prepared for that moment. His mind raced, but he stayed focused. All his police training kicked in. Skills he hoped he would never use: *Keep the suspect talking. Engage in a dialog. Make yourself as human as possible. Keep the situation calm. Don't agitate. Evaluate your injury. Get the subject close. Look for an opportunity. Wait for a distraction. When his attention is focused elsewhere for a split-second — make your move. Get out of the line of fire but expect to be shot. Take control of the situation. And never, ever, stop fighting.*

"You couldn't leave it alone," Mendoza said quietly. "You had to interfere. You had to stick your big cop nose where it didn't belong."

Jerrod nodded. He subtly moved his right wrist. It was painful, but no bones were broken. The numbness was subsiding.

"You harassed my family. All those calamities were caused by you. Stealing my money from the runners. The walk-in refrigerator failure. Purple feet. Half-price flier. Underaged beer drinkers. Efrain's arrest. Those weren't some coincidences. You caused them. Don't lie to me?"

Mendoza stepped closer. His voice was louder and more agitated.

"Yes, I was responsible," Jerrod said in a low and calm voice.

Deescalate. Don't aggravate. Get him closer.

"I'm sorry," Jerrod said. "It wasn't personal with your kids. I knew Maggie from school. We were friends. I was just doing my job."

Mendoza laughed. His voice lowered. He seemed to calm a little.

"Your job," he laughed again. "What, 'To serve and harass.' Is that your job? Is that what the taxpayers pay you to do?"

"They pay me to keep the peace."

"Keep the peace?" he said as his voice rose again. He moved a half step closer. His finger tightened on the trigger. "We had peace. You declared war."

"You're right," Jerrod said in a quiet voice.

Keep him calm. Get him a little closer.

"What are you going to do when I'm dead?" Jerrod asked in a quiet voice. "All the other cops know you were driving the Suburban. You shot a police officer. You're not going to get away. You should surrender now."

Mendoza laughed again. "Oh, you are a naive young man," he said. "Why would I surrender when I can just disappear. I'll just find a quiet place somewhere in Mexico. No one will know me, and I'll just fade away. You'll be dead and I'll enjoy the rest of my life. I have enough cash stashed away to last a hundred years."

"You're a religious man, right?" Jerrod asked. "You're a good Catholic. You love the church. You study the Bible. Murder is a mortal sin. You'll end up in hell."

Mendoza appeared caught off guard. His eyes drifted upward as he thought of a response. He quickly refocused. He was enjoying the cat-and-mouse exchange. He was used to being in control and had to have the last word.

"My faith allows for sin," he said. "Humans will be human. 'Free will' they call it. We make bad decisions and do bad things. Big and small. We just have to confess our sins. Perform an act of contrition. Seek forgiveness. Our sins get absolved. Heaven, not hell. You see."

Mendoza was calm. Still in full control. He stepped closer.

"Why did Hector have to die?" Jerrod asked quietly.

"Hector, Hector, Hector. Your little friend, Hector. He was an incredibly good runner. He was a leader to the other kids and could have advanced in my enterprise. But Hector had a problem. Sticky fingers. He helped himself to my money."

"How much did he take?" Jerrod asked.

"Very little, actually," Mendoza said as he moved closer. The muzzle of the gun was pointed directly at Jerrod's face. "He helped himself to small amounts. Ten here. Twenty there."

I wonder where he learned to do that? Jerrod thought.

"We set him up," Mendoza said. "We tested him one day and found the bag short. Oso and Efrain confronted him. He fought back and they roughed him up as a warning. For him and the other kids."

"But why did he have to die?" Jerrod asked as he felt his voice raise and he tried to control it.

"Simple. He did it again," Mendoza said. "He was warned. He took a beating. But then he did it a second time and he had to be eliminated."

"Did you kill him?" Jerrod asked.

"Sometimes the boss has to handle things personally," he said as he moved closer. "I had to set an example to everyone. My standards are high, and punishment is swift. Oso and Efrain brought him to me. He admitted stealing again. So, I shot him myself."

Jerrod felt white-hot with anger. He tried to suppress it. He looked up at Mendoza. The muzzle was six inches from his face.

Soon. Very soon. Time to make a move.

"You can't take a warning either," Mendoza said. "I had Efrain shoot out the window at your house. It didn't seem to have the desired effect. You get extra points for persistence, or I should say, stubbornness."

A bright white light from a distance flicked across Mendoza's face. He looked away briefly at the light source.

Now.

Jerrod grabbed the Colt with his left hand and pushed it toward Mendoza's face. Another fireball erupted from the pistol as a bullet traveled harmlessly into the air. He held the Colt and reached for the Beretta with his right hand.

"No," Mendoza yelled as he stomped the undercut heel of his custom-made cowboy boot down on Jerrod's hand. Bones crunched as the hand was pinned against the ground. The heel twisted. A two-inch U-shaped flap of tender skin peeled from the back of Jerrod's hand. Blood. Tendons. Raw meat. His right hand was useless. Mendoza stepped back and pulled the Colt away from Jerrod's grasp.

Jerrod and Mendoza had changed positions in the struggle. Jerrod was down on his right knee. Mendoza stood above him with every detail of his face exposed in the bright light. His glare was menacing.

"I guess Wheaton was wrong about you," Jerrod said. "He vouched for you. He said you were a valued member of the community."

"Andrew Wheaton," Mendoza said. "What a fine piece of work he is. Dedicated cop. Family man. Friend of the church."

Mendoza was loving the moment. The control. The power.

"Since you've mentioned the good captain, I guess you should know."

"Know what?"

"I've been paying Andrew Wheaton a thousand dollars a week for over two years. Every Sunday. He's on my payroll. He gives me information. He lets me know if any problems are coming my way. It was a particularly good arrangement... until you got involved."

Jerrod shook his head and the expression on his face twisted in disbelief.

"You look shocked," Mendoza said. "It appears I found something you were in the dark about. You look so disappointed."

"How did you convince him to join you?" Jerrod asked.

"It was very easy," Mendoza said. "He approached me. After he was passed over for chief-of-police."

"I have a little trouble believing you," Jerrod said.

"Well, you can thank Andrew Wheaton for Valdemar Reyes' untimely death," Mendoza said. "The captain alerted me to his little plan. I just couldn't let that happen. He lost some of my money and was hiding from me. All of a sudden, he was conveniently back in jail. He was trying to protect himself. He thought I couldn't reach him in there. He was wrong. Dead wrong."

"Motherfucker," Jerrod muttered to himself.

"It's over now," Mendoza said. "I'm tired of this. You can now die just like your friend... Hector."

Jerrod held his damaged right hand. Mendoza moved closer.

"Say your last prayer, Detective Gold," he said. "Or perhaps you have another witty piece of scripture in mind."

There was no prayer. Just images flashing through his mind. *Mom and Dad. Brother. Gram and Gramps. Baseball. Good times. The Corner. Gary Pell. The Kevins. AJ and Dave. Marko and Rusty. Craig and Willie. The Colonel. Hector. And Natalie.*

Mendoza moved closer. Jerrod bowed his head. He felt the cold of the gunmetal on his scalp as the muzzle was pressed against the top of his head.

It should be painless. Bullet straight to the brain. Just like Hector. Instantaneous unconsciousness. Sudden brain death. Any second now.

Jerrod held a vivid picture of Natalie's face in his mind as it happened.

CHAPTER 77

Jerrod used every scrap of energy in every muscle in his body to drive his left foot to the ground as he pushed the top of his scalp into the muzzle of the Colt. Mendoza frantically pulled at the trigger, but nothing happened as the pistol's slide was being pushed just out-of-battery.

Jerrod raised his left hand and grasped Mendoza's hand and the Colt. He pushed the gun up and away from his head as he continued to drive his legs up and got to his feet.

He let out a scream in pain as his mangled right hand landed a solid punch into Mendoza's solar plexus.

Mendoza gasped for breath after the blow to his abdomen as Jerrod pushed the pistol farther up into the air and twisted at it with his left hand. He swept Mendoza's legs with his right foot and the two men fell to the ground. Jerrod landed on top.

Jerrod struggled for control of the gun while Mendoza reached over for it with his left hand. Jerrod reached back and smashed his right elbow into Mendoza's face. His nose exploded into a massive river of blood and his left hand fell back to the ground.

"I'm going to—," Mendoza said as Jerrod interrupted his words with a second brutal elbow to the face.

Mendoza may have been trying to say he was going to kill him or that he wanted to surrender. It no longer mattered.

Jerrod twisted Mendoza's right wrist and the gun moved between them. Even with blood pouring from his shattered nose and laying flat on his back, Mendoza maintained a solid grip on the gun. Mendoza pushed the muzzle towards Jerrod's face as his finger futilely pulled at the trigger. Jerrod held the slide out-of-battery as he twisted the gun with all his remaining strength. The muzzle was forced away from his face and toward Mendoza's.

Mendoza choked on his own blood as Jerrod pushed the muzzle under Mendoza's chin. Neither man made a sound as Jerrod inched his finger inside the trigger guard.

The slide of the Colt snapped smartly back in-battery.

The two men locked eyes from inches away as Jerrod slowly pressed Mendoza's finger against the trigger.

CHAPTER 78

The explosion was deafening and the flash blinding as the 71 grain .32 caliber Full Metal Jacket bullet traveled the length of the Colt's barrel, pierced the soft skin under Mendoza's chin, sped through his tongue, penetrated the roof of his mouth, burrowed past the delicate bones of his sinuses, and through the base of his skull to settle in the left lobe of his brain.

Jerrod relaxed his grip and the Colt fell to the ground.

Mendoza's smug expression was forever gone from his face. It was replaced by the blank gaze of a dead man. A steady stream of blood pumped from Mendoza's wounds creating a growing wet circle, glossy black in the limited lighting, on the ground around his head.

Jerrod heard footsteps behind him. Someone running. Keys jangled and leather creaked. He looked over his right shoulder. A glint of a gold badge and a dark blue uniform. Marko ran toward him. A revolver in his right hand.

"Jerrod, are you okay?" Marko yelled.

"Yeah. I guess," Jerrod said as he moved off Mendoza.

Marko aimed his revolver at Mendoza and kicked the Colt away. He checked for a pulse.

"He's alive. His heart's still beating."

"He's gone, Marko."

Jerrod and Marko watched Mendoza's face for nearly a minute. His eyelids were open. Unblinking. His pupils fixed. The flow of blood slowed to a stop. His heart finally quit beating. It was over.

"He didn't get to confess," Jerrod said.

"Confess to what?" Marko asked. "The dope stuff? Hector?"

"No. His sins. He didn't get to confess his sins. He wasn't absolved. He's going to hell."

"Good place for him," Marko said.

"Indeed," Jerrod said.

Marko picked up the scuffed Beretta and placed it in Jerrod's holster.

"Lot of good that fancy gun did you," Marko said.

Jerrod smirked and said, "Thanks for everything. I owe you one."

"Yes. Yes, you do. Let's get you to the ER."

CHAPTER 79

"Mendoza told you Wheaton was on his payroll?" Sergeant Pete Hanson asked. "Are you certain about that?"

Jerrod sat on an ER gurney. He cradled his mangled right hand — which had been cleaned, sutured, and bandaged. A partial plaster cast stabilized fractured metacarpal bones and was held in place by an Ace Bandage.

"That's what he told me," Jerrod said. "He said he'd been paying Wheaton for information and protection for two years. Kind of explains things. Doesn't it? 'I personally vouch for him' and all that bullshit. You were there. You heard it."

"You have a point," the sergeant said. "Do me a favor and keep the Wheaton stuff to yourself. For now."

"Okay."

"I hate to say it, but you were right about Mendoza and the whole dope thing."

Jerrod smiled.

"But you were also wrong. I hope you're not expecting some kind of hero's parade on Main Street."

"Hardly. So, what happens now?"

"I don't know. You've created quite a mess."

"How's Craig?

"Craig's leg is in bad shape. He's getting ready for surgery now. The bullet's lodged in his knee."

"How about Rusty?"

"He'll be okay." He's got some scrapes and bruises. He's going to be sore for a while, but he should be okay."

"How about Oso?" Is he dead?"

"He's a different story. He got pinned in the Suburban when it crashed. We couldn't get him out of it. He yelled and spit and punched at the fire fighters and EMTs who were trying to help him. We had to get a tow truck to pull the Suburban away from the wall and cut the door away to get him out. He's going to live."

"Too bad," Jerrod said. "What about Efrain?"

"He was still in jail. We got his bail jacked-up and he won't get out."

The sergeant paused. "Jerrod, and I just need to say this for the record, you're an asshole. You violated a dozen policies and committed who knows how many crimes during your little, well, unauthorized operation. One bad guy is dead. Your fault. Three officers and another bad guy in the hospital. Your fault. A few cars crashed. Your fault. The whole damn PD working overtime. Chief on my ass. Paperwork for at least a year. All your fault."

"I—," Jerrod started to say.

"I'm not done," the sergeant interrupted. "Here's the dilemma I'm in. The way I see it, I have only two options: The first option is to tell the chief the truth. That is, you and all the others went freelance and created this whole elaborate plan yourselves. You worked off-the-books and on your own time. It all then dissolved to shit and led to the mess we're in now. On top of that, I get to admit I was clueless and had no idea what was happening around me. We all might as well just resign."

Jerrod nodded.

"The second option is to go with the flow. Imply to the chief this investigation was authorized and coordinated the whole time. Convince him we knew Wheaton was somehow involved with Mendoza, so we had to keep the captain out-of-the-loop. Then we had to act on short notice based on some 'reliable information' we had about the dope delivery."

"I like the second one best," Jerrod said.

"Fuck you, smart-ass. I wasn't asking for your opinion."

Jerrod grinned.

Now, if you'll excuse me," the sergeant said, "I need to go lie to the chief for a while."

"Thanks, Sarge. Really."

"Heal up and get back to work."

Jerrod laid down on the gurney.

What a week, he thought. He was exhausted and needed a rest. But rest would have to wait as he heard the thick metal band of a wristwatch shake in the hallway.

"How're you doing?" Willie said as he walked into the room.

"Hey, Willie. You okay?"

"Yeah. I didn't get damaged like everyone else."

"Good."

"That was some chase. A real E-Ticket ride, brother."

"It was," Jerrod said.

"I recovered the brick of dope that got thrown out of the Suburban. Looks to be high-grade Mexican brown. Unbelievable. You were right all along."

"Thanks. Let's go see Craig."

"Hey, guys," Craig said when Jerrod and Willie walked into his ER room.

The hospital bed was set upright and Craig's right knee was wrapped with enough white gauze bandages it looked twice its normal size. An IV line dripped into his right arm.

"How are you doing?" Jerrod asked.

"Okay. Now. They gave me something for the pain. I can't feel the knee. I can't feel anything." He grinned. "I kind of like it."

"I'm sorry this all ended like this," Jerrod said. "I had no intention for any of us to get hurt."

"I know that," Craig said. "It was a good plan. I just caught the 'X' that popped up before the 'H.'"

Jerrod smiled and nodded as he recalled their conversation from a few days earlier.

"I guess cigarette smoke isn't such a protective force after all," Jerrod said.

"I guess so. Time to change brands at least."

"You know Mendoza is dead and Oso's in custody, right?" Willie asked Craig.

"Yeah, Hanson filled me in on that," Craig said. "What happened to your hand, Jerrod?"

"It's nothing," Jerrod said with a smile.

"Yeah, right," Craig said.

Craig laid his head back on the pillow. The expression on his face became dour.

"My wife's pretty upset," Craig said. "Sandi told me she was sure I was dead when Hanson went to our house to tell her I got shot. She's always been afraid someone would come to the door while I was away at work."

"I'm so sorry, Craig," Jerrod said.

"Not your fault. We all knew what we were getting into. I'd do it again."

"Can I get you anything?" Jerrod asked.

"Bourbon on the rocks sounds good right now," Craig said.

"I bet it does," Jerrod said.

A male nurse dressed in scrubs and a surgical cap walked into the room.

"They're ready for you in the operating room, Mr. Wallace."

"Let's go," Craig said.

The nurse unlocked the wheels of the bed and pushed it toward the door.

"Hang on a second," Craig said to the nurse.

Craig held out his left hand to Jerrod and he took it with his left.

"The juice was worth the squeeze, kid."

Marko was with Rusty Browne in his ER room when Jerrod and Willie walked in. Katy Browne and their son were with them. Jimmy ran to Willie and jumped into his arms.

"Sorry about everything," Jerrod said to Rusty. He glanced at Katy, and she smiled back to him.

"I'll be okay," Rusty said. "Just a few scrapes... and a real good story. The Lord was looking out for us tonight."

Jerrod went back to his ER room and waited to get discharged.

Dave Yamamoto and AJ stopped in. Then The Kevins. All said they were glad to have helped with the operation and would do it again.

He thanked them all for the help.

Jerrod laid back on his hospital bed and was starting to fall asleep. He thought he was dreaming when he heard a familiar voice.

"That all you can do... *sleep*?" Natalie said.

He looked toward the doorway and saw her. Her arms were crossed. The swelling and bruising on her face had gone down. A small pink adhesive bandage under her left eye contrasted with her smooth bronze skin.

"I heard you got banged up a little. Willie called."

"Just a scratch. I'll be fine," he said. "I miss you."

"I miss you too," she said. "How's Craig doing?"

"His leg isn't good. They just wheeled him into surgery."

"He's in good hands here."

"Ready to come home with me?" he asked.

“I don’t know. I haven’t been there since the shooting. I’m not sure how I’ll do.”

“I can assure you the people responsible for the shooting are either dead or in custody,” he said.

Natalie looked down at the floor and rubbed the toe of her shoe at a spot on the vinyl. Her eyes glanced back up at Jerrod.

“We’ll see.”

CHAPTER 80

Sunday

The pain medication helped Jerrod Gold sleep for nearly nine hours. The ache from the hairline fractures to the bones in his right hand woke him up.

In his bed.

Alone.

Natalie had decided she couldn't stay at his house as her memories from the shooting were far too great.

The *Valle Verde Sun* headline read:

DRUG OPERATION BUSTED
LOCAL PROPERTY OWNER KILLED BY POLICE

The two-page article by reporter Bruce Witt detailed the VVPD investigation into the heroin overdoses, drug smuggling, car chase, and, ultimately, the shooting death of Armando Mendoza.

The article implied Hector Medina had been connected to Mendoza and his murder had been related to drug trafficking.

Sergeant Pete Hanson was quoted numerous times and stuck to the tidy, but mostly fabricated, version of the investigation. He had laid out a logical and believable scenario in which aggressive, diligent, and efficient police work led to the ultimate conclusion.

Jerrod was pleased the article did not specifically name the officers injured during the chase and aftermath.

The most telling omission from the article was the name of Captain Andrew Wheaton.

CHAPTER 81

Monday

They gathered in the gravel parking lot of the Catholic cemetery. A white hearse and six cars. A freshly dug burial site was visible near the lot. Green artificial grass covered the dirt mound. A blue portable shade had been erected that the overcast skies had made unnecessary.

Yvonne Medina walked over to Jerrod.

"We have only five pallbearers," she said. "Would you mind being the sixth?"

Jerrod looked at Natalie. She smiled and nodded to him.

"I'd be honored," he said.

Yvonne introduced Jerrod to the other five. All young Latinos. None older than twenty. Cousins or friends or classmates of Hector Medina. One of them may have secretly telephoned Willie Sanchez. One or more may have been intercepted by The Kevins and scared straight.

He would never know.

The funeral director asked if they were ready. A beautiful mahogany casket with brilliant brass hardware was slid smoothly from the hearse.

Jerrod took the last place on the right side of the casket so he could use his left hand. The five other bearers were strong and heft their portion of the heavy casket with ease.

The casket was silently carried to the lowering device directly over the open grave. Yvonne and Carmen Medina stood nearest the casket. The few other attendees stood behind them. Natalie joined Jerrod and they held hands.

A priest from Saint Daniel's performed a brief prayer in Spanish and Latin. The casket was sprinkled with holy water. Incense was waived. And Hector Medina was lowered into the ground.

Yvonne and Carmen each took a hand-full of the rich valley soil to the grave and paused silently before tossing the dirt onto the casket. Each of the guests, in turn, placed a portion of earth on the casket as they said goodbye.

Jerrod took an extra moment over the grave. There was no break in the clouds and no sliver of sunlight to warm him. "I'm sorry I didn't do more," he said as he let gravity take the soil from his hand.

“Let’s go camping,” Jerrod suggested to Natalie as they drove from the cemetery. “We both have the week off and I’d love to get out of town for a few days.”

“Okay,” she said. “Let’s go somewhere warm. The weather here is depressing.”

Natalie stayed in the Toyota as he gathered an air mattress, sleeping bags, and coolers from his garage. She simply could not go into his house.

They drove down the Pacific Coast Highway to a state park they had visited several times before. The coastal mountain range kept the fog away and the skies were clear and blue and warm.

Monday meant the campground was nearly empty. There were enormous oak trees. Hiking trails. A cool meandering river, and a private clearing. They sunbathed. Ate snacks. Drank good wine. Listened to soft music. And had minimal conversation.

That night, they cuddled together on the air mattress in the open bed of the truck and admired the stars they rarely got to see in Valle Verde.

“When are you leaving for San Diego?” he asked.

“Week after next,” she said. “I’m giving my notice at the hospital tomorrow.”

“How long is the program?”

“Two years.”

“You’ll do good there.”

“I hope so.”

Tuesday

The drive back from the campground was nearly silent.

Jerrod dropped Natalie off at her mother’s house. They hugged and said they would talk soon, but both knew their relationship was over and they would be permanently heading in separate directions.

He visited his mother and made-up a story to explain his hand injury. She wouldn't know the true details from Saturday night and how close to death her son had come for several years.

Wednesday

He went to Craig's home and was pleased to hear him say he was looking forward to healing and getting back to work.

Thursday

Jerrod made good on his promise and took The Kevins to a steak dinner for bringing in Val Reyes. He learned Captain Andrew Wheaton hadn't been seen around the PD all week and his office had been cleaned out.

CHAPTER 82

Friday was payday.

Jerrod Gold had grown tired of sitting around the house. His right hand ached and limited his activities. The stitches would be removed on Monday, but they itched under the cast.

He drove to the PD to get his check and found Willie at his desk when he walked into the bureau.

"Hey, stranger. Feel better?"

"Yeah, so-so. Where's Hanson?"

"Meeting with the chief. Again. He's been in there a lot this week."

"No surprise," Jerrod said. "Did I miss anything?"

"Stella called a few days ago."

"How is she?"

"Fine. Better than fine," Willie said. "She asked how you and Craig were doing."

"That's nice."

"Remember the dope money Val Reyes said someone ripped him off for. Well, Stella 'found' a gym bag full of cash. Over sixty thousand in used bills.

"And?" Jerrod asked.

"She asked what she should do with the cash."

"What did you say?"

"I told her to go back to wherever home was for her and do something good with it. That's what."

"Thanks for everything you did. I'll never forget it."

"No problem, brother."

Jerrod poured himself a cup of coffee. He tasted it and added more creamer and sugar to make it almost drinkable.

The Phil Collins song "In the Air Tonight" played on KHJB.

He sat down at his desk and looked at the unorganized mass of papers and files.

He looked across his desk at Craig's desk... with its full ashtray and its empty chair.

He thought about the people lost in the last couple weeks: Hector. Val. Craig. And Natalie.

As he sipped his coffee, it became apparent to Jerrod how near-brilliant Val Reyes' plan had been: He had staged the dope money rip-off, hid the cash, and turned himself in to get off the street while he worked a deal for a new parole elsewhere.

Stella obviously hadn't known about the cash until later because she was still hooking on the Friday night Hector Medina had been killed.

Val had shared just enough of his story right after The Kevins picked him up to get Jerrod interested. Val knew he had to stay in jail general population instead of protective custody to avoid being perceived as an informant.

Val told Stella about the stash of money during their jail visit and he had her come to the PD with the proposed deal.

He told his cellmate, Lucho, the story simply as insurance.

Val had planned to give up Armando Mendoza, Efrain Hernandez, and Oso, take the cash, and start a new life somewhere else with Stella.

The only thing Val hadn't counted on was Mendoza's ability to reach him in jail and have him eliminated.

Val Reyes, just like everyone else involved, had no idea Andrew Wheaton was feeding information to Mendoza. And Wheaton knew all about Val's plan. Wheaton was responsible for Val Reyes' murder.

Pete Hanson came into the office and was surprised to see Jerrod at his desk. "Just in time. I've got fifty new cases sitting here for assignment."

Jerrod held up his bandaged right hand. "I'm a little useless at the moment. What's up with the chief?"

"Just updating him on everything. Been a little hectic around here this week." The sergeant paused for a few seconds to gather his thoughts. "Where to begin? The bullet fired from Mendoza's pistol that hit Craig was a fluke. He had fired it into blinding light. He had a one-in-a-million chance of hitting anything. The bullet skipped off the asphalt pavement twenty feet away from Craig. It flew parallel and about four inches off the pavement, went under the car door and struck him in the knee as he crouched there."

"I talked to him the other day," Jerrod said. "He wants to get back to work as soon as he can."

"Craig's leg is worse than he's letting on," the sergeant said. "He may have more surgery and we don't know when, if ever, he'll be able to come back on the job."

Jerrod nodded.

"On the other hand. Rusty was off a couple days, but he's back now."

"Okay," Jerrod said.

"What else? The DEA took over the dope part of the case. It's a big deal and pretty much a state-wide operation now. They arrested

Mendoza's daughters and son-in-law. They searched their homes and businesses and hit the Mother Lode. Dope. Cash. Records. You name it. There was over four million in cash in a safe at Mendoza's house alone. The IRS will do a forensic audit of everyone involved and we'll probably never see them again."

"How about the homicides?" Jerrod asked.

"Interesting turns on those too. Since both you and Craig were out, the District Attorney's Office sent a few of their investigators — excuse me, *DA Inspectors* — to help out. I always thought those guys were prima donnas, but they were actually great to work with."

The sergeant pushed away from his desk.

"During the searches, they checked that west side barn out in the strawberry field. That's where the heroin was being processed. All the equipment and chemicals were there. They also found an area inside the barn with short rusty-gold-colored carpet, a roll of heavy clear plastic, and one .32 ACP cartridge case.

"Hector was killed there," Jerrod said.

"It looks like it," the sergeant said. "They found .32 ammunition in a cigar box at Mendoza's house and the crime lab said, preliminarily, the bullet recovered at autopsy from Hector was fired from the Colt handgun Mendoza had pointed at you."

"So far, so good," Jerrod said.

"The DA guys somehow got Efrain Hernandez to flip on the others. He admitted to all the dope stuff and to shooting your house. He admitted to beating Hector as a warning and to taking him to Mendoza at the barn the night he was killed. He confirmed Mendoza personally shot Hector."

"Did he have any information about Val Reyes' death?"

"He also confirmed Reyes was killed in jail. It was no suicide. He said Mendoza ordered him killed for losing his money. The SO has reopened that case."

"Okay," Jerrod said. "I've got a new theory about Val Reyes and that situation."

"Hang on to that," the sergeant said. "They've charged Oso with Hector's death. Even though Mendoza actually shot him, they still charged Oso with the crime. Murder, first degree.

"Nice," Jerrod said.

"Efrain cut a deal and is going to plea to a package of felony charges. Then he's going to testify against Oso and the others."

"How long is Efrain looking at?"

"He won't be out for at least twenty-five to thirty years."

"Wow," Jerrod said.

Willie shook his watch.

"How about the *other thing*?" Jerrod asked.

The sergeant's face became strained as he shuffled some papers on his desk.

"Willie, go get a cup at The Corner, okay," the sergeant said.

Willie said nothing. He grabbed his jacket and closed the bureau door behind him.

"That bad?" Jerrod asked.

"Yep. Here's how that went down: I told the chief about Wheaton and the money thing with Mendoza the night of the... chase... shooting... take your pick. He, at first, wanted to go arrest Wheaton himself."

"At first? He didn't?"

"Well, no. We waited for Wheaton to get home on Sunday and called him to the PD. He told him we were going to brief him on the... events... from Saturday.

"Okay," Jerrod said.

"We confronted him with the allegation. He didn't admit anything. But oddly, he didn't deny it either. It was a very strange interview. The chief suspended him on the spot. Took his badge, ID, and gun."

"What jail is he sitting in now?"

"The chief talked it over with the mayor and city manager. Now you have to understand how small-town politics work. They didn't want the scandal. So, Wheaton was, well, allowed to retire quietly. No jail. No charges. No nothing."

"You're fucking kidding, right?"

"I wish I was. That's what happened."

"No way. What's to keep me from running to the paper, the DA, or the Feds with what I know. With what Mendoza told me? With what Wheaton did?"

"Nothing to stop you, really."

"So?"

"Except for the fact your little operation was all done without authorization. It was creative, I'll give you that. But believe it or not, you don't just get to dream up plans, get officers injured, kill a bad guy, and have equipment mangled without some type of approval."

"What are the options?"

"Well, if you spill-the-beans on Wheaton, then you, me, Craig, Willie, Marko, and every other officer directly involved in this mess will probably lose their jobs... or worse."

Jerrod said nothing.

"You see, I had to authorize your little adventure after-the-fact. The chief's still in the dark about what really happened. He actually enjoyed all the positive attention the PD got. You've read the newspaper. You know how 'the department conducted an all-out investigation' and the other crap I fed them."

Jerrod nodded.

"In-house," the sergeant said. "The chief wanted to make a huge example out of Wheaton. But now he would just as well see this whole thing, especially the Wheaton part, fade away quietly into history. Do you understand now?"

Jerrod thought for a few moments. "No, I don't. That's all bullshit. Wheaton was dirty. Period. He tipped Mendoza off about Val Reyes' plan. He just gets to walk away from that? Murder? He probably gave Mendoza my home address so they could blast it."

"Jerrod, I don't disagree with you. Everything you just said is probably right."

"Then you agree."

"Okay. Tell me how you would prove Wheaton was dirty? Tell me how you would prove a respected career police captain took cash from a dope smuggler? A dead dope smuggler who can't testify. I don't doubt it happened, but we can't prove it did. And I seriously don't think Wheaton left a trail for us by making cash deposits to his Christmas Club account with the dirty money. Do you follow now?"

"We know he did it."

"And, again, I believe you're right. It all fits. Wheaton's constant questioning, snooping around, shutting down the Hector Medina murder investigation for a day, and directing me to keep you away from that case."

Jerrod rubbed his bandaged hand and took a moment to respond. "He shut it down? You're telling me Wheaton had us take that Sunday off and had the murder assigned to Craig? I thought those orders came from you?"

"Wasn't my idea. You just heard it from me. I drove my family back from Lake Tahoe, remember? I was ready to work as long as it took. Wheaton told me 'the overtime wasn't warranted' or some shit like that. And he said you were too close to Hector and wouldn't be objective."

"I'm sorry. I thought—"

“Don’t think anymore. You really don’t get it. Do you? You got the result you wanted — Mendoza’s dead, his lackeys are in jail, and his operation was shutdown.

Jerrod dropped his chin to his chest.

“We know how Hector died and who was responsible. We know who shot out your window. And you got to do it all your way.

Jerrod looked at his sergeant.

“Now we’re all going to move on... and that includes you.”

CHAPTER 83

On Friday afternoon, the black telephone sitting on the living room floor rang. She stared at the phone and debated answering it. One ring. Two rings. She picked it up on the third.

"Hello," Martha Figueroa said.

"This is the operator," the female voice said. "I have a collect-call from the Mesa County Jail. Efrain Hernandez. Will you accept the charges?"

Martha didn't answer immediately. She thought about just declining the call.

"I accept," she said.

There was a click, and a male voice came on.

"Hello, honey."

"Hello, Efrain. How are you?"

"Okay. I'm out for my hour. Protective custody sucks. Twenty-three hours in my cell and one out."

"That sounds rough."

"How's the baby?"

"He's really good. He's getting bigger every day."

"Give him a kiss for me."

"I will."

"I miss you."

"I miss you, too."

"I'll call tomorrow, okay."

"Sure."

Martha hung up the phone and held the receiver down for a moment.

She carefully took her sleeping baby from the arms of the man who had stood silently nearby as she spoke on the phone.

"Are you okay?" her brother asked.

"Never been better," she said.

"Ready?"

"Let's go."

Martha hadn't felt that good in years. She looked around the empty house and smiled. No furniture. No Efrain. No Oso.

She walked out of the front door. Locked it and placed the key under the mat for the owner.

Her brother's pickup was loaded with all her possessions. She was moving back to Turlock. A job was waiting for her, and she would start a new life with her baby. Her son would be in his thirties with a family of his own when Efrain got out of prison... if he even made it out alive.

She would never again be beaten or threatened or controlled by him. She would never again answer her door and accept paper bags from scared young men. And she would never again straighten the tangles of dirty currency, sort them by denomination into stacks of 100, and neatly bundle the stacks of cash with thick blue rubber bands.

Martha got into the truck, and they drove away. They passed the little neighborhood market two blocks from the house. She was familiar with the market... and the pay phone in front of it.

She had used that phone numerous times in the last week.

She reached into her pants pocket and pulled out a crumpled business card. A card once snatched from her hand by Oso. A card she had later found lodged along the sofa seat cushion. A card with the phone number for the young detective with the gentle voice she had called and disclosed the things she saw and did and overheard at home: Efrain and Oso in drunken conversations. Telephone calls she eavesdropped on the extension. Names and places mentioned — "Armando," "Hector," and "Bakersfield."

Her last call had gone through a police dispatcher in the early morning hours after Efrain was arrested. A kind and understanding man named "Al" answered. He said he would call the detective at home. The return call came quick.

She had told him one final thing: "Armando is picking Oso up at ten."

ABOUT THE AUTHOR

James C. Gray is a retired twenty-five year California law enforcement officer.

He lives with his wife, Cindy, in Northern Nevada.

Made in the USA
Middletown, DE
01 November 2021